This novel is entirely a work of fiction. The names, characters and incidents portrayed in it are the work of my imagination. Any resemblance to actual persons, living or dead, events or localities is entirely coincidental.

All chapter titles are quotes taken from Pat Conroy's *Lords of Discipline*.

To all who wear the ring.

GRAHAM MILITARY COLLEGE STAFF & ADMINISTRATION

President of the College	Major General John Gentry
Vice-President for Diversity & Inclusion	Matthew Malone
Commandant of Cadets	Colonel Jason Wright
Assistant Commandant for Assimilation	Lt. Colonel Esther Dehenre
Alpha Battalion Tactical Officer	Lt. Colonel Boyd Gibbs
Bravo Battalion Tactical Officer	Lt. Colonel Dudley Hart
Charlie Battalion Tactical Officer	Lt. Colonel Jackson Del Moss
Delta Battalion Tactical Officer	Lt. Colonel Eric Vincent
Commodore Advisor	Lt. Colonel Brandon Preston

CORPS OF CADETS TABLE OF ORDER & EQUIPMENT

Regimental Commander	C/Colonel Catherine D. Ward
Regimental Sergeant Major	C/Sergeant Major Bradford Klein
Regimental Executive Officer	C/Lieutenant Colonel Adam Fitzgerald
Regimental Adjutant	C/Major Dalton Buchanan
Regimental Academic Officer	C/Major Derek Gallagher
Regimental Athletic Officer	C/Major Eldon Miles
Regimental Religious Officer	C/Major Jack Steele
Regimental Operations Officer	C/Major Justin Hamilton
Regimental Provost Marshall	C/Major Nigel Montgomery
Regimental Supply Officer	C/Major Olen Smalls
Regimental Public Affairs Officer	C/Major Stanford Robbins
Regimental Human Affairs Officer	C/Major Vernon Knapp
Regimental Ops Clerk	C/Corporal Kent Knox
Regimental Admin Clerk	C/Corporal Myron Cantrell
Alpha Battalion Commander	C/Lieutenant Colonel Ryan Church
Alpha Battalion Executive Officer	C/Major Jared Tally
Alpha Battalion Sergeant Major	C/Sergeant Major Sidney Mack
Alpha Battalion Academic Officer	C/Capt Jeremy Walls
Alpha Battalion Athletic Officer	C/Capt Alan Hampton
Alpha Battalion Provost Marshall	C/Capt David Clay
Alpha Battalion Operations Officer	C/Capt Kenny Hester
Alpha Battalion Ombudsman	C/Major Kyle Wilkins
Alpha Battalion Ops Clerk	C/Corporal Booker Joyce
Alpha Battalion Admin Clerk	C/Corporal Noel Cross
Bravo Battalion Commander	C/Lieutenant Colonel Kevin Jordan
Bravo Battalion Executive Officer	C/Major Sherman Kerr
Bravo Battalion Sergeant Major	C/Sergeant Major Burton Hogan
Bravo Battalion Academic Officer	C/Capt Jeff Sweeney
Bravo Battalion Athletic Officer	C/Capt Kerry Cobb

Bravo Battalion Provost Marshall	C/Capt Marcus Burns
Bravo Battalion Operations Officer	C/Capt Kerry White
Bravo Battalion Ombudsman	C/Major Rayford Burks
Bravo Battalion Ops Clerk	C/Corporal Sam Stone
Bravo Battalion Admin Clerk	C/Corporal Anton Fischer
Charlie Battalion Commander	C/Lieutenant Colonel Shane Douglas
Charlie Battalion Executive Officer	C/Major Dane O'Neil
Charlie Battalion Sergeant Major	C/Sgt Major Everett Conley
Charlie Battalion Academic Officer	C/Capt Blake Watson
Charlie Battalion Athletic Officer	C/Capt Hector Alvarez
Charlie Battalion Provost Marshall	C/Capt Dwayne Bowers
Charlie Battalion Operations Officer	C/Capt Lyndon Fox
Charlie Battalion Ombudsman	C/Major Lucas Mosley
Charlie Battalion Ops Clerk	C/Corporal Michael Hahn
Charlie Battalion Admin Clerk	C/Corporal Wayne Bush
Delta Battalion Commander	C/Lieutenant Colonel Terrance Lloyd
Delta Battalion Executive Officer	C/Major Marion Kent
Delta Battalion Sergeant Major	C/Sergeant Major Philip Maddox
Delta Battalion Academic Officer	C/Capt Marc Harris
Delta Battalion Athletic Officer	C/Capt Adrian Morris
Delta Battalion Provost Marshall	C/Capt Bryon Doyle
Delta Battalion Operations Officer	C/Capt Hank McCall
Delta Battalion Ombudsman	C/Major Chris Harvatin
Delta Battalion Admin Clerk	C/Corporal Landon Wiley
Delta Battalion Ops Clerk	C/Corporal Steve Bass
Fourteenth Company Commander	C/Capt Steve Lowrey
Fifteenth Company Commander	C/Capt Avery Coleman
Sixteenth Company Commander	C/Capt Levi Bolton
Seventeenth Company Commander	C/Capt Sam Carpenter

FIFTEENTH COMPANY TABLE OF ORDER & EQUIPMENT

There are normally approximately 100 cadets in each company. Not all are listed here for the sake of brevity.

Company Commander	C/Capt Avery Coleman
Company Executive Officer	C/First Lieutenant Alex Corey
Company First Sergeant	C/First Sergeant Jose Trevino
Company Supply Sergeant	C/Sergeant First Class Tim Johnson
First Platoon Leader	C/First Lieutenant Will Davis
Second Platoon Leader	C/First Lieutenant Kenny Daniel
Third Platoon Leader	C/First Lieutenant Cecil Lucas
First Semester Company Clerk	C/Corporal Caleb Gibson
Second Semester Company Clerk	C/Corporal Spencer Lawson
Upperclassman	C/Private John Sherman
Upperclassman	C/Private Jared Royce
Upperclassman	C/Private Carlos Mathis
Upperclassman	C/Staff Sergeant Eric Goodman
Upperclassman	C/Staff Sergeant Allan Nelson
Knob	C/Private Phillip Doss
Knob	C/Private Jessie Bates
Knob	C/Private Dane Winters
Knob	C/Private Wade Holden
Knob	C/Private Clinton Callahan
Knob	C/Private Darron Singleton
Knob	C/Private Doug West
Knob	C/Private Karl Lawrence
Knob	C/Private Malcolm Parrish
Knob	C/Private Curtis Hatfield
Knob	C/Private Richard Tillman

Knob	C/Private Silas Durham
Knob	C/Private Ashley Allen
Knob	C/Private Reagan Pitchford
Knob	C/Private Kensley Bennett

Prologue

August 14, 2000

CAROLINE'S CORNER

Did women really ruin Graham Military College...or will Graham ruin itself?

Those of you familiar with my little corner of *The Low Country Gazette* - Charleston's hometown paper, know that each year, I select one matter of particular relevance to our fair state and city, to explore with all possible depth. While Graham Military College is certainly not new to those in the Low Country, Graham's recent challenges are—and so I have decided to make Graham this year's serial investigation.

To set the scene, just five short years ago, the South Carolina State Supreme Court ruled that Graham Military College—a state-funded school that welcomed only men into its Corps of Cadets since its founding in 1842—had to now admit women into its ranks. A college with an average enrollment of fewer than 2,000 cadets was suddenly thrust into the national spotlight as it served as the fish bowl for discussions on the merits of single-gender education, hazing on college campuses, and the value of military traditions.

After the ruling in 1995, the front pages of The Gazette were filled with updates on the protests and demonstrations on the steps of the court house, and in front of Graham College itself. Alumni and Graham supporters alike made an immediate call for privatization, however, after a year of intense fundraising, their efforts failed to raise enough money to walk away from the state coffers. The protest signs and fundraising drives went away, but the opinions and tensions did not - remaining just under the surface, bobbing up sporadically at larger Graham alumni events.

When General John Gentry, a retired U.S. Army Lieutenant General and Graham alumni, became the 18th President of Graham in 1997, his military service hadn't prepared him for his duties as President of this military college. Once called upon to make strategic decisions about the nation's security, he was now expected to herd and stifle the personalities and opinions of not only the cadets and alumni, but worse—of his own staff—lest Graham be deemed a failure and risk the loss of state funding, all under the watchful eye of the media.

As the sun sets over the banks of the Ashley River during a humid and breezeless Friday afternoon, General Gentry sits on the veranda of his campus-provided housing and awaits the start of another school year. When asked what his biggest goal for the school year is, he takes a sip of his sweetened iced tea and utters one word: "Graduation."

With a long sigh he adds: "We at Graham haven't been given a fair chance with figuring out how to assimilate women into the Corps. One day a cadet could walk to the shower with his bathrobe open and the next he not only was required to wear a full PT uniform but he had to tie the thing up too. But we've also had to cut things out of cadet life because of women on campus. I'm not saying women can't be cadets and part of the Corps. We just didn't have enough time to prepare and make it as successful as we wanted…as we know it can be."

Not enough time? Is five years not enough time to properly integrate women into the ethos of the Corps of Cadets?

Yet when I dug deeper, I realized what Gentry was talking about. He does indeed need more time to make assimilation successful. For starters, Graham has yet to complete a single academic year without losing women from within its ranks. Just take a look at this year's senior class: out of the twenty women who started in 1997, only eight remain at the start of this, their senior year. The subsequent classes that followed had similar outrageous attrition rates among the women—attrition rates most certainly not seen among the men. While some women chose to leave Graham for personal reasons unrelated to cadet life, the majority left Graham because it was not a "welcoming environment," as one former female cadet described it during her out brief. Yet what exactly constitutes a "welcoming environment" at a military college steeped in southern tradition?

To be fair, the school has tried its hardest.

Since the court ruling, women have been a part of all four classes, integrated into all four battalions, and overall have become as commonplace in all aspects of cadet life and around Charleston as Friday afternoon parades. Within the Class of 2001, eight women will finally wear the coveted Graham "band of gold."

Yet the landmark of graduating women cadets doesn't stop with rings. The Class of 2001 also has a female Regimental Commander, Catherine D. Ward. Many, including myself, thought this suspicious—and convenient. The first full class of women just happens to appoint a woman as the most qualified to lead the Corps of Cadets.

I will devote all of my time and energy to finding out for you what the future of Graham will look like at the end of this school year. Because if Graham Military College can't graduate a full class of women, can assimilation—and Graham itself—even survive?

Chapter One: *All was prelude.*

In four years, I will wear the ring.

I will march to the chapel with my classmates like all the senior classes have done since Graham's founding. I will sit with my company. When my name is called, I'll walk across the stage to receive the black velvet box cradling *my* band of gold. Afterwards, in front of the chapel, Dad and I will pose with our rings, together.

Finally.

I will run across the parade deck with the rest of my class, the heavy, humid October air in our lungs, the bright Charleston sun above us.

The pride in Dad's eyes again, finally.

The two of us standing there with our bands of gold glinting for all to admire.

I'll stand in front of the company number with my classmates for a photo, the lone woman in a sea of men.

"Attention to orders, attention to orders…" The loudspeaker bellows ominously throughout the battalion. "All members of the Corps of Cadets are to form up in company formation in their respective battalions immediately." I'm off my top rack before Ashley and Reagan even process the message.

"Did we just get called to a formation at 2350 hours on a Friday night?" Ashley asks, looking like she's in the wrong school as usual.

No, Ashley. It was Oz, the Great and Powerful, summoning you to his throne so you can receive your ruby slippers. I swallow the snide remark and choose to play nice. "Sounds like that's exactly what it was. We better hurry up and change and head to the squad room downstairs." Whatever this is about, being late isn't an option. (Being late is never an option at Graham.)

I'm not sure what either of my two roommates is actually doing here. Ashley is more of a question mark than Reagan, but they're both mysteries. For starters, they both thought it was a good idea to show up for Hell Week sporting long hair and pink luggage. There was no need to flaunt it—we stand out just fine without feminine luggage. Even after our knobby haircuts that make us look like 12-year-old boys, my roommates still try to act more Homecoming Queen than future military officer, constantly flirting with other cadets—even upperclassmen. It's probably because neither one of them comes from a Graham family. This place isn't in their blood, doesn't run through their veins like it does through mine and Dad's and his father before him. But Ashley is from Mount Pleasant, so she knew first-hand the amount of public scrutiny the school has been under the last few years. I mean, what other college freshmen saw their names printed in the morning paper the day they reported to college? You *want* to fly under the radar as a cadet—especially a female cadet, and *especially* now.

I hurry and change out of my blue cotton PT shorts and shirt with Graham embossed in large white letters, and into duty uniform—a white v-neck undershirt, light grey shirt, dark grey polyester blend trousers with a black stripe down each side, and black military shoes whose shine would make a mirror jealous. There've been complaints about the uniforms at Graham since assimilation, as the cut and style of the pants and shirt are clearly meant for men—shirt buttons on the right, belts threaded counterclockwise, that kind of thing. And our black, plastic name tag on the right-hand side of our shirt constantly juts out awkwardly due to our breasts. We're also required to iron military creases into our shirts that run lengthwise over our breasts like highway medians. Yeah, okay—awkward. But that's how it's been done for decades. Graham is about tradition and uniformity. Knobs especially need to blend into the pack. *Fade into the grey.*

I grab my buckle off the half-press. It's granddad's, and one of the only possessions I've owned that makes me feel…part of something greater than myself. And part of him. Part of Dad. I triple-check the sheen even though I shined it immediately after today's parade before wrapping it gingerly in a white shine cloth and securing in the top drawer of my half-press. No fingerprints or scratches. As always.

"Reagan…" Ash calls from her side of the room, rummaging through her laundry bag hanging on the side of her bed. "Do you have a pair of socks I can borrow? I can't find mine."

"Catch!" A black ball of cotton-wool blend flies across the room. "Thanks."

Seriously? You don't know where your socks are? It's October and we've been here for six weeks already. Our reporting instructions listed for us to bring ten pairs.

I'd hate Reagan less if she didn't constantly insist on helping Ash. Yeah, yeah, I know we're supposed to help each other out and have solidarity and share pants, but there comes a point where enough is enough.

Hurry up! I want to scream at them so badly. We're going to be late to the squad room, as usual. Yet I always have to wait for these two, or I'll be deemed a "bad" classmate. Does it matter that twenty-seven of our fellow cadets are waiting for me—for us—in the squad room right now, making the three of us collectively bad classmates anyway? Nope.

"Ladies…," I lament while standing at the door, cover in hand. The light from the ceiling reflects off my right toe with each tap, tap, tap on the hardwood.

"You could've helped her," Reagan says, tutting at me, "instead of complaining about how she's holding *you* up. You know Ash isn't as organized as you, Kensley. No matter how much we *all* wish we could be just like you." I bristle at the sniping. It's all we seem to do since we were forced to room together six weeks ago since we are an odd number and no knob can room alone. Now we're stuck with each other for nine months.

"You're right. Ash totally shouldn't know how to dress herself by now." My patience has its limits.

"Relax you two," Ash says. She's talking to both of us, but mouths "thank you" to Reagan when she thinks I'm not looking. "Anyway, I'm ready now. Let's go."

I roll my eyes at both of them as I open the door.

As soon as we cross the threshold of our alcove, we assume the brace position: chins in and oddly tucked under, arms by our sides, shoulders way back—probably further back than is healthy, if I were to ask a chiropractor. Thankfully, we only brace when we're on the galleries in the battalion, and in our rooms if an upperclassman is present. I couldn't imagine spending all day like that in class.

Out on the galleries, the battalion is a cacophony of slamming doors and leather soles on concrete. One behind the other, squaring any corners we encounter at a ninety-degree angle, we make our way across the gallery to the top of the stairs on third division. Before descending, I check to see if there are any upperclassmen, not out of fear of being asked some random knob knowledge this time of night, but because knobs must ask permission to use stairs if an upperclassman is on them.

All clear.

As we make our way down to second division, I see that while most upperclassmen are wearing duty pants, some didn't bother to put on their duty shirts. Instead, they wear their white v-necks and cheat the system by wearing zipped-up field jackets over top. I don't get it. Yes, we're having some random formation at nearly midnight on a Friday, but how tough is it to put on the correct shirt? And they claim women ruined this school. I do another check at the top of the second division stairs. A flurry of profanity runs through my head when I see an upperclassman standing directly in our path. His back to us. *Just turn a little so I know*

who you are. Please, please, please. No, not that way. Why are you talking
to Mr. Sherman anyway? Come on, we're already so late. Ah...got you—

"Sir, Mr. Royce, sir," I bark loudly. "Cadet Private Bennett, Cadet
Private Pitchford, and Cadet Private Allen request permission to drive
your stairs, sir."

Silence.

I hate when they make me repeat it. As if he didn't hear me. As if
he didn't hear the female voice reverberating within the battalion walls,
piercing the night. No matter how much I try to lower the octave, it
remains distinct. I resent feeling like an outsider when all I am doing is
following their rules.

"Sir, Mr. Royce, sir. Cadet Private Bennett, Cadet Private
Pitchford, and Cadet Private Allen request permission to drive your stairs,
sir."

"Drive." Royce doesn't even look at us. Probably doesn't even
know my name. I only know his 'cause we're forced to learn the names of
all upperclassmen in the company.

Before Royce can finish the word, we fly down the stairs, across
first division and into the squad room, where our classmates, as predicted,
have been waiting for us. Thirty knobs are now gathered in a room ten feet
wide and seventeen feet long, along with two full presses, two half
presses, two desks, and a bunk bed—affectionately called a "rack."

From somewhere in the abyss of grey comes, "And *that's* why they
shouldn't have let women into Graham." I swallow my anger at such a
cowardly remark made from the safety of the unknown. I'm tired of being
lumped together with Reagan and Ash or the other women in other
battalions. We aren't all the same, I want to tell them, just like all of you
aren't stellar cadets either. It's just easier for some of the underperforming
guys to squeeze by because they've got upperclassmen looking out for

them and because, well... we just can't seem to blend in no matter how much we try. We're always being looked at.

Judged.

I say nothing, because either way I lose. Besides, I'll outrank whoever it was—and I have my guess—by next year anyway. I'm not only going to graduate from Graham; I'm also going to shoot for the highest rank I can get. First step will be company clerk next year.

"So what do you think this random formation is all about?" Bryan Doss asks no one in particular. He gets no response, not out of rudeness but because we're all too tired right now. And a bit unnerved. Each one of us is trying to find a spot in the room to focus our eyes. Staring at each other would just be creepy, but with so many bodies in a small space, it's a challenge. Suddenly the tell-tale sound of the screen door opening screeches against the silence; before we can blink, the solid wooden door of the squad room comes flying towards us. As if catapulted by the same invisible force, the 15th company first sergeant, Jose Trevino, comes bursting in. Instantly, we all pop to attention and brace.

You would think a six-foot-tall Hispanic-American from Texas would be out of place in a small military college in the southern part of the United States, but you would change your mind if you met Trevino. He exudes patriotism with his impeccable military style, and the bearing that has just a hint of cowboy swagger.

"Happy Friday night, knobbies! Hope ya'll are shined up and didn't decide to try to pull one over on us," he remarks in his indistinguishable Texas drawl, turning over Leek's brass buckle looking for any smudges or scratches for which we would all get blames. (You never want to be the knob near the door.) Before he can advance to the next knob, Tim Johnson, our company supply sergeant, pops his head into the room and in his best command voice yells "Roll out!" We shuffle past Trevino before he can object.

Bracing, we proceed onto the gallery, grey ants flooding out of an anthill, being careful not to bump into Trevino on the way out or each other.

For a college that encourages an almost fanatical sense of unity among classmates, they divide us at every opportunity—physically, that is. From day one on campus, every cadet is assigned a squad. There are seven cadets per squad, and five squads form a platoon. Three platoons equal a company, four companies forge one battalion, and four battalions comprise the entire Corps of Cadets. All two thousand - give or take a few, of us living, eating, sleeping—*existing* together in four grey castle-like fortresses that to outsiders resemble a prison.

During formation, we each assume a position "on line," which for some of us means standing on an actual line on the gallery floor, where we march in place until the order to form up is delivered over the loud speakers.

"Mark time, maaaaaaaarch," Trevino's Texas drawl commands as he walks past us. There's an edge to his voice tonight. Perhaps he's upset that Johnson called us out to formation? Both are vying for 15th Company Commander next year, and obviously one will miss the mark. We march in place, lifting our knees as high as we can.

Bracing. Marching. Bracing. The fibers in my thighs grow hotter with each step.

"Knees up, chin in, Bennett!" Trevino whispers in my ear. (Whispering, I've found, is much more terrifying than yelling.) He must not realize that this is how high knees go when you're my height.

The long note of the bugle signals us to formation on the quad.

Knobs scramble to find their spots on the quad, while the upperclassmen meander to theirs. In less than a minute, four companies assemble in perfect rectangles within the four battalions. Unfortunately, because I'm the shortest cadet in my squad, I was put at the end, but at least they didn't put all three of us girls into one platoon.

"Fifteenth Company all present or accounted for," Avery Coleman, our Company Commander, reports to the Delta Battalion Commander. Before the others can finish reporting their accountability, the Battalion Commander shouts, "All Company Commanders and First Sergeants fall out on me immediately!"

As the company commanders and first sergeants huddle around the Battalion Commander in the sally port, the rest of the companies remain in formation on the quad. Some of the upperclassmen break their military bearing and look around, straining to hear the hushed, animated conversation happening in front of us in the sally port, gesturing to each other in confusion.

When the huddle breaks, four different commanders and first sergeants simultaneously instruct us to form around the company number painted in periwinkle blue in big block letters in each corner of the battalion.

"Bring it in, knobs," Coleman, standing on the stairs leading to second division, demands. We shuffle closer to the company number and each other, being careful not to step on anyone's shoes. We're close enough to know who forgot to put on deodorant. Again.

"To get to the point because it's late and my classmates and I would rather be enjoying our Ring Night: The administration is conducting a Corps-wide investigation into events in the Field House. Regardless if you're Corps Squad or not, you will be interviewed at some —."

"*What?* Aside from my swim test knob year, I've never been inside the fucking Field House," an annoyed voice shouts from behind us. *You and me both, buddy.*

"I get it, Carlos! I'm not excited about this either, but the faster I get the rest of the instructions out to you tonight, the faster we can move on. Now as I was saying, even if you're not on Corps Squad, you'll be interviewed. The investigation is being led by our very own Delta Battalion Ombudsman, Chris Harvatin. He and some of the other ombudsmen want to first separate everyone by class. I'm not sure—."

"This is *FUCKING* bullshit," he interrupts again; a couple of other voices now join in his low protest behind us.

"I didn't call for the investigation. So - chill. the. fuck. out, Los." Coleman's voice no longer hides her irritation. "Moving on…all seniors are to report to Tew Hall, juniors to Anderson, sophomores to Grinalds, and knobs to Lackey. Everyone will find out more at their respective locations. Bennett, Pitchford, and Allen, stand by while everyone else is dismissed."

No, no, no! Don't let it be what I think it is.

A low groan of profanity-laden protests accompanies the upperclassmen out the battalion. My male classmates form a single-file line on the galleries to begin their walk to Lackey Hall.

"Knobs, as I'm sure you've figured out, all the women in the Corps are meeting with Lieutenant Colonel Dehenre in Barton Hall. Meet in the conference room. You three *better* step it out to get over there before I do. That'll be all," Coleman instructs briskly.

Of course. All female cadets will report to some separate location on campus. That's been typical during these first years of assimilation— like our concerns and needs are different from those of our male classmates, and we need private, women-only, "safe" space to let them be known.

"Barton Hall?! That's halfway across campus," whispers Ash next to me. I hate that she thinks it's okay to just whisper to me or Reagan when we're out on the galleries. If she gets caught talking, we'll all end up doing extra pushups or running the stairs.

"*Shhh*. Suck it the fuck up and deal with it," I say as I lead them both to the galleries and out the front sally port.

Outside the battalion, the campus is abuzz. The October air hangs heavy with the rancid smell of the paper mill up river. The normally dark, square fortresses that house our classrooms and rooms are lit brightly from within, surrounding the parade deck at the center of campus with a soft halo of light. Beads of sweat roll down the center of my back in the humid Charleston night, gathering at the small of my back and no doubt leaving an embarrassing dark grey stain on my shirt and pants.

As we approach Barton Hall, junior and senior women of the Corps are entering through the front steps—a privilege reserved only for that select group of upperclassmen. I make a hard left to walk between two buildings, enter Barton through the back door, and walk straight to the conference room on the first floor.

Since there aren't many of us, and it's assumed knobs will stand anyway, the room is sufficient but still crowded. And stuffy, as the air conditioner shut off hours ago to preserve energy throughout the weekend. A heavy, mahogany wood table with seating for twelve dominates much of the room. Dark oak paneling and black velvet drapes only add to the ominous mood; it's exactly the type of room you'd expect to see at a military college.

I move to the right, while Ash and Reagan—always together, like some oversized amoeba—move left. At least we beat Coleman despite her ability as a senior to walk across the parade field. I stand between two other knobs from Second Company yet who don't look familiar to me. A brief glance at their name tags over their right breast pockets doesn't help. Probably losers like Ash and Reagan anyway. I smile politely, nevertheless, before retreating into silence like the rest of the knobs here.

Coleman enters and quickly joins four of her female classmates - all seniors, which includes the token female Regimental Commander, Catherine Ward, at the front of the table. The Regimental Commander is the leader of the Corps of Cadets and the highest ranking cadet, who represents the school not only at parade every week but at various functions. If they *had* to choose a female RC, Coleman would've been a better pick. I focus my eyes on a spot on the carpet in front of me and let my tired mind go blank. It's easier than letting myself remember what happened six weeks ago, but that's all my brain wants to do lately, in the few quiet moments I can spare.

"Okay, ladies. Quiet down please. I want to make this quick," Lieutenant Colonel Esther Dehenre, the Assistant Commandant for Assimilation, announces softly at the front of the room, clapping her hands as if addressing a kindergarten class and not a room full of military cadets. "The school is conducting a Corps-wide investigation into an allegation that the Field House was being used by members of all classes, and by both genders, for…." She pauses, though I'm not sure if it's for effect or because she's uncomfortable. "uhm…sexual activity." Her face flushing crimson.

As if on cue, gasps of frustration, outrage and annoyance fill the crowded room.

"Quiet down, everyone," Ward bellows, her posture commanding instant obedience.

"Thank you. The investigation will be led by Cadet Major…," Dehenre flounders, closing her eyes briefly to search for the correct name. As the clock ticks closer to midnight, I can't blame her.

"Chris Harvatin," Ward supplies to her in an audible whisper.

"Right. Thank you, Cathy. Naturally, Colonel Wright will oversee the investigation, but we in the Commandant's Office felt it best if the interviews were led, and managed, by a cadet. Every cadet, regardless if you are on Corps Squad or not, will be asked the same questions. Are there any questions at this time from you ladies?"

No one moves.

No one breathes.

No one dares to make a sound.

The room suddenly feels even more oppressive.

"Nothing? Okay, well, right." Dehenre shifts from side to side. "I'm sure you have a million questions. Remember what I always say: *our time together is a safe space for you to speak freely, regardless of your rank or class year.*" Dehenre's condescending, kindergarten teacher grates on my nerves like chalk on a blackboard. I don't understand why we had to be told this news by someone on staff in the Commandant's Department. The Corps structure is designed for us to govern ourselves and why are we not with our classes or even our companies?

Before I can fully register the motion of Reagan's hand flying up into the air, Dehenre calls on her.

"Ma'am, can you tell us anything more about the allegations? Are they *suuuurrrre* female cadets were involved, and not just girls from the College of South Carolina here in town. I worry that we," she gestures to the room in general—to all the women within it, "will get blamed for everything. The incident, the investigation, ruining Ring Night…" Reagan 's voice trails off. Her brazen questions aside, she brings up a point I didn't consider: What if the Corps, and of course the alumni, really do blame the female cadets not just for the investigation, but the incident itself? No matter how much I try, by default I'm part of that category too. Why didn't I think of that sooner?

"Let's not get ahead of ourselves here, knob. No one is blaming anyone for anything," Ward tries to assure her—us; herself. "We don't know much right now. Which is why we have to conduct a Corps-wide investigation." She goes on to say pretty much the same thing Dehenre already did—that we'll all be treated equally, in that we'll be asked the same questions by the cadet leadership conducting the investigation.

The room falls silent again.

Feeling the awkwardness and heaviness of the room, Dehenre ends the meeting and wishes us a good night. "Remember ladies, email or call me if you want to chat. Day or night."

Snippets of conversation from the upperclassmen accompany us out the door, as we head towards the rear of the building. They all seem to share the general sentiment that a Corps-wide investigation is not only ridiculous, but the timing verges on suspicious, given this year's investigative focus of Caroline's Corner and the LAMC Foundation.

Delta Battalion's is blanketed in near darkness and only the type of quiet that is associated with the midnight hour, as we return from our meeting in Barton Hall. The calm before the storm perhaps? We pass through the sally port and quickly make our way to our room, hoping not to be seen. Despite the constant tension among us, I still sense a silent, unifying dread hanging among us.

Sleep—even if just a few hours—is the only thing on my mind right now. The Parents' Day activities for Saturday are still in full effect: open barracks at 0900 hours, Parade at 1100 hours, lunch, then march over for the home football game. If we win, we'll get an extra hour of general leave, which after tonight would be fantastic. I could really use the extra time at Tad's. I wonder if Max will be there?

"Knobs!"

"Ma'am, yes, ma'am," we respond in Pavlovian unison before even coming to a complete stop at the top of the stairs on third division. How the hell did Coleman beat us back to the Battalion?

"You sure took your sweet ass time getting back here."

"Ma'am, no excuse, ma'am," Ash whispers.

Coleman ignores her response. "Looks like you guys are scheduled to talk to Harvatin on Monday afternoon." She thrusts a crumpled sheet of paper forward. "The times are listed next to each of your names." She crosses her arms. "I don't like surprises. Is there anything I should know *now*?"

Eagerly, I take the paper. "Ma'am, no, ma'am." I hope I just responded accurately for all three of us.

"Try not to embarrass me, knobs."

"Ma'am, yes, ma'am," we respond, but Coleman has already disappeared down the stairs.

"Geez, she nearly gave me a heart attack standing in the dark like that," Ash says, once in the safety of our room. "It totally reminded me of Hell Night." Drama queen.

I read the paper in my hands, eager to change the subject. "Okay. Looks like Ashley, your interview is at 1500...then I'm at 1530...then Reagan, you're at 1600."

"We could all walk over together after class," Reagan suggests, looking at Ash.

For once, I actually would prefer their company.

Chapter Two: *I had become so accustomed to the shouts of the cadre that I no longer even heard them.*

I couldn't concentrate during my Monday morning classes.

Lunch was a blur yet comfortingly routine.

And now sitting in Professor Francis' Algebra class, the minutes seem to slow down as they move closer to my interview. Why are only the female knobs from 15th Company interviewed today? Are the girls being singled out? Does Max know about this? I've only been to the Field House once or twice since I've been here. It's a building used almost exclusively by the cadet-athletes on Corps Squad. A building I most *definitely* avoid. Why bother attending Graham if you're going to be on Corps Squad and miss half the Corps events anyway as they are always out for practice or some random team events? The rest of us get stuck with picking up their slack.

Once class is over, I head downstairs to meet Ash and Reagan by the side door of Harris Hall. *Please let them be on time,* I pray silently. My unease is put to rest when they're already waiting for me. Single file, we make our way to Barton Hall. Just like the other night, we enter through the back yet this time we head straight to the conference room on the second floor. Reagan and I take a sit on the hard wooden bench outside the room. Ash knocks on the door exactly at 1500 hours and is swallowed up with one step forward across the threshold.

We sit in silence as expected of knobs.

Waiting. Trying not to look nervous or worse, guilty.

The hallway is busy with cadets of all classes, administrative assistants, and military staff walking about. Aside from housing instruction for all four ROTC branches, Barton is what breathes life into the "military" pillar of Graham; it's what makes Graham a leadership laboratory. Colonel Wright has a staff of several Assistant Commandants who mentor and guide leaders like Coleman or Trevino in their cadet positions. Most of the Commandant's staff are Graham alumni, who wanted to give back to the college after their retirement from the military.

Without warning, Reagan jumps up from her seat. "Oh my god, Ash! I've been so stressed. How was it? Where the questions hard?" I look at my watch. What the hell? Her interview only took fifteen minutes. And she emerged...*smiling.*

"Keep your voice down, Reagan. We're outside the Commandant's Office," I whisper through my teeth. *I swear these two.*

Ignoring me as usual, Ash replies at the same volume, "It was super easy. We aren't supposed to tell anyone what we were asked but you shouldn't worry, Reagan. By the way, that Harvatin guy is totally *hot.* He's in our battalion. On staff. That's who Alexandra was talking about on Saturday at the Solomon's."

"Oooh, that's *him,*" coos Reagan. "Does he really look like—."

"Are you guys fucking for real right now?!" I seize both of them by an arm. "This is serious! Graham is conducting a Corps-wide investigation into sexual activity on campus and all you two can think about is how *hot* some upperclassman is." They stare at me in confused silence. I try to bring a sense of logic into the mix and add, "Reagan, you said yourself at the meeting with Dehenre that you didn't want the girls to get blamed. Well if someone overhears you guys talking like this, they surely are going to blame us and assume we knew where the key was hidden."

Fuck.

"Key? What key, Kensley?" Reagan asks, catching my slip, as she crosses her arms across her chest. "How did *you* know they asked me about a key? They just started the interviews and we weren't suppose to tell *anyone* about the questions we were asked. We have an *Hoooooonor Code* here as you know." Despite the continuous bustle in the hallway around us, the tap, tap, tap of her right shoe on the linoleum floor is the only sound I hear.

Fuck, fuck, fuck.

The wheels in my brain churn quickly, desperately trying to grab onto a thread of logic with an anchor. Trying not to sound too nervous or rattled, I say, matter-of-factly, "We aren't the first girls - and maybe even cadets, to be interviewed. Someone mentioned it. I can't remember who," I reply dismissively, waving my left hand. I'm not waiting another fifteen minutes with these two out here and decide to - brazenly skip ahead of Reagan on the schedule. "I've got to go in now." I shoot at Reagan before I can think, I am skipping ahead of you. At least *try* to keep your gossiping to a low whisper, huh?"

I don't wait for them to retort and raise my right fist to place a singular knock on the wooden conference room door.

A solitary male voice is heard from the other side. "Enter."

This conference room is smaller than the one downstairs, but decorated the same. Dark table in the center. Dark wood paneling on the walls. Heavy drapes. I turn my gaze towards the only other person in the room, but my eyes can't seem to bring his features into balance given the lightening. *I can't entirely trust Ash that she got the upperclassman's name correct.*

I take one step closer, unsure as he didn't give me any directions yet standing near the door doesn't make sense either. (Sometimes I hate being a knob - you are damned if you do and damn if you don't.)

"Come, come, knob," he says nonchalantly as he motions with his right hand while barely looking up from the papers in front of him.

I descend further into the room with each step. As I get closer to the round table he is sitting at, I can see that he's relaxed - almost slouching in his chair. But I know it's him. For once Ash got it right.

Chris Harvatin.

Asshole.

Aside from being a senior in Delta Battalion, he's also in my English Literature class. He's never said anything to me, of course. But that doesn't matter. It's always the same feeling when his type is in the room. A sense of loathing for women at Graham, disdain because he feels he had less of a Graham experience because of us, punctuated with a touch of indifference exemplified through his complete ability to ignore any woman cadet. The irony isn't lost on me that *he* is the one leading this investigation or wait…maybe that is the point. Put a cadet in charge who hates women at Graham and that report will pretty much write itself. Invisibly, I shake the thought out of head before it grows roots. Although, since it has only been four years since assimilation, you couldn't throw a rock at a formation without hitting a cadet in the eye who feels the same way as Harvatin.

I let out a small breath and move my left hand ever so slightly to brace myself against the chair. Waiting for him to give me my next command. There are no discernible noises in the room. It's like being underwater, but somehow I can hear the sound of my own breathing. The air is heavy with the smell of plough mud, salt spray and the bitterness of wax myrtle from the Ashley River. (Damn, that smell is everywhere!)

"Cadet Allen" His voice guides me to the surface like a Siren.

"Sir, no, sir." This won't go over well.

His head jerks up from the papers on the table in front of him. He does a double take fro the paper to me to the paper to me.

"Sir, *no*….sir?" he asks confused putting extra stress on no.

"Sir, no excuse, sir." I mean, technically it is one of three acceptable knob answers. And explaining to him that I was tired of waiting with my gossiping roommates in the hallway was certainly not going to win me or women at Graham any favors.

He shrugs, "Whatever. It's all the same. You don't have to stand at attention throughout the interview. You can sit at the table if you'd like. I want you to be relaxed," Harvatin's cool voice explains.

I nod in acknowledgement. Silently relieved.

No longer framed by the light from the window, I notice his dark-as-night eyes staring cold and empty at me.

Let's get this over with.

I slide into the dark wooden chair at the table.

Harvatin gestures at the piece of paper in front of him. "I'm going to ask you about ten standard questions. Just so you know, everyone in the Corps is being asked the same ones. Not by me *obviously,* but by their Battalion Ombudsman." He flashes a devilish smile as he briefly looks up. I think he's one of those guys who desperately wants you to think he wants women here for the sake of the administration yet everyone knows he doesn't or he would've had a better position senior year than Battalion Ombudsmen. Clearly someone within Barton Hall had a sense of humor when they handed out cadet rank the year prior. Ombudsmen are supposed to be an advocate for cadets, so they've got to be approachable. Softer than the average cadet. Friendly. Even to knobs. *What goes around, come around, douchebag.*

"We're talking to all of the women in the Corps first, but I don't want you to be alarmed." The freshly awarded band of gold on his right ring finger catches a speck of sunlight from the window as he talks and gestures with his hands.

I tune out the rest of his canned introductory statement that he reads in a forced upbeat voice. Does Harvitin remember we're in History of Southern Lit together? I sit one row to his left, three seats back. He probably hasn't noticed. Professor Gish barely refers to me by last name, as I rarely participate for fear of drawing attention to myself - a lone knob, and a woman at that, in a class full of upperclassmen.

It only takes fifteen minutes for him to ask the ten interview questions.

I don't remember the questions.

Or my responses. Mostly, yes or no.

Probably because it doesn't matter anyway.

Harvatin takes one last look at the checklist in front of him. "Okay. That about wraps it up."

I can't decide whether to be amused or alarmed that I want him to have more questions. *Live with no regrets*, Desiree and I always say. I let out a sigh. "Sir, was that all…?"

He hesitates for a moment, a tiny glint in his eye. "Yep. But if you think of anything else, that maybe I didn't ask—anything at all, no matter how insignificant you think it is—don't hesitate to email me via campus email."

I nod, hoping I've sufficiently hidden my disappointment.

"Or you can just hit me up in Gish's class." Guess I was wrong.

"Sir, yes, sir."

As I push open the door to trade places with Reagan, Ash jumps up to greet me "*And*….how'd your interview go?"

I look at her in bewilderment, "Why are you still here?"

"I was…was waiting for you guys. Thought we could walk back together when Reagan is done."

"Um… I've gotta get back to the battalion." Bless her heart. Sometimes it's hard to be mean to Ash. But then I remember, we're at a military college, five years after assimilation. In the South. And sweetness wasn't on the packing list.

Chapter 3: *There was something wicked in the air.*

The status of the investigation gnaws at me. True to the Honor Code none of us shared our interview with each other. Although we rarely get to interact with other women knobs in other companies, I had secretly hoped we would actually have another all women's meeting.

"Hurry the *fuck up*, Callahan," Nelson sneers at his end of the table, bringing me back to lunch mess.

Good Coleman hasn't arrived yet to take her place at our end.

"I'm thirsty." The sound of his fist against the table serves as punctuation yet not before he manages to bulldoze all of the table's silverware, plates and glasses forward into a jumbled pile in the middle of the table. I suppress an eye roll as we stand behind our chairs waiting for the "rest" command by the Regimental Adjutant. (And they say women are dramatic.)

The entire Corps eats all three meals at the same time, together. (After marching to the mess hall, of course.) We sit at tables of fourteen, divided into two sections, each managed by a mess carver - a senior or higher-ranking junior cadet, at either end. Knobs are responsible for most of what does or does not happen at mess. I, along with three of my classmates, sit at Coleman's side of the table. We're like air traffic controllers. Knob knowledge coming in from the left from her or the other upperclassmen at the table, while at the time serving dishes land in the center of the table, silverware and empty glasses refilled at breakneck speed. Plates, silverware, glasses are in their appropriate spot and filled accordingly— for the upperclassmen and us. Wadies—a term of endearment for the women that work at the mess hall—carry large silver trays containing two serving bowls of each dish from the warming cart positioned along the walls of the mess hall to the table. Since we are a family, we eat family style of course. The food may change but it is always the same routine. As soon as we arrive for our meal, we load everything from the metal trays onto the table without a moment's hesitation. There are some days when the four of us are so busy directing plates, silverware, food and knowledge, we barely have time to eat ourselves. (Thank goodness for the hidden stash of food in our room, illegal but oh-so-delicious.)

"Make me a peanut butter and jelly sandwich." Coleman's face carries a stony expression as she takes her place as mess carver. at the head of our side of the table.   My guess is she isn't happy about today's main course: fish. Or maybe she's just particularly annoyed by the constant smell of stale frying grease and bleach hanging in the air.

"Get that other crap away from me." The plates, glasses and serving dishes crash together in an orchestra of annoyance as she pushes them to the center of the table.

"Ma'am, yes, ma'am," we say in perfect unison and almost near harmony.

I serve as personal waiter, of sorts, for Coleman as I sit to her immediate right. Not only do I have to dilute her iced tea with just the right amount of water - take care not to spill a drop of water on the table, but I also have to anticipate her needs before she does. I sometimes don't know what *I* want, let alone what another human being wants. And sometimes she's just faster than I can manage.

"Tooooday, Bennett," Coleman laments as I fumble with the bagged white bread and peanut butter jar. I smash the two bread slices together and hastily but gently, place the sandwich on Coleman's plate. "Take your sweet ass time, why don't you!"

I hastily finish the peanut-butter and jelly sandwich and gingerly place it on her plate with my napkin'ed hand. Approval is given through silence as she picks up the sandwich and slowly eats it piece by piece.

Thankfully, Coleman isn't up for testing my knob knowledge today.   I take a few bites of the rice and fish while stealthy looking around the table to make sure no one is missing or needs anything. Bates punches my left leg under the table, our agreed-upon signal that all of us knobs are done eating and ready to go. Unfortunately we're stuck in our seats until the Regimental Adjutant finishes any announcements at the podium at the front of the mess hall.

Buchanan's throaty "Dismissed!" booms overhead throughout the mess hall. The four of us pop out of our chairs, grab our covers from underneath, and head back to the battalion and afternoon classes in our ubiquitous single-file line.

He's already there when I arrive to Professor Gish's class, History of Southern Literature. There, sitting on top of his desk. Laughing with two other upperclassmen. His broad shoulders squared towards me. His right leg swinging casually, the sharp crease of his grey pants cutting like a knife into whatever it pleases. Into me. A crimson hue smacks me in the face. I duck quickly into the classroom and slide into my seat in the back of the classroom, hopefully unnoticed. This might be the one time where being the only knob and girl in a classroom full of upperclassmen has its advantage.

"Alright, everyone take your seats," Professor Gish directs as he walks to the front of the room. "I want to talk about our class trip in January before today's lesson." History of Southern Literature is a two-semester course, where the second semester is devoted primarily to the study of one southern author or poet. The independent study section starts off with a weekend trip to Savannah. Probably a lot more enticing if you're an upperclassman, but for a knob, a full weekend away from Graham just means you're likely to be called a *shitbag* by your classmates, who believe you've searched high and low for a means to shirk your duties as a knob, cadet, classmate. People are quick to forget that aside from a Band of Gold, Graham also awards its graduates a legitimate bachelor's degree.

"I'm passing around a sheet of paper for everyone to write down your author of choice and the one work of theirs you'll focus on. For now, I'll let you choose, but remember—I've been teaching here for fifteen years. Try not to be lazy and predicable. Or boring."

It takes a certain type of person to choose to be a professor at Graham. While their days certainly aren't filled with marches to meals, physical fitness or Friday afternoon parades, they are required to wear a uniform and most importantly, tolerate myriad reasons for students missing classes or assignments. Someone was called to the Commandant's Office, or they were up all night on guard duty. It's a military college's equivalent of the dog ate my homework. It's not the kind of thing any of our professors would have to put up with at a traditional college.

"This is an upper-level English class, gentlemen. I expect not only for the work to reflect that," he pauses to pull more papers out of the black bag on his desk, "but I also absolutely expect assignments to be handed in on time. No excuses. And no exceptions. In the packet coming around now, you'll notice the due dates. Commit them to memory aaaaand write them down." A low groan erupts from the room.

I take the paper from the upperclassman next to me. Neither one of us attempts to make eye contact with the other. In the two months we've been in class together, he's never spoken to me. Or looked at me. Actually, none of the upperclassmen have spoken to me unless they absolutely have to. I'd like to think we've reached a silent understanding of acceptance, but really I know they think by not speaking to me, I don't really exist and therefore they can claim that there are no women in *their* class.

I quickly scribble my selection onto the paper in blue ink. Cormac McCarthy's *Blood Meridian*—selected specifically for its intensity, violence, and male main character. There's no way the upperclassmen can ridicule my choice, nor will Gish find it predictable.

I cautiously tap the upperclassman in front of me on the shoulder to hand him the paper. "What. The Fuck?" His bright green eyes reflect his contempt as he whips his head around. "Don't ever touch me again, knob," he sneers through his teeth.

A single drop of sweat slides down my spin. "Yes, sir." I swallow hard and try again. "Sir, yes, sir."

He snatches the paper from me like a viper as the room fills with a low hiss—the Graham mark of disapproval. Snakes hiss to warn you; upperclassmen hiss to tell you you've already gone too far.

"Cool it, Eric. Save it for the barracks," a crisp, firm voice speaks from a row over.

"Don't be a tool, Chris. If I'm not allowed to touch a knob…then sure as shit *it's* not allowed to touch me."

"Gentlemen…*is* there a problem?" Gish asks from the front of the room, his glasses perched on the tip of his nose.

"No, sir," the upperclassman replies. Chris smiles at him, as an ombudsman is expected to do. "No problem here. Just a little misunderstanding," he finishes.

"Alright then. You might as well hand that paper back to Thirteen-oh-five." Turning his gaze and attention to me, Gish continues."Thirteen-oh-five, unfortunately I'm not going to allow you to choose your own author and work. You'll be reading Pat Conroy's *The Lords of Discipline*. I think you'll find rather significant symmetry between Will McClean's depiction of the integration of African-Americans at the fictional military college in *Lords* to, well…*your* current situation, Thirteen-oh-five. I think you could bring a pure, honest, intimate perspective that I haven't seen before. One that—."

I tune out whatever else Gish is going to say about why he wants me to read the book. *This book.* To devour every word. Soak it in. Tear it apart and build it back up to a story befitting the present. I'd gladly do that —and so much more, with any other book but this one.

Not with this book.

Please.

———

It was one of those quintessential hot and humid South Carolina summer afternoons. A constant see-saw of confusion between the blast of cold air on your skin one minute and suffocating soupiness the next. We still lived in Columbia then. Dad, wanting to stay close to his alma mater, convinced my mom—a native New Yorker—that life without four seasons would be like being on vacation every day. "After a stressful day, you can just sit out on the porch. Read a book. Sip something cool. Take in the air. You don't have to close your eyes and imagine being some place else." Clearly he was brilliant as a negotiator both in and out of the court room, because she agreed.

It was three weeks before the start of freshman year. High school. Pep rallies. First love. Football games. First heartbreak. The SATs. Cliques. Driver's Ed. College applications. Prom. Graduation. All part of the road to maturity, to adulthood ahead of me. I was just passing through the kitchen for a snack before heading to the mall with "my pack," an affectionate (I think) term coined by Dad for the group of four girls I had been spending all my time with since the days of nap time and recess. Mom pushed a colorfully wrapped square across the kitchen island.

"What's this?" I asked casually after swallowing my mouthful of peanut butter and jelly sandwich.

My mother's face, ripe with schoolgirl giddiness, stood betrayed by the well honed prosecutor's voice. "Something I've had lying around for awhile. I just never knew when to give it to you. But today…today is the *perfect* day." She pushed the package towards me across the granite.

"Okay, mom. I get it. I should open it *now.*" I wiped my fingers, tacky with jelly and gritty with peanut butter, on the back of my shorts. "You had the store wrap this, didn't you?" I asked with a teasing smile. My mom is good with words, not crafts. Her presents were always wrapped by store clerks with commercial perfection. From the weight and feel of it, I knew it was a book. I carefully pried the tape at the seams.

Mom's excitement boiled over. "Oh for god's sake, Kensley. Just rip the paper off already," as she shifts with anticipation.

"So predictable. Presents are supposed to make the receiver happy, not the giver." I did as demanded and tore the colored paper off in one swoop, leaving naked in my hands a fresh, new hardcover edition of *The Lords of Discipline.*

Confused, I stared at the book and then at mom's beaming face. "Thanks, mom. But…but I already have a copy. Remember, Dad gave it to me in third grade when I won that reading award…?"

"Yes, yes, I know. And I also know you lied to your father and told him you read it."

Embarrassment colored my cheeks. Busted.

"Don't worry." She conspiratorially touched my forearm. "I never told him. I'm giving this to you *again*, because today…*today*, Kensley, the South Carolina Supreme Court announced Graham has to admit Shannon Faulkner, not just as a day student but as a full fledged member of the Corps of Cadets."

I was stunned. I'd only passively been following the plight and court case of Dad's alma mater in the news. Due to her male-sounding first name, Shannon Faulkner was accidentally accepted to Graham; when the school realized she was a girl, her admission was revoked, as Graham —although a state-sponsored school, was still all-male, as it had been since its founding in 1842. For three years, Shannon had been fighting the system to regain her admittance. And today…

"Do you know what this means, Kensley?"

I nod slowly, overwhelmed with this roadblock now lifted.

"It means you can go to the same school as your father. And your grandfather. I mean, only if you want to, of course. Don't feel like you have to. I don't want you to feel pressured into going there now. I—*we*, your father and I, will be proud of you wherever you decide to go to college. It's just such a new possibility now. I don't—."

"Mom."

Her rambling stopped mid-sentence. We stared at each other in heavy silence, realizing perhaps the burden I would face - the one all of the women who decided to enroll during the first few years would face. The heavy burden of setting a good example, of not being a stereotype, of showing that women can survive and *thrive* in the Corps of Cadets.

I didn't decide to enroll right then.

Or even that day.

Or that month. Sure Graham had a lot to offer, but nothing that ever enticed me. I heard enough of Dad's reminiscing. Uniforms, marching, inspections. No thank you.

Yet two years later, after everything changed, it was my only option.

The night my mom gave me the book, I drank in every word of *Lords*, barely coming up for air. My eyes burned deep into the night from the small, black type on the cream colored pages. Heavy with fatigue, drops of tears cried out for me to stop. To take a break.

But I didn't.

I became Will. I checked between the pages of three hundred eight and nine of *The Decline of the West* by Oswald Spengler. I watched as my roommate was drummed out of the Institute. I delivered a cold salute to

General Durell at graduation. I always had the option to end it by just closing the book.

But now…I don't.

Gish wants me to snarl my life with Pearce, the first African American cadet at a fictional military college, as a cheap way for me to talk about the things you're not supposed to talk about if you want to fit in —*assimilate*—at Graham.

He wants me to stand out from the grey. After everything that's happened, it's the last thing I want to do.

Chapter Four: *There are a few holier-than-thou deviants among us.*

"Bennett, stop by my room at 0745 to wrap my sash for today's inspection," Coleman says just as I'm leaving breakfast mess.

It's Saturday. One of those Saturdays hated by Graham cadets. Instead of starting General Leave to do nothing at all, we're stuck on campus for a major room and personal uniform inspection by senior military officers of Barton Hall, for the first part of the day.

"Ma'am, yes, ma'am." Always dutiful. I'm Coleman's mentor knob—part of a long-standing Graham tradition where upperclassmen take a knob under their wings and teach them about the inner workings of Graham, and also to ensure they don't get hazed by upperclassmen. I had the cadet stuff down pretty quickly; it's the politics of the Corps that I need help with in order to make rank. In order to show the school women belong here; in order to make my family proud as I continue our own legacy.

Reagan's in the room, halfway through her uniform metamorphosis, when I get back from mess. I quickly throw off my duty uniform, only to button and zip it again before hanging it in my full press, and redress in SMI uniform—heavily starched, white cotton pants and a salt and pepper wool tunic-looking thing. (Whoever thought wool was a good idea for Charleston was clearly masochistic, primed for military college.) Reagan and I take turns helping each other put on the ceremonious cross-webbing attached to our "butt box"—an empty black cartridge box named so because it's supposed to sit well, directly above your butt. In the front, the cross webbing is bound together by a two-by-three-inch, highly shined brass plate, which has an unfortunate resting place smack in between my breasts. I put on my waist belt, also constructed of white webbing, as well as my white gloves. I smooth out any wrinkles in the reflection in the mirror.

I take one last look around.

Everything is where it's supposed to be according to Blue Book regulations. After all, we did spend three hours last night cleaning and polishing every corner of this room over and over again.

Ash freezes my hand on the door handle. "If you're going to Coleman's room…wait for me, *please*?" The politeness isn't enough to cover her pleading. "I've gotta go to Corey's for his sash wrap."

If at all possible, knobs avoid being on the galleries on their own. I lean against the sink by the door, indicating my reluctant acceptance and let our an annoyed sigh. Part of the Corps politics is being a team player with the other women too.

Ash hurriedly throws on her uniform, possessing all the clumsiness of a newborn filly. Her cross webbing is twisted on her back and her shoes would only be considered shined if an actual flashlight cast its beam on them. I asked her once during those first few days why she came to Graham; she was obviously confused by the haircut, the uniform, the marching, the constant smell of brass-o on her hands. "Athletic scholarship," she whispered in the dark after taps one night. It explained everything.

Most of the women at Graham right now are on Corps Squad. The school did a heavy recruiting campaign for women athletes in an effort to not only boost numbers but also increase the flow of Title Nine funding. When Coleman's class first started in 1997, the only sports available were track and cross country. While Graham has several more women's teams now, volleyball and cross country are still the two that bring in the most women athletes. I don't understand why anyone would choose to come to Graham and then be on Corps Squad—male or female. Aside from the constant harassment from the rest of the Corps for missing out on formations, parades, and other Corps events, I would think it'd be tough to juggle academics, practice and games, not to mention the cadet stuff you *can* attend. But I suppose the combination of love of the sport and love of Graham and its traditions is enticing. In the end, those on Corps Squad receive same the ring the rest of us do. For better or worse.

I make it to Coleman's room five minutes late. Damn it.

No words greet me. Just a cold, hard stare that conveys one word: disapproval. Words easily get swallowed up in a sea of grey, yet the pointed looks from upperclassmen hit you like a twenty-foot wave, leaving you gasping for air. For anything.

"Bennett! What the fuck. Are you listening?" Coleman's voice pulls me back to the present.

"Ma'am, yes, ma'am," I reply, not really knowing what I just said yes to.

"Let's get moving. I need to be downstairs for formation in five minutes. And you were late." She points towards her desk. "My sash is in the white box on my desk, and the safety pins and name tag are next to it." Only senior rank holders and juniors in certain positions wear a sash instead of waist plate or butt box.

I retrieve the ten-foot long, six-inch wide wool-blend maroon sash from her desk and begin to wrap it around her waist, taking care that once completed, the bottom tassel hits at her knee and the top tasseled end hits mid-thigh. I secure the overlapping corners with two large safety pins. Any type of movement causes the sash to loosen and sag. A name tag is used to pin the layers together and also to prevent movement but it is so much more than that. It is a link to those that came before you. It's bad luck to use your own name tag. Graham tradition is to wear the name tag of someone you respect, but the name tag has to be handed down to you. Maybe Coleman will give me hers when she graduates?

The final piece of the ensemble is her sword, also passed down from cadet to cadet per Graham tradition. Another link to those that came before us.

"Ma'am, will that be all, ma'am?"

Before Coleman has time to figure out if she needs anything else, the door opens without a knock, admitting the Regimental Commander. My muscles tense. I suffocate the memory from Hell Night.

I want to leave this room.

Now.

I hate this bitch.

With her sweet tea-infused North Carolina accent, Ward exclaims, "Hey Avery! You won't believe this. I was in the admissions office in Anderson Hall yesterday and I heard—."

Coleman raises her hand, stopping Ward mid-sentence, then points at me.

Standing by the empty desk. Bracing.

"Oh…I clearly didn't see the knob in the corner. Did I interrupt a 'mentoring' session of some kind?" Ward asks, her words wet with sarcasm.

"No, Cathy." Coleman rolls her eyes. "Bennet was just giving me a sash wrap for SMI."   Turning to me, she says, "That'll be all, Bennett."

***

The first part of SMI is the physical inspection of our uniforms while standing in company formation on the quad under the unforgiving Charleston sun, all of us just trying to think of anything but the sweat accumulating in every corner of our bodies. The slow trickle of sweat beads rolling down the center of our back and accumulating at our lower back.

A shadow falls over me. Major Hunt, the Delta Battalion Tactical Officer, steps in front of me. He looks me over from cover to shoes without a micro-expression on his face. Coleman standing next to him holding her clipboard at the ready - posed to take down any demerits he bestows on me for anything out of place.

Adrenaline brings a soft quiver to my knees. I know better than to lock them, or I risk cutting off the blood supply and passing out. Falling head-first onto the red and white squares in front of *everyone* to see. It'd be the only thing I would be remembered for throughout the next three years and more fuel for those - cadets and alumni, who think women don't belong at Graham. My mind echos with the common refrain - *too weak, not tough enough, ruined the system, ruined our school.*

Think of something else, Kensley....anything.

"Impeccable uniform, Cadet Bennett."

Like a slap, my mind snaps back to reality.

Absofuckinglutely!

"Sir, thank you, sir." I bite the inside of my cheek to keep from smiling at my gaudiness and steal a quick glance at Coleman, who's expression doesn't betray approval or disapproval.

Once the entire company is inspected, we head to our rooms to wait for Major Hunt and other cadet leadership to walk through. Being on third division, I already know we'll be waiting for at least forty-five minutes. Waiting in our rooms wouldn't be so bad if we could sit down or turn on our computers. But no one dares to move anything after our marathon cleaning session. Ash, an extrovert, can't stand the silence.

"We're going to our host family's house after this. Soooooo looking forward to it. I'll probably sleep for like three hours today," she drones on. "You?"

"I've got to go downtown to get some things. Then I'll probably go to the Corbitt's. I think Max is meeting me there."

I regret mentioning Max the second his name passes my lips.

A chorus of girlish oohs and aaahs explodes like fireworks across the room from the two of them. "What's going on with you two anyway? I know you normally just meet at your host family's house but I've seen you chat in the library and in the halls after class too."

TMZ would be proud, Ash. I don't know why I have to constantly explain to them that I am not interested in dating a cadet. My objections are met as usual by eye rolls, but at least it kills the subject and brings the welcomed silence back.

To keep busy, I remember to spritz a bit of furniture polish all around the room. Some upperclassmen told us to do that before each SMI. "A clean smelling room is automatically a clean room." I don't question wisdom handed down from generation to generation.

Finally, Major Hunt, flanked by Coleman, Corey, and Trevino, enters and begins to inspect our tiny alcove of a room. We brace instantly, watching in silence as they each maneuver around the room like a dance taking care not to bump into each other or us. They each run their white gloves over the light above the sink, across the railing between our bunk beds, and across the top of the door. I hold my stare straight ahead as Coleman checks to see if all the zippers are zipped on our uniforms in our full press.

"Looks good, knobs! Keep it up," Major Hunt says matter-of-factly as they exit. I hate how two hours of work is rewarded by just two minutes of time.

"So…we didn't get any demerits, right?" Ash asks once the door closes.

"Nope. Feels good, right?" Maybe now they understand why I wanted to clean the room so thoroughly last night.

Reagan glares at me. "You are always such a fucking show off, Kensley."

I open my mouth to retort yet on second thought decide it isn't worth it. She isn't worth it. I doubt she will come back to school after Christmas furlough anyway.

I bolt to the bathroom as soon as the lone bugle note marks the end of SMI, sparing some understanding for the guys who pee in the sink in their rooms. When I get back, Ash and Reagan are already gone. Typical. The room is sprayed with a confetti of webbing and stray uniform items discarded in a rush. *They'll never learn.* I neatly lay my white webbing in the top drawer of my half press so it doesn't get dirty, and wrap my breast plate in a polishing cloth to keep it from getting scratched.

We still have to wear our uniforms out into town. Not until I'm a senior can I wear something a bit more comfortable, albeit still a uniform —grey pants and a blue blazer. As cadets, we're required to follow the "two bridges" rule: we can only wear civilian clothing if we've crossed a minimum of two bridges. Two bridges, and you're part of normalcy again. Well, at least most of the women have to follow that rule. We are constantly in the spotlight. Someone is always looking and waiting for us to fuck up. The actions of a college student used as fodder for the justification as to why Graham should be private and all-male.

I've got fifteen minutes till the next bus downtown arrives in front of the main gate at Graham. Plenty of time to get there at the pace we're forced to walk around campus. I send Max a quick email letting him know I'll be at the Corbitt's around 1400 hrs, and hustle to make the bus.

———

The bus drops me near the open air market, smack in the center of downtown Charleston. I walk through even though I don't ever buy anything yet I do like to people watch. Tourists in their tennis shoes and shorts, clutching crumbled sweaty paper maps in one hand and an unruly toddler with the other. Pumpkin spice lingers in the air. The midday fall sky is a soft blue that bleeds into purple and red earlier and earlier as the days grow shorter. Looking at the various trinkets makes me forget for a moment that I'm a cadet. I feel like just another person bustling about, doing whatever it is an average person does on Saturday morning.

But I'm not like everyone else.

I'm a Graham cadet. I have to be here. For Mom. For me.

I may be able to pretend for a moment that I'm just like everyone else, but it doesn't take much for me to notice the people staring at me, whispering behind their hands. The stark reminder that not everyone in Charleston is happy to see forced modernity at their beloved institution. Women are still an anomaly at Graham, and therefore a tourist attraction when downtown. Something to be gawked at. There's constant pressure to be perfect. At academics, physical fitness, in public, and most importantly, cadet life. The only thing to do is to hold my head high, as if it doesn't bother me. And to keep walking.

I quickly make my purchase and head back to the number 171 bus stop in front of Showers and More—a big-box store that sells body wash, lotion, hand soaps and the like. No matter how many times I've been here, the bright blues, vivid greens, and deep reds of the liquid-filled plastic bottles and jars are for the first few seconds foreign to me, a stark contrast to the grey and black and white of Graham. We aren't really supposed to wear perfume, but no male upperclassman is going to point out if we smell good. And besides, body spray isn't a perfume.

"That'll be eight dollars and fifty-five cents, si—oh sorry, I mean, ma'am." The clerk's face reddens at the mistake. "Not something we're used to yet," she says softly without making eye contact.

I nod and smile, a southern smile that is sweet on the surface but sharp and biting underneath. *What a lame ass excuse.*

I check out with five minutes to spare before the number 171 bus transports me back towards campus. This time, however, I exit the bus two stops before the front gate and walk half a mile down Beauregard Avenue, a side street lined with live oak overflowing with Spanish moss, towards the Corbitt's house. Every out-of-state cadet is given the option of a host family during their first year, to ease the transition. Born and raised until my sixteenth birthday in South Carolina, I bristled at the idea at first. I hated being categorized as an out-of-state cadet - a foreigner again, a distinction that only further alienated me from the good 'ole boys in the Corps. But my current residence is New York City, so there was no getting out of this one.

Host families are a kind of sanctuary. A place to relax, if even for a moment. To watch some television. To change into sweat pants that don't have a Graham logo on them, or the last four of your social security number and surname sewn into them. A place to do laundry with non-industrial soap. A place to meet other cadets from outside of your own Battalion. A place to eat whatever you like. A place to be you.

"Hellloo?! It's me. Is anyone here?" I shout as I let myself in through the wooden front door. Host families are generally Graham alumni, though on occasion are Graham faculty and staff. And they always host more than one cadet.

"In the den!" Max calls. Max Brown. Knob. Classmate from Ninth Company.

Max is enjoying a bowl of pistachios on the dark colored couch, while Tad is leaned back in the 1970s-style recliner, out of place in the modern room. Neptune, Tad's Doberman mix, sleeps on his back in his bed by the window.

"Hello there, Cadet Bennett." A sarcastic grin punctuates his greeting. Tad's a '65 Eighth Company grad who elected not to go into the military but remained in the private sector instead, much like my dad. Originally from North Carolina, he attended law school in San Francisco after Graham. It was an eye-opening, interesting time for a Southerner and graduate of a military college. He always jokes that he was accepted there to balance the anti-war protests on campus. Eventually he became a judge in the 9th Circuit, only to retire two years ago and settle down in

Charleston. He and his wife, Gwendolyn, have one son and one daughter, neither of whom decided to attend Graham.

"Hey Tad. Sorry I'm late. Had to run some errands first." I plop next to Max and steal a handful of pistachios, realizing only now I forgot to get lunch downtown. "Anyone else here?"

"Stacey and Dean where. But…they went to Mt. Pleasant. And then I think they're getting stuff for dinner tonight. We voted without you to have spaghetti and garlic bread. Hope that's okay with you?" Tad adds with a raised eyebrow.

I roll my eyes. "Sir, yes, sir." I'll take anything not served in the mess hall on a silver tray. while sitting on the front 3 inches of my chair.

Stacey Martin and Dean Gilmore are both sophomores from 5th Company. Usually the school tries not to put knobs from the same company together in the same host family, but computer glitches happen. I haven't talked much to Stacey this year, as she keeps mainly to herself. I do know that she wants to go to law school after Graham, which is why I assume she got paired up with Tad. I haven't heard anything good or bad about her as a cadet. My guess is that she's not pursuing rank, and therefore no one in the Corps cares about her.

"I'm sorry your father didn't make it down for Parents' Weekend," Tad says solemnly, cautiously. I bite the inside of my cheek to counter the warmth filling my eyes. "I know it was your first big weekend at Graham. Having him here would've been extra special. I know it's hard to see all your classmates with their parents, giving room tours, eating at the mess hall, taking lots of pictures." He pauses for a moment, searching for something more upbeat to say. "There are two more big weekends still ahead of you—Homecoming is just around the corner, and Corps Day in March."

I can only nod. I don't want to talk about my dad not coming down. He knows what the inside of the barracks looks like. What the food in the mess hall tastes like. Besides, I didn't really *need* him to be here last weekend. I think.

Taking my silence for exactly what it is, disappointment, Tad quickly adds, "And besides, the only Parents' Day that matters is your senior year when you get your ring."

I inhale deeply to keep my voice from betraying me. "He wanted to come, but he has a big case right now. Bad timing and all. He said he'd be here for Homecoming though, since it's his twenty-five year reunion, too."

"I have laundry in right now but it should be done in about fifteen minutes if you want to throw yours in, K." Thank you, Max, for the life raft to this conversation.

"Ugh. I forgot to bring my laundry bag. Busy week and all."

"*Oh yea*?! Busier than usual?" A sly grin passes across Tad's face. "It shouldn't be… 'cause I know after they allowed women into Graham, standards went down. At least that's what I read in the paper, so it *must* be true."

Ah yes, Caroline's Corner. That weekly fluff piece in the local paper. What does she know about being a woman at Graham? She has no experience as a cadet. Her latest piece quoted some random girl that started with Coleman's class. I don't think anyone had heard of her before. She claimed that everyone at Graham was "mean" to her—even the professors—and that Graham was "too hostile to foster a successful academic environment." Someone who speaks out against the college and their peers isn't worthy of being a Graham grad anyway. It's obvious she's just looking for her fifteen minutes of fame, not to mention someone to blame for her personal failures. For her weakness. The truth is, not everyone is cut out to be here.

Dad told me his knob year roommate "couldn't hack it so he had to pack it" before the end of first semester. Graham demands a lot of a person, period. Better she found out early and bounced. Not everyone is going to make it for one reason or another —something I knew even before reading *Lords*.

I let out a dry laugh. "No one paid attention to that article. You know the real tension on campus is the—." I catch Max's eye before finishing.

Right.

Tad doesn't know about the Field House incident or the ensuing Corps-wide investigation. How in the world did this not leak to the alumni network yet?

"Oh, pray tell. The lawyer in me is all ears."

How can I play this off? How in the world can I play this off? Fuck.

"You know how it is so close to Christmas," I pivot. Poorly. "Thirty knobs trying to decide how to decorate the company with Christmas lights and other holiday decorations *always* causes tension." I add an eye roll for extra dramatics. "When's dinner?" Terrible change of subject but it's the best I got.

"Okay. I get it, kiddo. I was a cadet once. Sometimes it's best that what happens in the barracks, stays in the barracks," Tad say's as I escape upstairs before I slip and say something I shouldn't.

Thirty minutes later, the old wooden stairs creek under Max's socked foot. Thank goodness he didn't make it too obvious and immediately follow me. He's going to make a great foreign correspondent one day with instincts like that. We met at the Graham beach house at the end of Hell Week. Knobs are bussed there the day the rest of the Corps returns to campus, to keep us out of the way as they unpack, unload, and move into their rooms. We spent most of the day sleeping and worrying about our return to campus that afternoon. Up till then, we had only been around the cadre - those training in how to train us. Yet the return of the

Corps means more eyes on us, more judgement, and more faces and names to memorize. When the moment finally came for us to march back into Delta Battalion, hundreds of bodies were draped over the railings on all four divisions, hungry and eager for their first glimpse of us. Fresh meat. AC/DC's *Welcome to the Jungle* serving as the appropriate soundtrack for the moment.

"That was close." Max sprawls flat on his back on the beige carpet.

"Um…no kidding. Did you know before today that Tad, or better yet *none* of the alumni, seem to know about the 'incident'?"

Max shakes his head. "I sometimes forget how cut off from the world we are. No phones in our rooms, no television, slow internet connections, and of course no time to read the paper."

"Except for knob knowledge."

"Right. There's that. But something like this would've—*should've* —made it through the alumni network who is *always* hungry for Corps gossip."

"Now that I think about it, Jeremy would've sent me whatever he saw bouncing around the alumni bulletin boards if something leaked." Jeremy Rowland conducted my first interview for Graham during the application process. He was against assimilation at first, but something changed his mind. Selfishly, I'd like to think it was seeing that in the end, girls who choose Graham are no different than guys who choose Graham. But he probably just realized he should be on the right side of history.

"Yea, I agree. The LAMC foundation would've been all over this in a New York minute," Max adds. He's right. If you didn't know better, you'd think the LAMC Foundation is the official alumni association of Graham. Since the South Carolina Supreme Court's ruling, the LMAC Foundation has never missed an opportunity to set up a tent at a football game seeking donations or capitalizing on a moment when a woman cadet made a mistake. The worst part? For the last four years, they've had an inside man on campus. No one knows who it is, but conventional wisdom says that the speed at which LAMC members learn about every little incident on campus must mean their source is a member of the Corps. Except it would mean that that cadet was already reporting to the LAMC Foundation since he was a knob.

Knowing better, I ask, "How have things been with Malone in the company?"

Frederick Malone. Son of Matthew Malone, President of the LAMC Foundation. The Corps' pride and joy. Malone was the favorite choice for Regimental Commander for this year's senior class: Perfect grade point average. Regimental Clerk for both semesters his sophomore year. Regimental Sergeant Major his junior year. He checked all the boxes and then some. Yet the one box he couldn't check—the female one—kept him from being this year's Regimental Commander. Rumor on campus is that he bombed his rank board interview. Walked in there arrogant, sure of himself. So when he was offered Charlie Battalion Commander, and learned Ward would be RC… he turned the rank down out of protest, spite, and principle. The position was beneath him. (His words.) So now Malone is a senior private, stripped—in his mind—of his rightful rank.

I guess Malone thought the administration would cave and make him Regimental Commander, in light of his dad's position with LAMC and all the money the Foundation has raised over the years. He miscalculated. Now, in an ironic twist, his bare uniform shoulder boards make Malone a martyr in the eyes of alumni and cadets.

Max gives me a displeased look and adds sarcastically. "Um… well, we don't talk much. Him being a senior and me a knob and all."

"That's not what I meant and you know it." I flash Max an ironic smile. "What I meant was, have you overheard any chatter on the galleries?"

Max shakes his head.

"What about rumors?"

Again, Max shakes his head. "No more than the usual gossip."

We sit in silence for a few seconds.

"Wait." I turn to Max with a sudden thought. "Were you guys told at your meeting not to say anything to anyone outside of the college?" Dehenre definitely didn't warn us.

"Well, sort of." Max nervously plays with the threads of the carpet. "I mean, it was just…sort of implied. Plus, who would I talk to about an investigation about the Field House?" Max pauses. "But, then again, I don't know what the upperclassmen were told at their meetings. Plus, who knows…given the high profile nature of this, maybe Colonel Wright or even General Gentry talked to Malone in private."

Maybe. Maybe the Commandant of Cadets and President of the College talked to a senior private alone, about an incident that prior to that night they didn't know anything about. It wouldn't be beyond the realm of possibility. Through his previous year's position within the Corps, Malone did report regularly to them.

But it still doesn't explain the complete radio silence on this across the alumni network. This is *just* the type of thing the LAMC Foundation would use as an additional talking point in their never-ending diatribe about why Graham should revert to being all-male. And probably make a bumper sticker or two with some catchy phrase like - *Save the Males.*

"Maybe they're saving it for later…?" Max muses. "Lieutenant Colonel Preston showed me an internal memo the other day. It said this is the last year the Department of Justice is giving the LAMC Foundation to raise enough money to privatize Graham." Max was the editor of his high school school paper in San Francisco. Here, he's on staff at *The Commodore*—Graham's paper. Being the only knob on the *Commodore*'s staff has been a rough battle for him, kind of like me being the only knob in Gish's class. All of his story ideas have been shot down by the upperclassmen. I hate to see him frustrated. But he does get to learn about internal Graham politics and Corps gossip.

"*Privatize*?!" I let out a shaky laugh. "Geez. Pretty sure that fucking ship has sank." I swallow my annoyance. "Look, obviously some women don't belong here. I can certainly name a few. But the same can be said for male cadets. What would that even look like? It would be a logistical nightmare." I begin to pace back and forth in the small room as my mind races through a maze of possibilities. "I could potentially *not* have a college to return to next year, Max! What the fuck. Is this a *real* memo?" This can't happen. It can't be an option. I need Graham so I can make things right.

"K, let's not have the logic train derail," Max nearly whispers.

I take a deep breath and rejoin Max on the carpet.

"It just isn't going to happen, K. These guys have been fighting for privatization for five years. And look how far they've gotten. There would have to be some major scheming to create the perfect storm to energize the fundraising." He pauses, eyeing the door. When he continues, his voice is all but a throaty whisper. "You promise you won't say anything?"

I lower my voice to match his and cock my head. "About what?"

"What I'm about to tell you."

I nod.

"Preston showed me that internal memo because he wants me to write a piece about the LAMC Foundation. He hasn't even shared the idea with the editor of the paper. And I'm not sure how I'm going to pull it off, honestly. As soon as I start asking questions and requesting interviews, the cat will be out of the bag. Plus…*hello*, I'm a knob." He pauses. "But Preston said there's something not right about the timing of the discovery of the Field House scandal. Like, it just came out of the blue. Who reported it? Why was the investigation launched in such a dramatic manner on Ring Night of all nights? It completely took away from the Class of 2001's night. "

I stare at him in disbelief…and *astonishment.* Max can't be part of the investigation. He just can't. And he certainly cannot write about it.

For the second time tonight, I'm forced to steady my voice. "Wow! That's awesome, Max." I try to feign support. "What a great opportunity for youHave you made any discoveries yet?"

Max shakes his head. "Preston just told me about this on Wednesday. All I've done is brain storm." He holds up a blue spiral notebook. "In between sweep details, knob runs, and heel-and-soling my shoes….and oh, going to class and studying." We both laugh at the absurdity of Preston's request. A knob investigating the largest alumni group at Graham is impossible on practically every level. Maybe Preston assigned the task to Max cause he wants it to fail?

Alone with my thoughts later that night in the battalion, I relive my conversation with Max. He never really gave me his true opinion about the Field House investigation. Maybe that was by design. *Maybe* he thinks Graham should privatize. What did he say exactly… *The LAMC Foundation should've jumped all over this.* That sounds like he sides with them. I told him how I feel; that's when he should have offered me his opinion.

Stop, Kensley. He is your friend and classmate. Not everyone hates women here.

But he does have Malone in his company—a company that hasn't had to assimilate any female cadets. It's so easy to give into peer pressure when we live and study together twenty-four hours a day. We all make choices based on the context of our environment.

It's what you have to do to survive.

It's what you have to do to be part of the Corps.

Chapter 5: *Our survival lay in our solidarity.*

"Bennett! Did you pick up the sheets from the laundry yet? Remember, we want to work on the banner this afternoon during general leave. Homecoming is this weekend... so we don't have a lot of time to get this done," Callahan barks at me as we all are gathered in the squad room before formation.

For every big weekend—Parent's Weekend in October, Homecoming in November, and Corps Day in March—knobs are required to make a company banner to hang from fourth division during open barracks. We're supposed to come up with a unique design that embodies the spirit of the company. I have yet to figure out what 15th Company's spirit is. If you asked the rest of my classmates, it would be "just the good ole boys," but generally no one asks anyone or comes up with any ideas. They just end up painting the banner with a flag of South Carolina and then the names of all seniors from that company. Back in the "old Corps," there was an unspoken tradition among Battalions and Companies to see which knob class could come up with the largest. At some point, the administration ruled that the banner can be no larger than four queen-size bed sheets sewn together. I guess competition between the companies got out of hand. As if banner size reflected... well, never mind.

I know I dropped off the sheets last Friday to the tailor shop on campus before parade last week. The seamstress said they'd be done by Tuesday—.

Shit.

Today is Wednesday.

Fuck. I forgot to pick it up.

"They said it wouldn't be ready till after lunch today." I lie to save face. "It's on my to-do for after class this afternoon." Another lie.

Clinton Callahan is not a classmate you want to look weak in front of. *Ever.* He's also from a Graham legacy family, except his roots run deeper than mine. Probably all the way to the founding of Graham. I think nearly every male Callahan in his family tree is a Graham alumnus. Growing up, Clinton probably didn't even know there were other colleges in the United States.

Although we don't have class leaders as knobs, Callahan has sort of taken on the de facto role. Everyone, including upperclassmen, accept him, and routinely goes to him when information needs to be passed to all of us. Knob life definitely seem easier for him. He hasn't officially said it, but I know he wants to be company clerk next year. The company commander selects two sophomores for the position, one for each semester. Military bearing and appearance and grades are taken into account, but there's a bit of favoritism involved—and popularity. It's not a beauty contest; the clerk interacts with nearly every single person in the company at one point or another—dropping off company mail, reminding people of training schedule changes, and of course carrying the company guide-on during parades. Depending on who from the current junior class will be selected as Company Commander next year, means I will have a fair or no chance at all. Or better said - some juniors will be more accepting of having a female guide-on bearer next to them at parade.

Callahan is my biggest competition for the position of first semester company clerk—the preferred position as it comes first. Personally, I think he's a pompous ass and we won't ever be anything close to acquaintances, but I have to get him to at least *accept* me. He has to believe that out of all the women at Graham, I am the one most worthy and …tolerable. That I'm *just* like him. I've got to do one more push up than him, run one second faster, ooze the smell of brass-o. I can't slack off for any reason. I need him on my side. It'll soften the blow for him, and the others if,—no, *when* I'm company clerk first.

I decide to pick up the sheets immediately after lunch. With the tailor shop right behind the mess hall, I can drop them off in my room and still make it to my 1300 class. Yet the lines at the tailor shop aren't playing ball with my grand plan. I get in what appears to be the mildly faster-moving queue and try to contain the urge to tap my foot in annoyance.

"Psst, Kensley," Max whispers from the other line.

Geez. He's no better than Ash. I acknowledge him with a nod. Last thing I need is to get busted for "chatting it up" with all these upperclassmen around. Out of the corner of my eye, Max's mouth is forming a bunch of words while pointing to the door. He's obviously not giving up. Peripheral lip reading isn't my strong suit, either. If I just ignore him, he'll figure it out.

"I have a pick-up for Bennett," I tell the tailor shop attendant when its my turn.

"Last four of your social, sweetheart." Her southern twang making you feel less like a stranger.

How could I forget? "One three oh five," I recite robotically.

After a few minutes, a brown paper package containing four sewn-together white bed sheets sits tucked under my arm. I check my watch and realize I'm definitely going to be late to Gish's class—the one class I don't want to be late to. And definitely not with this package in hand as Professors aren't keen on cadets being late to their class for Corps business.

"What are you scowling about?" Max asks, waiting for me between the double doors of the building. Whatever it is, I'm sure it can wait.

"I wasn't scowling. This is my normal face."

His facial expression makes it clear that he doesn't believe me. But he doesn't challenge it and gets to the point. "Listen, I need to talk to you. We've both got class now and I assume you guys are painting your banner this afternoon too?"

I nod.

"I would've talked to you at Tad's over the weekend but you didn't show up. But this is important. Can we meet during ESP tonight?"

This is going to interrupt my study time and finals are just four weeks away. But Max is being insistent, and arguing with him will only make me more late. Besides, maybe it's about the secret investigation he's doing. Definitely need to meet Max for that.

"Okay, do you want to come to my room at 2000?" Normally knobs don't go to each other's battalions. Too risky. You could be asked knob knowledge by upperclassmen you don't know. Max hesitates, as the same thoughts percolate in his mind, but the budding investigative reporter and the inability to come up with another private places to meet, overrules. "Yeah, I'll see you at 2000."

I get to Gish's class out of breath, damp with sweat, and fifteen minutes late. A sharp pain in my right shin reminds me that our black leather uniform shoes offer little cushioning.

"Welcome, Thirteen-oh-five! Hope my class didn't interfere with tea time at the president's house. But I see you brought a present to make up for it." I freeze at the back of the room. Wow, Gish holds a grudge. I've only missed his class once, when Dehenre made all female knobs meet at General Gentry's house during the second week of school. You can't say no to the president of the college. The judgment of eleven set of eyes accompany me slowly to my desk.

"Wellll, Thirteen-oh-five? Did it?"

"No excuse, sir." I slide into my seat and drop the package on the floor next to me with a flat smack. The sweat from my arm has left a gangly imprint on the brown paper.

A look of disappointment washes over his face. "Fine, Thirteen-oh-five. Take the easy way out. Get with one of your classmates about the assignment I passed out before your arrival." Not surprisingly, an audible hissing takes hold of the room as soon as Gish uses the word "classmate."

I keep my head down to hide the flush crawling up my neck. To hide the hurt their rejection causes. I'll be damned if I let them see their childish antics bother me.

I keep my head low and pen moving for the remainder of the class. I was already late so I don't need further harassment from Gish or the upperclassmen.

"Hey Bennett, Gish was just messing around with you," Chris says as I rummage through my knobby bag after class is dismissed. "He isn't strict on the military protocol stuff like some of the other teachers." What the fuck. Chris waited until nearly everyone left the classroom before speaking to me.

Speaking. To. Me.

He takes a step closer to my desk. "He was disappointed because he wanted you to reply with something creative. That's why he was so harsh."

My mind is frantically searching for a clever rejoinder—or really any response that won't make me sound like an idiot. Or a knob. This is some sort of test, right? I come up empty. But I've got to keep him in conversation. Here. Now. I nod and smile, almost mad at myself for acting like Ash about this ass.

He smiles back. Lunch does a somersault in my stomach. Oh god, I hope I don't smell like knob—a mixture of sweat and boiled laundry. (Right, cause everything else about me screams girls.) I cast the thoughts aside quickly.

He's an upperclassman. And a dick. That's what I need to remember.

"Since you missed the beginning of class," a wink flutters my way, "I'll be happy to meet up later and give you all the details. I'm having an early dinner with my dad downtown tonight. I can swing by your room around …say 2000?"

I nod, unsure if I should respond with a preferred knob answer.

"Perfect. I'll see you then."

***

"*Finally!*" Callahan says, throwing his hands in the air like the drama queen he is.

My classmates, dressed in physical fitness uniform, look as if they've been waiting for hours in the squad room. Really, I know it hasn't been more than ten minutes.

"Wait, where are Allen and Pitchford? They better be coming to fucking paint, too." Hunter disparagingly shakes his head before I even respond.

West throws more fuel onto the fire. "Yea, this is bullshit. They already didn't help with the banner for Parents' Weekend. Shitbags!"

Others follow suit in solidarity.

"Well, Bennett?" Callahan glares at me. As if all women are telepathically connected and thus know each other's whereabouts at all times.

"Um…what's today…Wednesday?" Stalling for time. "They're at volleyball practice. They have an away game this weekend, so Coach Megan called for a practice session this afternoon."

"What? I'm on Corps Squad and I'm here. So why the fuck aren't *they*?" Hunter is only sort of right. He *is* Corps Squad, but he plays baseball, which doesn't start practice until January. (Even I know that.) And besides, Parrish and Singleton aren't here either because of some Army ROTC obligation. But no one seems to ask about them.

I just shrug and say nothing to defend them.

We head outside to the rear sally port between 15th and 16th Company, which is rarely used as a means to enter or exit the Battalion.

Cadets just store bikes and kayaks there. We spread out the banner on the red concrete and begin dividing up tasks. More accurately, *Callahan* divides up tasks for us. Since Callahan and Lawrence came up with the main design for the banner, they're blocking it out on the sheets. It's a simple skull and cross bones at the center, but the numbers '0' and '1'—the senior class's year—are replacing the bones. How creative but I guess it is a step up from just the flag of South Carolina. The names of all the seniors are going to be stenciled on either side. I know it's futile to argue with Callahan, or anyone else, about the design—or lack thereof. While some of us work on the stenciling, others untape and retape the stencils together to form the names of the seniors - we were only able to get two packs of stencils. We work mostly in silence as expected. Only the occasional whisper of "Pass me the next name," or "Pass me the black marker" or "You're in my space" breaks our rhythm. We work until evening formation. The finished banner will be kept—*where else*—in Callahan's room until Saturday morning.

After dinner, I settle into my desk. Headphones. Classical music. Spanish homework. Although who am I kidding? I can't focus knowing Chris will be here in ninety—no, eighty-nine minutes. Right here in my room. But I have to try.

"You aren't going to study in the library tonight?" Ash asks. "What gives?"

Play it cool. "Oh, you know …sometimes I like to break routine. Plus, I read a study the other day that it's good for the brain and learning process to change your environment every now and then." I don't even believe my own bullshit. And clearly Ash doesn't either because she gestures to Reagan with a raised eyebrow. But they leave me be.

Lost in verb conjugation, I miss the knock on the door. Which is why it's particularly surprising to see… *Max* standing in front of me.

Chapter Six: My hands smelled of Brasso and Kiwi polish.

Shit!

My embarrassment in Gish's class, combined with my brain's inability to make sense of my hate and like for Chris, led to me double-booking myself. Lucky for me, Max is fifteen minutes early. I got this.

"Hey, Kensley. I got here a little early. Hope that's okay."

"Absolutely. I've got a ton of homework to do anyway, so the earlier is better." I choose my words carefully. "So what did you want to talk about?"

We're both just now realizing that meeting in my room wasn't the best idea. Max tosses a sideways glance in Ash and Reagan's direction, while my roommates do a poor job of pretending not to be interested.

"Hey Reagan...um, will you go with me to Dane's room to get biology notes?" Reagan suddenly asks.

"What? *Now?*"

"Yes. I can't seem to find mine."

Ash tosses me a wink as she and Reagan walk out the door. My lips mouth "thank you" before my brain smacks me to reality.

Of course, they leave the door slightly ajar per Blue Book.

I waste no time. "Okay, they're gone. What did you want to talk about? I got the impression it's was pretty urgent."

Max takes a few seconds to get back on track. "So far, only the women in the Corps have been interviewed for the Field House scandal. They've all been asked the same mundane ten questions that don't provide any new—."

"Any new information," I finish for him, gesturing for him to get on with it already. "Remember, *I'm* a woman in the Corps too. I was already interviewed."

"That's not what I meant. I meant all of the women from all four classes."

"So." I take a second to think. "Wait…you're saying that no *male* cadets have been interviewed?" Max shakes his head. "How's that possible? It's been like, five weeks since the scandal broke. Even with classes and parade, there should've been enough time. More than enough."

He shakes his head in equal confusion. "I don't know, K. But that's not what I wanted to talk to you about actually." He leans up against the half-press as he settles into the conversation. "Preston told me that his contact at the *Low Country Gazette* gave him a heads up today that another editorial will come out in the paper this weekend."

"During *Homecoming*?" A shiver runs down my spine. Perfect timing for max readership. "Do you know what it's gonna say?"

"Not directly. Preston said it includes interviews from two other female cadets who left within the last three years. They're going to talk about some sort of game the upperclassmen made them play at mess." He's lowered his voice practically beyond a whisper as if the walls had ears. I lean forward—faces nearly touching—to make sure I catch every whisper.

"*Game*? What does that mean? What's the school saying about this? That makes no sense—."

A knock at the door.

Reflexively, I shout "Decent!"—an indication that everyone in the room is dressed and it's okay to enter. I realize a second too late who's standing on the other side of the door.

Fuck.

Instantly, Max and I brace as Chris walks into the room.

Why has everyone conspired to mess up my timing today? Late, early—what happened to right on time?

I hope Max is current on his knob knowledge and push-ups cause this could go bad quickly.

Chris's face is expressionless. "Knob! I need to ask you some more questions about your interview the other day."

"Sir, yes, sir."

"Alone." He casts a firm stare at Max. "Beat it."

"Sir, yes, sir," Max says, grabbing his cover and knobby bag off the half press in one swipe.

Whew. That was easier than I thought.

"Wait! You're not in this battalion, knob... " Chris jerks his head to look at Max's name tag. *"Brown."*

Busted.

"Sir, no, sir. This cadet private..."

"I didn't ask you for your family history, knob."

"Sir, yes, sir." Max learned his lesson and stops there.

"What the fuck are you doing here? What class do you have together? Do you know who I am?" Chris quizzes Max in typical knob-knowledge fashion by firing off questions quicker than anyone can reply. Multiple questions are asked at the same time to heighten stress and increase confusion. It's even more intense when multiple upperclassmen are asking questions at the same time. Instinctively, the fight-or-flight response kicks in. Some knobs shut down and stop responding entirely, retreating into themselves like turtles and not responding at all. Others attempt to beat the upperclassmen at their game by striking back with one of the three acceptable knob responses, only to realize too late, once frustration and fatigue have set in, that they're always a swing behind the pitcher. Faces turn red on both sides. The interrogators raise their voices. Profanity is interspersed with every other word. It's an unwinnable game for knobs no matter how you choose to play it.

Max chooses to swing. "Sir, no, sir."

"You don't know who I am? Are you fucking kidding me?" Chris's spit splatters the left side of Max's face. "You dare to come into *my* battalion unprepared? Clearly standards over in Charlie Battalion are slipping. You know what, I'm not even going to waste my time on you, smack. Get the fuck out of my sight before I drop you for push ups."

Max scrambles to leave the room as quickly as possible choosing this time to not play the game.

"And don't let me catch you in this fucking Battalion again!" Chris shouts after him.

Alone with Chris, I just now realize how fast my heart is beating. For Max? For Chris? I stand there, continuing to brace.

The silence breaks. "You can stop bracing for now. I can't have a conversation with you like that. In fact, just act normal."

Normal? *What the hell is normal?*

I give it my best shot. Well, I at least stop bracing.

"Why was he in here? Are ya'll friends? I hope I didn't interrupt anything there, Bennett?" Chris says more rhetorically, looking around the room.

"Sir, no…no." The normal conversational diction sounds almost foreign to my ears but at least I still responded the right way. "We're at the same host family. He was just here to ask me a question. I didn't know he was coming." I lie. Well, technically I just forgot.

"Oh, okay," Chris says flatly. "Is this your family?" He's pointing at the photo collage in the eight-by-eleven frame on my desk. (We're allowed to have only one frame as cadets.)

"Yes." I smile at the reminder of one of the few good memories between us of late. "That's me and my dad on top of the World Trade Center last summer. Class of '75. He's a corporate lawyer in New York. He's coming down for Homecoming this weekend. It's pretty exciting. It'll be the first time he'll see me in uniform. I mean, he's seen pictures, obviously. But it's different in person. Plus I can show him my room. Okay, also not exciting for him since he's a grad and all. But maybe we can even take a photo in front of the company letter. And he'll get to see me march in parade. Not that he hasn't marched in his own parades plenty of times…"

The flow of words surprises me. Maybe its because I am so rarely asked about anything personal. About me. It's always about academics, knob knowledge, the next thing on the training schedule. It can be all consuming to the point you end up a supporting actor to Graham. To its traditions. Its ethos. Its history. No matter how much you want to forge your own path and traditions, we all fall silently, and comfortably, inline.

Chris continues to inspect my desk. "I remember the first time my father…well, my *step*-father, came to see me during my knob year. He married my mom when I was about nine or so. My real dad died in an accident a few years earlier. Warren and my mom met in business school in Raleigh. Mom was getting her MBA and Warren—." Chris pauses. "Actually, I don't really know why he was in Raleigh. Anyway, he's the one that first told me told me about Graham. We even visited campus at the start of high school together." His eyes grow bright at the memory. "Some sort of bonding thing."

I nod for him to continue. Briefly forgetting my status at Graham, basking in the conventionality of a college senior talking a college freshman.

"Even though he's my step-father, Warren had a strong influence on me. You can just *feel* the kind of man he is when he walks into a room. He isn't just physically in the room; he *owns* the room. He makes you want to listen to him. He's everything a Graham Man should be. Integrity, duty, honor—aren't just words to him. They're his life. He learned all of that here." He gestures his arms wide across the room to emphasize the point. "And I knew that if I wanted to be like him, I *needed* to become a Graham Man as well. Easiest choice in my life."

The structure of Graham—academics, physical fitness, military life, and spiritual life—is designed to mold each cadet into a Whole Man. Upon graduation, those pillars are embodied in his actions and life. They're the same in all Graham alumni, so if you only knew one thing about a person—that he's a Graham grad—by default, you'll know everything about him. After the school became co-ed, the term was changed to Whole Person, so as not to offend or make women feel unwelcome. I still say Whole Man, like most of the guys. I'm not being defiant or trying to exclude women; it's just silly to change when "man" is clearly used in a general sense, to refer to human beings generally. (And maybe a part of me is being defiant. It is just a word after all.)

We had a discussion about this once during one of our all-women meetings. Some sophomore in Second Company accused me of giving into peer pressure. "You're only agreeing with terms like that to fit in, Bennett," she said, her voice nearly fanatical as it took on a higher pitch. "The only way for them to recognize that we're here to stay is by getting rid of words like that. They're antiquated. Even those outside of Graham know that." True or not, what does *she* know? She's not from a legacy family. She can't possibly understand anything about traditions. Not everything has to change just because women are suddenly at Graham. Tradition is what makes this school what it is. It's what ties me to everyone who wore the ring before me.

I nod at Chris, hanging on to every word like my life depends on it. My left hand reaches for something behind my ear. Phantom hair, clearly. I can't believe I just did that. I'm a cliché. *Get it together*. You're being ridiculous. He's an upperclassman. You're a knob. And he's still an asshole regardless of how nice he appears to be now.

"I don't know why I just told you that." Chris clears his throat. "I just want to make Warren proud, I guess."

I don't realize what book he pulled from the top shelf until he's already holding it. "Sucks Gish wouldn't let you choose your own author for the class."

I stand paralyzed as Chris opens the front cover of the hardbound copy of *The Lords of Discipline* and reads the inscription. "*To my loving daughter. Always follow your heart, your passion, and your soul no matter where they may lead. Because in life, we take risks not to escape life but to ensure life doesn't escape us.*"

Tears stream down my face at hearing the words written by my mother five years ago. Her words, in his mouth, brought to life. Here in this room. A room she would've been proud to see me stand in, on a campus she wanted me to attend when she pushed the book toward me across our kitchen counter in Columbia. A risk she would've wanted me to take, and one I took to bring back life. To bring *her* back.

"Oh shit. I'm sorry… I-I-I…"

"It's okay." I take a seat on my bed, not caring that I'll mess up my perfect hospital corners. "I'm sorry, actually. I was just…just caught off-guard," I mumble through the snot and tears. I wipe my wet cheeks with the palm of my right hand. "I hadn't read the inscription since she gave it to me. Hearing the words out loud was …so *unexpected*. Surreal. Like from another time. Another life."

"Did she…did she, um…*die*?" Chris's voice is low and cautious, uncertain of the terrain.

Avoiding his eyes, I nod. The mattress sags beside me under his weight. The twin metal bed frame lets out a shriek. Almost a warning.

We sit side by side for a few seconds, both of us staring at the world hidden in the polished wooden floor in front of us.

He breaks the silence first. "It's tough. Losing a parent. But…but I can't imagine what it's like when it's so recent. And then…then to be at Graham."

I let out a low wail. My face seeks refuge in my hands—to hide my embarrassment and to catch the waterfall of snot, tears and inarticulate sounds. Chris's right arm envelops me and pulls me close. I bury my face in his shoulder, inhaling the smell of soap, deodorant, and... *him*. His hand on my shoulder seeks to add futile comfort. I'd forgotten what it felt like to be touched by someone. *Anyone.* I lose myself in the comfort of his touch, his care, his pureness—only to be jarred back to the now by the crackle of the loudspeaker outside.

I pull away from him quickly and stand up. I could get a million tours for this. "I'm so sorry. That shouldn't have happened. I just got lost in the moment—."

"Hey…hey, it's okay." He stands up to face me. "Emotions happen. We're all human. Besides, I'm the Ombudsman. I'm supposed to be the upperclassman you feel comfortable with. You should've seen me when my dad first died."

He flashes me a smile in the hopes of lessening the tension.

"It seems like your mom really wanted you to be here, right?"

I nod.

"All of this would be easier to deal with if you weren't here at Graham. But it is what it is. And you'll make it through okay. I know you will."

I answer him with a slight smile.

"Remember, I'm always here if you need to talk. You're only a knob for nine months." His left hand gently touches my right shoulder. "But the Corps can be pretty unforgiving. They love nothing more than to feed on some gossip. So, prob best we just communicate via Instant Messenger if you need to talk."

I nod.

"Life can be tough for a knobette." He chuckles at his presumed cleverness. "I get it though. Perception is reality and after all."

I nod in confusion as he walks out onto the galleries, the blue wooden door closing behind him with a soft thud.

Chapter Seven: *To the audience in the reviewing stand, the companies presented an image of absolute stillness, order, silence, and discipline.*

I arrive in the squad room just as Callahan is finishing his instructions to our classmates. "…Okay, so then at 0730 everyone needs to hang their blankets from their division. Make sure they're spaced out evenly. It's gotta look shit-hot guys. We'll hang the Company banner right before the gates open for Open Barracks."

"What are we doing tomorrow?" I obviously know tomorrow's Homecoming. The day Dad will be here. But I wouldn't put it past Callahan to change what he's told us *all* week the day before.

Callahan lets out an annoyed sigh. "You should've fucking gotten here sooner, Bennett. And maybe taken some notes from when we talked about this shit earlier in the week. You know we're supposed to be in the squad room fifteen minutes before each formation. This isn't Day One of cadre."

Callahan's bravado is met with approval from a couple of unnamed snickers in the back of the room.

"No need to be a dick about it, Clint. You know damn well I have to give Coleman her sash wrap before Parade, so it's not like I was late because I couldn't decide what to wear."

"Big deal. I gave Trevino *and* Johnson a sash wrap and *still* got here before you did. Maybe you just don't know how to give a good sash wrap," Singleton chimes in. "Maybe you are better at *giving* something else."

The room erupts with laughter.

My cheeks burn with heat in an instant.

My heart races as the anger boils.

If I say nothing they win. Yet I don't want to miss an opportunity to show my classmates that I can accept their criticism and jokes - no matter how crass. I take a gamble, "It's clear one of us has had more practice at '*giving* a sash wrap'"—thank you, air quotes—"as you, Darron being from the big city and all."

The room erupts in laughter. *Mission accomplished.* Another small victory.

The laughter stops abruptly with Callahan's annoyed look and crossed arms.

The room is bathed in tense silence for a few seconds before Wade comes to my rescue. "Basically, we've got a douche detail—I mean uhm…*hydro* detail," he corrects, using the newly sanctioned, politically-correct term for a wet sweep detail, "after parade today. Then we're free to go on general leave. Tomorrow we need to do our normal sweep detail in the morning, hang the blankets, and put out the shakos. I think you heard the rest, Bennett."

A douche detail—new Corps terms be damned—is no different than a regular sweep detail, except we add water. It's a necessity, since the galleries get dirty with just about everything—dip, dirt, the contents of someone's cup. Once we've dry swept the galleries, two cadets fill up large plastic trash cans with water in the bathroom. We always use the men's bathroom because they have open showers, versus the individual showers in the women's bathroom. We dump the warm water onto the galleries while a procession of brooms follows obediently behind, sweeping vigorously back and forth, ensuring every inch of the galleries from top to bottom is drenched. It's rigorous, back-breaking stuff, but if we all work together, it's over pretty quick.

I nod. "Thanks. When did you guys finish the banner?"

Callahan and Singleton look at each conspiratorially before Clint says, "We finished it in my room during ESP last night. It was pretty risky and difficult because we couldn't fold it out all the way."

"Yea, and the room smelled like permanent marker all night," Darron adds unnecessarily. "Gave me a fucking headache. But it's done. So don't worry about—."

The door flies open.

"Roll out, knobbies!" Trevino's Texas drawl commands. "Parade time."

***

Ash and Reagan are long gone by the time I get back from parade. I don't bother questioning how they got back to the room and changed before I did; I'm just glad they're gone and I have the room to myself to check my Instant Messages. I wiggle the mouse to wake up the computer and enter my password. I've taken to staying signed into my account just in case technology fails me. You never know who might send a message. Ever since that night that Chris stopped by my room and we had a normal college moment, he's taken the habit of IMing more frequently. A lot more frequently. He asks about my day and tell me about his.

A smile illuminates my face before my brain registers why.

You're probably out doing some knob duties, but I wanted to wish you a good evening before I head out. Having dinner with Warren and my mom in Mt. Pleasant. Chat soon.

I take a minute to think about what to write back that won't sound cliché. It has to sound adult. And of course it has to convey that I appreciate his note. Don't get me wrong, Chris is still an ass when others are around yet that's where the double standard comes into play. Guys like Callahan can just chill in an upperclassman's room as a knob but the minute a women does it, the rumors are born and multiply into perceptions that become reality that cannot be shaken for the rest of the time at

Graham. Like Coleman always says - *he who gets the story out first controls the narrative.*

After several false starts, I settle on something basic and mundane, "Hope you had a great dinner. I'm sure he's proud seeing you in your uniform. Excited for the same with my dad tomorrow."

I lock the computer before putting it to sleep.

I change out of my physical fitness uniform into my leave uniform —white pants and a grey wool blouse. I grab my bag of dirty laundry and cover before heading out. Since Dad won't be here until tomorrow morning, I'm meeting Max at Tad's for dinner and a movie. Since our last conversation got interrupted, we never really got to talk through the latest developments with his investigation that LTC Preston assigned him.

I walk past the tour walkers on my way out of the battalion just as a few drops of rain begin to fall, though the smell of damp grass already hangs heavy in the air. Tours are awarded for only the most serious of Blue Book infractions, like leaving Graham outside of General Leave hours or hazing. Not only can you not go on general leave until you've completed your assigned tours, but you walk back and forth on the quad—rain or shine—for fifty minutes at a time, for all to see. Worst of all, walking tours is a sure-fire way not to get rank.

"Is that you, Kensley?" Max yells from the den before I'm even fully through the front door. I'm soaked to the bone; the rain went from a drizzle to a downpour when I was halfway to Tad's.

"Sure is. Where's the fire?"

"What took you so long? I'm starving. We were going to order pizza but were waiting on you because I wasn't sure what you were in the mood for."

We just had pizza last week. "Why are we having pizza? Again. Gwendolyn didn't make anything? By the way, who else is here?"

"Nope. And it's just us. Tad and Gwendolyn went to some alumni thing downtown. She did make stuff but it's for tomorrow's tailgate and I was given strict orders not to touch any of it. Or let anyone else touch it either."

"Fine. I just want cheese. Nothing else. I mean it, Max!"

"You aren't still holding onto *that*, are you? It's not my fault they got the order wrong. I'll ask them to do half *just* cheese, and half pepperoni."

Max places the pizza order while I go into the laundry room to start my first load. Since we aren't allowed to have civilian clothes, laundry is pretty simple. White v-neck shirts are washed with white socks, and everything else is dark. The only thing I try to take to the laundry on campus are my white pants and wool blouse. They must use some alien technology starch because I've never been able to replicate the crease they create. You could almost cut a person with that crease. And it conveniently holds for several wearings.

I keep a couple items of civilian clothes here. Nothing elaborate: a pair of flannel pants and a tank top. It's nice to be comfortable, to feel the soft flannel on my skin. It reminds me of home. And then I've got a flowery wrap dress for that "just in case" moment. I have yet to figure out what that moment would be at Graham, given the two bridges rule, but I still felt compelled to buy it at the store last month. *Just because.* The truth is, it's been tough to find a balance at Graham between being a girl and a cadet. I'd never admit it out-loud if someone asked me, because any kind of wavering about cadet life is a weakness, a vulnerability to be exploited. And I feel like right now Graham only accepts two kinds of women cadets: the ones that are no bullshit, swear with the guys, run with the guys, use "old Corps" terms like dousche deal and under no circumstances date a cadet; and then there are the ones that are the exact opposite of that. There is no in between. After all, everything's a competition. Everyone's a rival. Everyone's looking and judging and looking and judging, which means there's never a safe moment. Some pieces need to stay hidden away —like the piece that would love to wear a dress and put on makeup once in awhile. Or want to be seen.

Sometimes I wonder if I'm the only girl at Graham who feels this way.

I slam the top of the washer shut and shake the thought out of my head. It's not forever and there is an ending.   It is only four years.

When I join Max on the couch, he gives me a pizza update. "They said it would take like forty-five minutes. Friday night and all." Anticipating my protest, he points to a cheese and cracker platter on the side table.

"Wow! I didn't know you could cook. You're so domesticated. Do the girls at the College of Charleston know about you?" He flips me the bird as I reach for a cracker and some sort of white cheese, cut up in irregular squares. "What movie did we decide on? Or are we just going to flip through the zillion channels like we always do?"

An unusual amount of silence passes. I elbow Max in the ribs. Cracker crumbs fall down his shirt like a trail of ants.

"We never got to finish our conversation from the other night 'cause that jerk upperclassman came to your room." His voice is calm but monotone. "I totally knew who he was, by the way. You know I memorized all of the guys on staff for *all* the battalions. Plus he's good friends with Malone, so I've see him in my company area plenty of times."

Jerk upperclassman? From what I remember, Chris didn't ask Max anything out of the ordinary. In fact, he told him to leave. Never dropped him for pushups.

"Did you mean… Harvatin?"

"Yep. That dude. I don't trust him, K," Max says flatly.

79

"You met him for like, five seconds, Max. Don't be dramatic." I pause. "Plus, he was supposed to be a dick to you as you were in *his* Battalion. If I went into your Battalion during ESP, or any other time during the day, I *definitely* would have been running the stairs or satellites or both."

"Dramatic?" He turns his body towards me. Suddenly the couch feels very small. "Jesus fucking christ, Kensley. I *am* calling a spade a spade. I had to run the stairs in full uniform before parade today cause that dude told Odom that not only was I in another battalion during ESP, but that I was in a *girl's* room." Max's nostrils flare with rage.

I wipe my hands on my sweatpants. "You don't know that he told your Company Commander you were in my room. Maybe you weren't shined up during formation or didn't know your knob knowledge at mess. Chris isn't even from Charlie Battalion. He's from *my* battalion, so the likelihood of him knowing Odom is slim." I just can't see Chris telling Max's Company Commander about him being in my room. Yes, it's rare for a knob from one battalion to go to another, but it is not unheard of. Max's reporter mind is making analytical leaps. Clearly he misjudged.

"What do you mean, they *couldn't know each other*. They're fucking classmates, Kensley. They've been at this school for four years together. And Odom told me himself. Why aren't you on my side here?" He gets up and sits on the other couch across the room and we sit in silence for a few minutes. Arms crossed, he suddenly asks matter-of-factly, "And since when do *you* refer to upperclassmen by their first name?!"

I ignore the question and attempt to misdirect, "I don't want you to think that everything is a conspiracy. I think this thing that Preston has you working on has got you paranoid. You're overanalyzing the—."

"Ohhh, I see what's going on here. You have a crush on Harvatin. Or should I say *Chris*, since clearly you're already on a first-name-basis with the guy? Did you Google everything about him yet?"

"Don't be a dick." My voice shakes slightly, whether with rage at my failed misdirection or embarrassment I can't be sure.

We stare at each other in frustration. We've reached that delicate moment in an argument between two people who know each other's vulnerabilities, each other's faults. Who know exactly what to say to fan the ambers while at the same time both know what to say to end the argument with a draw.

"Look... I'm sorry," Max starts. "I was just trying to tell you about my day and finish the rest of our conversation. Maybe I'm just tired because I had to run up four flights of stairs five times before parade today. It's cool if you like the guy. Not my business." Max gets us to a draw.

"Thank you," I whisper to my lap. "I'm sorry, too. I should've listened to you first before making an assumption. I'm sorry you had to run stairs. I should know better. It's not like...it's not like I don't know the unwritten rules at Graham." I take a sip of the room temperature tea from the cup next to me. "And I don't *like* the guy. It's just nice to talk to someone sometimes." I flash Max a smile. "How's the secret investigation going? You never got to tell me the rest of your thoughts the other night."

Max leans forward, his enthusiasm for the topic overpowering any lingering awkwardness between us. "Right. I realized that in order to tackle this story, I need to understand the LAMC Foundation first. So I did some research online. *Lots* of research. There wasn't a ton of stuff out there about them, but they've been around for the last five years - really ever since the South Caroline Supreme Court decision. And since they need to raise money, they've held public fundraisers where they take pictures for their website and newsletters. Usually they just have like two fundraisers a year. But…" Max pauses for effect. "Over the last six months, they've held three times as many. And they've reached out to a ton more Graham alumni clubs across the U.S. Like even doing speaking events or whatever."

I listen intently, nodding every so often.

"It's clear they've changed their marketing and messaging strategy. But a drastic change like that requires funding especially to spiff up the website and fly across the U.S. The website didn't say how much they've raised this year but all of the monies they have - and will raise is going to be set aside to make a play at privatizing Graham. I think there's a…"

"Privatization? So…so this is really a *thing*?" I remark uneasily.

Max looks at my sympathetically. "Yea, K. I mean…there are still so many unanswered questions but I really do think this is a *thing* this time around. I think there's even a silent donor paying for the marketing and the travel. There's no way the LAMC Foundation could raise this much cash and still do this much advertising without a big donor. And still have money left over to make a real play at privatization. If I can find *that* donor, then maybe we can stop them."

I pull my legs up against me on the couch and stare at Max in silent disbelief. Timing couldn't be any worse if what Max has found so far is true. Is it possible for the LAMC Foundation to really succeed this time and privatize Graham? What would happen to the women in the Corps? Would we be transfer students? But to where?

The hunger growl of my stomach pulls me back to the present.

"Damn. That's really good work, Max. Was there any clue on the webpages or newsletter as to who the man behind the curtain might be? Any new faces over the last six months that you didn't see before?" I ask not wanting to burden Max with the college status of 80 or so women within the Corps, I focus on his work.

Max shakes his head. "I saw some new faces in the photos but no one with the money to fund the marketing strategy." Max gets up and sits next to me again. "Look… I know it's easier said that done, K…but I wouldn't worry about Graham privatizing. It would be super bad publicity for the school. People forget that this place is also a college that awards degrees—degrees that grads need to take out into the world to get real jobs or commission into one of the four services. I'm sure it would cause some problems with people's commissioning status's to just change schools no matter where they are in their academic track." I nod not knowing what to say. "Maybe you can ask your dad if he's heard anything. He's pretty active in the alumni network, right?"

Dad and I have never really talked about assimilation. After mom died, we actually didn't talk much about anything at all. We moved from Columbia to New York, and life was supposed to start anew. But it didn't. He remained distant and immersed in his work. I thought getting into Graham would be part of that fresh start—a means for us to connect again. Yet when I showed him my Graham acceptance letter, he just handed me a check and went back to work.

I place the dusty memory back where they belong and center my attention instead on the now. "I just don't like that the *Low Country Gazette* decided to do an editorial right now. It's bad timing and fuels the fire."

"Yeah… And it's free publicity for the LAMC Foundation."

The doorbell rings. Finally.

"We'll have to endure a couple editorials, I expect. Which is why I need to find the man behind the curtain sooner rather than later." Max's voice trails off to the front door.

The man behind the curtain. For now I'll settle for the pizza guy behind the door.

Chapter Eight: *What happens tomorrow night that could be worse than what happened today?*

After Saturday morning breakfast, as planned, we hang the dark blue cotton blankets over the railings on each division in preparation for open barracks for Homecoming. It's a tedious task as each Graham crest has to be centered and aligned with the one next to it. It is even more tedious as a knob because you can't just have one of us stand in the middle of the quad and yell up to the others - "a little to the right." Instead one of us is always folded over the railings like the blanket itself and hope that our peripheral vision is accurate. Since each company in the battalion is responsible for its own section of divisions, we don't have to use too many of our blankets. The key of course is remembering to get your blanket back at the end of open barracks. If not, you'll be making a trip to the cadet store on campus to purchase another.

The Company banners go up last, usually just five minutes before open barracks. For dramatic effect, of course. For open barracks, our rooms don't have to be as clean as they do for an SMI day—just neat and orderly. Generally only parents, family, and friends of the current occupants visit a room; there is the occasional stray alumnus who will stroll in to relive his college days. We had two wander into our room during open barracks on Parents' Day Weekend and as soon as they crossed the wooden threshold, a flood of lost memories physically transported them to days of grey uniforms, early morning physical fitness formations, and nightly taps. Their faces convey a longing and appreciation for the past, when those around you grew from classmates to brothers.

Ash and Reagan are sitting at their desks, surfing the Internet. In stolen moments like these, I wonder if we would have been friends at another college or if maybe, just maybe, we could still be friends here at

Graham. Some of the other women have seemed to fair okay. So why can't we? I let out an audible sigh. Who am I kidding? I don't think we're destined for sisterhood, now or in the future. No one would fault them if they quit. I certainly wouldn't. I wouldn't even miss them. No one would. The only evidence that they even existed here would be their cadet ID cards on Trevino's bulletin board, a macabre memorial to those who will not wear the ring.

I briefly glance at the desk clock. Only five minutes till open barracks.

Instead of meeting in the front sally port, Dad said he would just come up to my room. It's too awkward to walk next to him, bracing. Awkward for me, not him. He'd probably want to talk to me while we're walking to my room (like he doesn't know better), pointing out where so-and-so used to live, or how the walls were painted a different shade of light tan when he was a cadet.

The unborn memory brings a smile to my face.

"All-in?!" Dad's baritone voice booms into the room almost before he does.

He came.

"You made it!" I wrap my arms around him as tight as I can. The many years and long hours behind a desk have been hard on him despite the pedestrian-friendly streets of New York. He's not super overweight, but the doctor has told him he could afford to lose about twenty pounds.

"Hey, kid. Let me take a look at you." He holds me at arm's length. "You've lost weight. Are they feeding you in the mess hall?"

"Hello ladies!" Dad says to Ash and Reagan across the room before I can respond.

"Hello, Mr. Bennett," they respond simultaneously. "It's *so* nice to finally meet you."

"Please call me, Gary. You guys have to call enough people Mister and Miss around here. Kensley has told me much about you guys already. I feel like I know ya. I'd love—."

My poorly disguised cough interrupts him, but it's better than a laugh. I always knew that parents lie. At least to other people to be polite. I've *maybe* mentioned them once to him. And only in the context of me having roommates.

Dad is unfazed by my interruption. "I'd...I'd love for you to join us for dinner after the game tonight. On me of course!"

What, what? No, no, no. This is my time with *my* father. Graham is the one thing we've had in common in years. This is the first step to making things right between us again.

"Oh, that's so nice of you, Mister Be...I mean, Gary." Ash's grown-up voice sounds worse than her girlish giggle. "But we already have plans with some other girls in our class. A lot of their parents couldn't make it, so we're having a *Sex and the City* binge-watching night at my house in North Charleston."

My dad's raised eyebrows appear to freeze in place.

"Oh, oh, it's totally innocent. Don't let the title fool you. A lot of our classmates haven't seen it yet so we thought this would be something fun for us to do. Order pizza, eat candy...talk about boys," Reagan adds, shooting me a vindictive look. "Wait...it takes place in New York. Do you know Sarah Jessica Parker?" Before my dad can respond, Reagan launches into a monologue on the character she plays, her obsession with shoes, and of course Big.

My dad manages to squeeze into her monologue as Reagan took a breath, "Well, that sounds like a nice time, ladies. Certainly don't let me keep you from any classmate bonding." He turns to me, "My feelings wouldn't be hurt if you'd rather join them, Kensley. It's my twenty-five-year reunion so I'm sure I can entertain myself - and we do have some reunion stuff planned. Plus I still have a legal brief to finish for this case that's about to go to court."

I shield myself from the impact of his words as much as I can. He came all this way and still doesn't want to spend time with me. "That's very considerate of you, Dad. But you already traveled all this way and since I probably am not coming home for Thanksgiving, I'd rather spend time with you." Besides, Reagan and Ash never once mentioned this watch party to me before. Clearly they too are not accepting applications for new friends. At least I now know the feeling is mutual and we don't have to pretend anymore.

He shrugs unassumingly. "Okay. It's up to you but you can always change your mind. Now you didn't answer my question, young lady. Don't think I forgot. Are they feeding you in the mess hall?"

"Yesss, Dad. Of course they're feeding us." I smile. "We march to the mess hall three times a day just like back in the old corps," I respond almost sarcastically.

"Thanks for stating the obvious. I was a cadet once too you know. A few years ago," he pats his stomach, "but I still remember. They aren't playing games during meals, are they?" Suddenly I feel like I'm on trial as his voice takes on a prosecutorial tone.

"What? I...um, don't understand what you mean."

"I know you read the paper, kid. And so do I."

Right. That fucking editorial. Last week's Caroline's Corner was about supposed games former cadets were made to play at mess under the direction of upperclassmen. Something about one knob chewing food and then giving it to her classmate. I barely took notice since both girls ended up leaving Graham anyway. It's unspoken tradition to not take notice of those that leave before the end of knob year. The only reminder that they were once at Graham is their cadet ID card on the back of someone' clipboard - a reminder flashed to those left behind at unexpected moments.

I waive a dismissive hand and with an eye roll add, "Ugh…I *did* read it. I just let myself forget it almost immediately because it's sooooo ridiculous. Even if it was true, I don't know what those girls hoped to gain."

Sometimes it's hard to keep track of what I can talk about. And with whom. Max is doing a secret investigation about the LAMC Foundation that no one can know about. Even though they're public, the sources for the editorials are a mystery—especially since it's clear that Caroline has an inside source. A source who's on the side of the LAMC Foundation. Yet so far, the only connection is that the Foundation commented on the claims by those two cadets in the editorial last week. Yet that would be just the type of thing the Foundation would want, no need to comment on. Two former *women* cadets speaking out about their time at Graham. Those ridiculous claims that they were made to eat each other's chewed up food at mess knob year. A better story for an editorial would be the Field House scandal. Yet Max said that he - and so were the upperclassmen, not to talk about it with anyone. They didn't tell the women that—which still seems strange. Maybe… *maybe* the school knows what the *Low Country Gazette* is going to print in advance. It would make sense as Graham has had plenty of bad press since Shannon Faulkner's lawsuit. Who could forget the picture on the front page of the *Low Country Gazette* with the upperclassman in a red sash with his arms spread wide in victory and the battalion behind him an eruption of elation? That could explain why no one from the administration commented on the claims by the two girls Caroline interviewed. They're waiting to comment on a story that really matters. The bottom of my stomach falls out.

"You okay there, kid? You look a little pale." Dad rests his hand on my shoulder.

"Yeah." My voice shakes slightly as I mute my thoughts. "I probably haven't had enough water today. Let's not talk about the editorial. Those girls don't matter. They chose to leave Graham." I pick up my cover and head for the door, "We should go take a photo by the Company Number."

As he turns to leave the room, his eyes catch the picture of us on top of the World Trade Center on my desk. All three of us. My room and me suddenly a mere reflection in his sadness. The space between us visible again. An insurmountable wall.

I can't let Ash and Reagan see the tension between us. "Daaaad..?" I awkwardly croak. "Let's go downstairs."

"Oh…yes. Let's um, take that photo."

The battalion is a different place during open barracks. It's foreign to see people in civilian clothes walking in and out of rooms and across the quad as if it was any other college. Children run about playing, unaware of the otherwise earnest mood. Their laughter reverberating throughout the battalion. It is nice though, to know that some of those in civilian clothes are grads who've returned to reunite with their past and us - the future. They'll always be a part of something here.

Once down on first division, we wait on the galleries as other cadets take a photo in front of the Company Number. Some with their families, some with just their fathers, some with their roommates.

As Trevino and his parents finish their picture, I whisper to Dad next to me, "That's my company first sergeant."

Dad just nods and smiles.

Disappointment washes over me. He doesn't care about my cadet life. Or me at Graham. Or me. He steps toward the company number just in time for me to swallow the first trickle of tears.

I'm not sure if I can stop bracing for this one moment. It's hard to tell if anyone is looking because there are too many people around. Maybe it'll be okay for this one moment. Because it's still an important moment for us. For Dad and me. I am trying so hard. For our future. Feeling gaudy, I relax my shoulders and let out my chin as soon as the civilian stranger Dad handed the camera to counts to three.

We walk to the front sally port. Eager to hide my earlier disappointment and to salvage this trip, I go into cadet mode. It's simple. It's safe. It's familiar. "Okay, so we've got parade at 1100. Then lunch. And then we have the march over for the home game. I assume the game will be over by 1600. Do you want to meet at Tad's at 1700 and then we can go to dinner?"

"Whoa…slow down there, cadet private Bennett." I catch the smile across his face. And mine. "It's nice to see you've acclimated to Graham rather quickly after…well, after…." His voice trails off and both of our smiles disappear.

We stand in the front sally port for a few minutes in weighted silence.

Hoping the familiar will do the trick again, I ask hastily, "Did you bring the red hat to wear during parade?" No way I would spot him from the stands without something unique. Large weekends always draw large crowds - usually in the school's colors: periwinkle blue.

He pulls a crumpled red baseball hat out of his pocket. "Bet you thought I forgot. Okay, I can see the to-do list running across your forehead. I'll sort of see you at parade but I will definitely see you tonight as planned," he adds with a wink.

After a brief hug, I turn to go back into the battalion. Before I turn sharp right, I remember to take a quick glance at the company banner waving at me from across the battalion. I hadn't seen the final design since Callahan worked on it in his room. Looks like the guys managed to only affix the top half to the railings, leaving the bottom to flail in the wind like one of those wind figures you see at used car dealers. I guess they forgot to measure out the proper length of rope to secure the bottom corners.

Measure twice cut once. Fucking idiots.

We most certainly are going to get yelled at, and probably dropped for push-ups, before parade - with a sprinkle of a sweep detail after parade. Especially since the other three companies managed to secure all four corners of their banners.

Just as I'm about to take another step, my mind processes the glaring error on the banner. *Two* glaring errors to be exact.

I freeze in the middle of my pivot.

I can't believe they did this. I knew they were up to something. I just fucking knew it. Callahan and Singleton were so secretive with the banner. Why didn't I double check it? Did the others know?

I wonder if anyone has noticed.

Of course people have fucking noticed, Kensley. Don't be naïve.

Everyone has noticed at this point. The banner's been hanging for nearly two hours.

I fly to my room as fast as I can. The door is already open, as Ash and Reagan are being entertained by Wade and Dane. What a surprise. Oblivious as usual.

"Have you guys seen the banner?" I demand, catching my breath.

"What?" Reagan continues to stare at her computer screen.

"Did I fucking stutter?"

"Look, Kensley... it wasn't our idea, okay? Callahan said he was *ordered* to do it. He wouldn't tell us by whom. We didn't have a choice," Wade clearly heard me *and* knew what I was talking about. Coward.

"He's right," Dane chimes in. "Don't be mad at us. What were we supposed to do? Make a second banner?" Makes that cowards.

"Don't get mad at Wade, Kensley," Ash says, defending Dane without knowing from what.

"Unless you know what you're fucking talking about, stay the fuck out of it, Ash." I slam the drawer of my half press shut in anger at them.

At the school. At myself. There's no point in trying to explain how wrong this is, regardless if they were ordered to do it or not. I have to talk to Coleman. Now. Except I dont know where she is. I fumble with my wrist watch.

10:25 hrs. Perfect. I'll do it in a few minutes, when I give her a sash wrap before parade.

The breast plate slips out of my shaking hands and tumbles to the floor, ringing out a low chime as it lands on the hardwood floor.

"Fuck!" My right fist interacts violently with the top of my half press. That's definitely not the best idea I've had in a while. I know without looking that the breast plate is scratched. Fuck it. I pick it up and wipe it on my pants before snapping it into place. I straighten my dress blouse, grab my cover, and storm out the door. (Reagan and Ash can get themselves to the squad room.)

My knock—two knocks, to be exact—on Coleman's door are met with silence. Maybe she didn't hear me. The banner's shadow waves on the wall next to me. Mocking me. Reminding me that I should've done something to stop it. That I should have known better. That even though women assimilated into Graham four years ago and there are women among various class years in all of the companies and in various leadership roles, women still aren't accepted. No matter how hard we try. No matter how hard we use their language. We undergo a different system - one that lasts for all four years.

I knock again.

Nothing.

I stand there for a few seconds doing nothing. Nothing at all.

The shadow waves again. The seconds tick by.

I take one last deep breath, press the door handle down and push the wooden door forward.

The room is dark. And empty.

Coleman isn't here. On her bed is the white box that normally holds her sash. Also empty.

Of course she wouldn't want a sash wrap from me today. Or probably from anyone in the company. It betrayed her. It let her think that she was accepted, that she was part of it just because she marched at the front of us all.

I stand motionless in the center of the room. Frozen for a second time that day.

My mind races.

Maybe I should've paid better attention when we were making the banner. I am *her* mentor knob after all. I need to talk to her. But really what would I say to her? Tell her I'm sorry? Sorry for what? I have been trying so hard to break into Graham that I missed the open door in front of me. The door that ushers me onto the path of those few women who have come before me. I could explain to her that it wasn't my fault. Callahan designed it. I could try to tell her that my male classmates did this because it's easier for them to lump all women into one box. Just like Ash and Reagan bring me down, Ward brings her down. Coleman has to know everyone hates Ward, regardless if she is the RC.

That's why this happened.

Yes. A bad few ruined it for all of us. It's why I haven't walked through the open door. It's why I continue to pound on the closed one.

The bugle sings out its one note across the loud speaker summoning us to the squad room. Robotically, I make my way to the squad room. The shadow waves one more time as I turn to walk down the stairs.

Most everyone is already in the squad room, including Ash and Reagan. A soft hum of inaudible chatter hangs in the room yet it is just idle chatter. No one is talking about the banner. I stand by the sink next to the door, saying nothing, arms crossed in silent protest. Callahan darts an "I dare you to say something" yet satisfied look over at me. I choose to ignore it. He's not worth it. And I am out numbered. You can't change the mind of guys like that. And the ink is already dry on the banner anyway.

Suddenly, the screen door screeches. Yet instead of the door flying open, it opens without flare to reveal... Coleman.

Alone.

She takes one step into the squad room and shuts the door behind her.

We all brace.

"Relax, knobs." Her face is a hard shell. Unrevealing. "Seriously, stop bracing, knobs. Right now!"

We hesitate. It could be a trick. Yet one by one, as our eyes dart at each other, we slowly begin to relax our shoulders. At first just a little. Then a little bit more. Until we're all just... standing in front of our Company Commander as equals. Well, not quite.

Coleman lets out an audible sigh. "Okay, knobs. You know what you did. I'm not going to stand here and yell at you. Or make you run the stairs. Or even take you out for a run after parade. I know someone in my —our—company told you to leave my name and my classmate's name off the banner."

She pauses for a beat, "If you didn't like that women were at Graham, then you should've applied elsewhere. Look around this room. You have three female classmates in your own company, whether you like it or not. Whether your family or the alumni like it. I don't need my name on some oversized piece of fabric to tell me that I'm part of this school. I don't even need my ring for that. I know it in my heart. And so does my classmate." Her eyes meet all of ours head-on. Almost like a challenge. She doesn't blink. Or smile.

No one seemed to have moved a millimeter since she started her speech.

"I hope that one day you'll understand that Cathy and I don't need your validation. We don't need your acceptance to be part of this school." The screen door screeches again. Coleman steps out of the way to let Ward enter. I swallow hard. Coleman doesn't even look at me as she nearly steps on my shoes to get out of Ward's way. Guilt and disappointment reflexively cast my eyes downward.

Ward stands next to Coleman in equal challenge, as she continues. "Let me leave you with this. Think about if your mother, your sister, your aunt…, your best female friend called you to tell you this story about what happened to her at work or at school. I bet you'd be pretty pissed off for them. I bet you'd want to do something about it. Come to her rescue. Think about that, knobs the next time you're asked to exclude people."

None of us respond. Mainly because we aren't sure *how* to respond. Any one of our three knob answers would be like pouring salt into a wound.

Instead, Ward and Coleman exchange a glance that only friends - classmates, can understand before turning to leave the room.

Chapter Nine: *The meeting we held in the room that night was both dismal and funeral in tone.*

"So why aren't you going to New York for Thanksgiving furlough again?" Ash suddenly asks as we're getting ready for the last parade of the first semester. "I would sooooo love to go to New York."

"Oh…um, my dad is busy with this huge case." I respond as I look up from my laptop. It's the only lie I could think of in the moment. "And I've got to start on my project for Gish's class," I add. Procrastination can be kept at bey only so long. Besides we'd probably just sit in silence in opposite ends of the apartment anyway, if Homecoming was any indicator.

"In a city of eight million people you don't have *anyone* else to visit except your dad…?" Reagan turns her whole body away from me. It's obvious from the uncontrollable jolting of her shoulders that she's suppressing her laughter.

"Who cares. At least you wouldn't be here," Ash adds as an attempt to keep me from noticing Reagan.

I ignore them both. If I don't I'll dive head first into the reason why we left South Carolina for New York midway through high school. "Um, no, smart-ass. The main reason is that it's just a lot of travel for a short amount of *actual* vacation. It's like a twelve-hour drive from here. Plus this time of year New York is stuffed full of tourists."

"Whatever," Reagan says sarcastically across her shoulder.

"Not like you guys are doing anything special. I assume you guys are *just* staying here?"

"Of course." Ash is oblivious to the sarcasm. "It's going to be great! My grandparents are coming down from North Carolina on Wednesday, and then uhm…I think some cousins are coming too. From out of state. I can't remember from where though… My mom and grandmother make this huge dinner—more like a late lunch on Thursday, so the boys can watch the game. We'll have everything. Turkey, obviously, cranberry sauces, pies. You know, all of the usual stuff. Then we just sit around and catch up. And sleep." They both look at each other in shared future memory.

I nod and smile. "That sounds great, Ash." I actually mean it. I would give anything to have that kind of normalcy again.

"This year Reagan's family is going to come over, too. You know cause we're classmates…" Ash stops herself from finishing the rest of her thought. Realizing too late that she just said out loud what we've all already know. Have known since the first day of Hell Week on that sweltering Charleston morning in August.

Ash and I stare at each other as if we are in a stand off. She looks like she wishes she could melt into the furniture. I know my expression is blank, unfeeling, unwavering. Reagan's shoulders stop jolting and she turns around. Two girls—*three,* in the same uniform. With the same short boyish haircut. In the same company. Girls who should've been compatriots. Who should've leaned on each other for support, for empathy, for understanding, for a helping hand.

We've done none of those things.

Instead, we've become opponents. Each standing on opposite sides of the room—filling the space between us with loathing, competition, vengeance and jealousy. I still standing in front of the closed door and they perhaps having walked through that open door created by those before us.

"Is that what time it is?" I ask rhetorically, pretending Reagan's digital desk clock surprises me while really serving as a conversational pivot. *And you made me miss my chance to chat with Chris before parade,* I want to scream at her.

I shut my laptop, grab my cover and rifle and walk out the door. "I have to get to Coleman's room for her sash wrap."

I knock on Coleman's door and enter before I get the all-clear.
Shit.

Staring me eyeball to eyeball is Ward.

I'm paralyzed.

Her cold, hard stare clearly conveys that she holds *me* personally
responsible for her name being left off the banner. As if her name not on
the banner could be counted as revenge for what she did. *Not even close.*

She stole my ticket into the boys' club. She ruined my chance to
prove I can be part of the Old Corps. To be part of this school. To belong.

"Oh. It's you," Coleman's icy voice coats the room. Obviously
Coleman blames me for the homecoming banner. "All of my stuff is in the
usual spot. Let's hope you can manage a sash wrap." Coleman turns to
Ward. "Tell me about the *rest* of your meeting with Dehenre."

Ward darts her eyes at me. "Um, well…"

"Don't worry about her, Cathy. I know you've got some concerns
but she knows to treat this room like Vegas. Right, Bennett? Especially
after Homecoming…"

"Ma'am, yes, Ma'am."

Ward still hesitates, pensively starting at me as if she's deciding
whether to purchase a sweater on sale.

"*Fine*. If this gets out, I know who to come for." Her rueful smirk
is sharpened to points. *"Again."* I swallow hard and bite my inner lip.
Exactly what I'm talking about. You're a bitch to everyone. That's why
you're responsible for Coleman's name being left off the banner. I
retrieve Coleman's sash, safety pins, and name tag from across the room.

"Anyway, Dehenre gave me this big lecture about how as RC, I
should make more of an effort to reach out to other female cadets. Of *all*
classes. So that they can see me as… *human*," Ward explains, leaning back
on her elbows on Coleman's bed.

"Is she for real? Human? What the fuck does that even mean? You're the RC not a camp counselor. I'm sure they've never said that to other RCs before." Coleman's voice conveys annoyance mixed with confusion. (I agree with her. As much as I like knowing Ward was reprimanded, it sounds like a double standard.)

Ward nods. "Trust me, girl. I told her that. I also told her that my schedule doesn't permit that. Since the start of the school year, the administration has me attending the normal events the RC attends. but then because I'm the "highest ranking female cadet"—an oft repeated refrain—"I've got a ton of other events on top of that. Like we're all on Manor Farm just here to pose for pictures. Oh and while all of that is going on, I am also supposed to be going to class and studying. Don't get me wrong, Ave—I'm damn proud to have earned this rank, but sometimes it…it gets so fucking annoying."

Earned? Who are you kidding? Everyone knows that Malone should've been RC. Not
Ward. She was the Delta Battalion Supply Sergeant last year—a non-leadership position. The school just wanted to reward her with a higher rank than Coleman because she smiled pretty for the media. Even as a poli sci major, she got crappy grades. (You *can* learn a whole lot at those all-female meetings.)

Coleman nods and remains in receive mode.

"The all consuming pressure to be perfect, Cathy! It's never ending." Ward lets out a frustrated sigh. "I feel like my words, actions, … *shit* even my tone of voice, are constantly picked apart by like vultures on a carcass. Everyone is just *waiting* for me to fuck up so they can say - see, told you she - or better yet, the school wasn't ready to have a female in a leadership position this high." She takes a deep breathe to reload. "I earned this fucking position. I interviewed juuuuust like everyone else and if the school didn't want me, then they should have selected someone else! They're stuck with me just like I am stuck with them. So why not make the best of it?"

Ward leans forward and rests her head in her hands. "It's so hard to know who to fucking trust these days. I hate this feeling of constant paranoia. And we aren't even…" The last of Ward's words drown in her tears.

Forgetting I am trying to wrap her sash, Coleman moves towards Ward and sits next to her on the bed. "Damn, girl. I am really sorry."

Silence fills the void of the unspoken.

"I really thought you had it all together. That you figured out how to thrive up there in the ivory tower as RC. That you somehow figured out how to not need their validation. That you tapped into a fuck you attitude." Coleman scoffs. "Meanwhile I am over here trying not to loose my shit for most of the day - balancing school, company bullshit…and don't *even* start talking to me about graduation. Or life after Graham."

Their simultaneous laughter evaporates the heaviness of the moment.

"Thanks, Ave." Ward wipes her tears with the meaty part of her palms. "You know, knowing what I know now about Graham and our time here…I would still do it all over again. Same place. Same time." She pauses for a beat. "I really do love this place."

"Me too, Cathy. Me too," Coleman whispers into the room.

"Fuck…I have to be back over in Bravo Battalion in like ten minutes for parade," Ward suddenly exclaims realizing the time. "Okay..okay….so back to my convo with Dehenre before I forget. Let's see…oh right…the whole be more human part….so after some back and forth, I ask Dehenre straight up what she really wants me to do. I mean, that is really what that meeting was for, so just get to the point. So she tells me that the real issues are the editorials. They're bad press for the school, writ large." Her shoes stomp loudly as gets up from the bed.

"No shit, Sherlock," Coleman interjects. "I don't even remember Callie and the other loser they interviewed. Move on with your life already. Stop whining to the press about it."

Exactly my thoughts. Those girls Caroline interviewed remind me of Ash and Reagan. Peas in a pod. It's never too late to quit, ladies.

"Agreed. Dehenre then tells me—," Ward moves conspiratorially closer to Coleman, so close that I could wrap this one sash around them both, and whispers, "she tells me that this year the school is taking the LAMC Foundation seriously."

"Seriously in *what*?" Coleman tilts her head to the side. "Being dicks? Cathy, you gotta let Bennett finish the sash. I've gotta be downstairs in like twenty minutes. Lieutenant Colonel Vincent is making all Company Commanders give weekend safety briefings before Friday parades." Ward takes two steps back.

Those safety briefings are lame. Upperclassmen have said they're another way women have ruined Graham, made it soft. Like no one knew before the brief not to drink and drive, or engage in otherwise reckless behavior.

"My bad." She laughs her annoying laugh. "You mean you aren't totally tracking the major fundraising the LAMC Foundation has been doing since August? It's like all over the alumni bulletin boards.

Coleman shakes her head. I quickly stop my head from shaking too before either of them notices. Wait, didn't Max tell me a few weeks ago that the LAMC Foundation seemed to have a new marketing manager? Or at least an influx of money to build a better marketing campaign. *The man behind the curtain.* Shit. I don't remember all of the details.

"Oh. Maybe all of those events that I *have* to go to are useful. It seems like at every single alumni event I've been to this year—whether here in town or out of state—there's at least *one* table with LAMC Foundation members and their propaganda. They've always been polite to me in conversation, but I've definitely overheard them at their tables." She pitches her voice low, imitating a stuffy, harrumphing alum. "Graham would be better off all-male again. There's value in single-gender education. Assimilation has brought nothing but bad press to our school. Standards have gotten sloppy. Blah blah blah. All stuff we've been hearing since we reported three years ago."

"Same old bullshit," Coleman chimes in supportively. Rolling her eyes for added emphasizes.

Max would be really interested to know this. If only I could ask a question or two.

"Yea. Dehenre then tells me that starting next semester, Malone's dad is going to be part of the President's Office. They're creating a special position for him. Something to do with diversity. Dehenre didn't know the exact title. Of course she's concerned because the LAMC Foundation may be rallying behind Fred not getting what *he* thinks he deserves. He's like their poster child *against* assimilation." Ward fidgets with her own sash, brushing a speck of white lint off of her dress blouse.

Coleman waves her hand dismissively. "Whatever. That dude also needs to move the fuck on. He could've been Charlie Battalion Commander; yet nooooo….that was beneath him. He *chose* to be a senior private. No one forced him."

True. No one forced Malone to be a senior private, but maybe if he was Regimental Commander, the school wouldn't even have to wonder if Graham will revert to being all-male again. Enough of the status quo would have been left intact that some of us wouldn't have to worry about whether or not we'll have the chance to graduate.

Ward rolls her eyes. "He's such a douche. We're in Spanish class together. He makes it a point to sit as far away from me as possible."

"Even though this is very interesting," Coleman gestures for Ward to get to the point while glancing at the clock. "What does this have to do with you being more...*human*?"

"I know, I know. Parade. But this all ties together. Dehenre said that we need to step up our marketing campaign, too. The women here ..."

"Marketing campaign? We aren't fucking puppets. We are cadets *and* college students!" Coleman interrupts furiously.

"Don't get me started, Ave. I wanted to give that woman a piece of my mind. Apparently, we need to be seen doing more stuff together - the women. With male cadets too, of course. So the public can see we're fully integrated and accepted or whatever."

"What image does she have in her mind? Oh I know... we could highlight the Field House scandal. Male and females cadets were doing stuff together there!" Coleman laughs. I prick myself with a safety pin.

"Ugh...don't remind me of that shit. Chris," I turn my head so they don't notice my flush, "said he couldn't finish interviewing everyone he needed to yet, I told him to get me something by 30 January. *Someone* has to know something substantial. I don't know why he is taking so long."

"Shocker. He's dragging his feet," Coleman laments while placing her sword in its sheath. "Are you guys talking again, by the way? Not about school shit... but *you know*." Coleman pauses for a few seconds. "I know you don't want to hear it—but he *still* owes you an apology, Cathy! You guys were friends at one point. Like for three fucking years! And then when his boy, Fred didn't get RC, he just dropped you. No warning. Just iced you out. Like it was convenient to be friends with a girl before yet now it suddenly wasn't.

Ward raises her hand at Coleman. "I got it, Ave. Can we not talk about this right now. It really doesn't bother me. We are cordial with each other. Besides, when someone shows you who they are, believe them."

"Fair point," Coleman offers. "Okay, okay. Let me ask you this then—back on topic. Do you think the Foundation has a chance of raising enough money to privatize?"

A few seconds pass. "No...no, I don't. There'd be a legal battle again, someone would sue for sure. Plus, what would happen to the girls that're already here?" Both turn to look at me in unison. Without thinking, I meet their gazes head on before they look away. "But I suppose *we*—you included, could do more to at least try to get to know the other women more."

Coleman smiles and sighs. "You know I hate doing all-girl shit. Always have. The school knows it. And Dehenre *definitely* knows it. But since you asked me nicely and it *is* our senior year...Fuck it. What do you need me to do."

"I'll send you and our other six classmates an email this weekend. I'll leave out the LAMC Foundation stuff though." Ward waves her index finger at Coleman. "That's between us. Remember that!"

"Ma'am, yes, ma'am," Coleman responds sarcastically with a grin.

Ward walks out of the room flipping her the bird.

———

After parade, Max and I had planned to get supplies to make the Thanksgiving headdresses. For Graham's Thanksgiving feast, knobs make headdresses for their mess carvers. The bigger the better, naturally, plus they have to be handmade and personalized. Knobs are always Indians with one lone paper feather. It's supposed to be a group project among all of the knobs on mess, but after what happened with the banner, I'm not taking any chances. Not surprisingly, neither Callahen, Bates, nor Tillman put up much of an argument when I said I'd handle Coleman's. They can handle ours and the two sophomores on mess. Let's hope they don't fuck that up.

But just in case, I'm getting supplies for those too.

I check my IMs before heading to Tad's.

Hey there…haven't heard much from you in awhile. Are Ash and Reagan giving you a hard time? Want me to take care of them. ☺ *Definitely need a break from marching in a box. Off to meet F for dinner before I hit the books this weekend. Want to get a head start on finals. Shoot me a message over the weekend so I know you're doing okay. Talk soon.*

A warm smile consumes my face at the normalcy. Thank goodness Ash and Reagan already left. I wouldn't be able to hide it.

I grab my laundry bag to wash at Tad's and head out of Delta Battalion. The battalion is bathed in the soft, yellow light of the emergency lamps spaced evenly along the top of the galleries. I like the battalion like this. It makes me feel like everything is going to be okay. Like everything makes sense. It makes Graham almost …*bearable.* As if I actually do really belong here. That I'm here for duty or honor or country - or all three, when really I'm here for *me.*

Chapter Ten. *So the fearful order lived again.*

We assemble in the squad room dressed in a hodgepodge of uniforms on Saturday morning. Some choose to wear their general leave uniforms, like me. Others are still in the physical fitness uniform, like Ash and Reagan.

"Alright. I'll make this quick." Callahan booms authoritatively as usual. "Let's do a quick sweep and trash detail on your respective divisions. Then you can go on General Leave. If you want to go to mess for breakfast, meet back down here and we'll all march over together."

It's generally a good idea not to go to mess by yourself as a knob - even on weekends. Since we don't march to mess on the weekends, it's open seating. Basically, we just fill in at the next empty seat, mixed in with never-before-seen knobs and upperclassmen. It's a quick way to turn a simple Saturday morning breakfast into a game of Russian Roulette.

"Also, everyone remember to finish your headdresses." He turns squarely to me. Hands on his hips. "Kensley, are you *sure* you have Coleman's covered?"

"Sir, yes, sir." *Dick.* I couldn't resist.

The room fills with a low flood of laughter.

"Why the fucking attitude? It was a serious question, Bennett." I don't answer, which only infuriates him further. His face's crimson hue angry. "I don't want *your* Company Commander coming in here crying again about some bullshit."

"*My* Company Commander? I didn't realize 15th Company had more than one. It must be sooooo fucking exhausting to be you!" My words run reckless of their leash. "Do you even believe the bullshit that comes out of your mouth, or do you just pretend to believe it to win favors with upperclassmen and your family?"

I regain control of them in the silent stillness of the crowded room.

Callahan takes one step towards me.

My heart knocks against my chest.

My throat dry.

My stomach the scene of the Olympic gymnastic try-outs.

Yet I know better than to move even one eye lash.

"Fuck. *You*, Kensley!"

I let out a quite breath to steady my anger. The heat and rawness of his words still faint on my face as he turns, cool and refined, to the rest of the knobs. "Anyway, if you want to go to breakfast, meet back here in thirty. Then let's do this all over again tomorrow. Any questions?"

———

Maybe it's time for a little girliness on this headdress. Among this grey. I'm thinking glitter. Pink construction paper. The works. I was on the fence about it before, since female cadets already stand out for so many reasons. Longer hair, even with our knobby haircuts. Breasts that make our uniforms fit awkwardly. I've seen some of the upperclassmen wearing makeup and little studs in their ears—all within Blue Book regulation, of course. At first I was against it. Like I always tell Ash and Reagan, if you wanted to wear makeup, you should've gone to another college. But other times, guys like Callahan make me want to be a girl even more. How dare he volley cheap shots at me on a Saturday morning in front of the rest of the class? And I am not even surprised that Ash and Reagan just hid in the back of the room and said nothing. Cowards.

Fuck it.

Thanks to that little display, he and everyone in the Corps will be able to see Coleman's girly headdress from across the parade deck. The only one whining will be Clint. Besides, I need to try to get back into Coleman's good graces somehow.

I head to Tad's as arranged. Max and I are already planning to spend all day today building our headdresses. The glue will have plenty of time to dry and we can go back to the store on Sunday if we need to for any last minute additions. I'll be working on Coleman's and Max is on Malone's. I'm glad 9th Company made Malone a mess carver even though senior privates aren't supposed to have any interactions with knobs. Just because he doesn't have rank, doesn't mean that Malone isn't a leader.

The smell of glue greets my nose as I enter Tad's house. Clearly Max got a head start on his headdress.

"Hey Max. Sorry I'm late." He's bent over his creation, gingerly trying to glue together the inside wooden frame. The enclosed terrace on the side of the house is littered with craft supplies leaving me unsure of where to step.

"Hey, K. No worries. I just wanted to get started as soon as I could. Don't want to spend the whole day putting this shit together. We deserve some rest, too." Rest. What a comforting thought. I'd given anything right now to be able to stop ruminating for at least a few hours. Watch some mindless television. But I can't afford to rest. There's always something you could be doing as a knob - studying, shining-up, ironing.

I nod. "Couldn't agree with you more. A break from General Callahan would be an added bonus."

Max shoots me a questioning look.

"He made us report to the squad room prior to the sweep detail for accountability. Then he had the balls to ask me in front of everyone if I was *really* working on Coleman's headdress. Like, have I ever not done something I said I was going to do?" My hands gesture wildly. "Seriously! Who does he think he is? Oh…and the best part is when I told him I had it covered, he goes, 'I don't want *your* Company Commander whining about something.'" Max laughs at my imitation of his southern accent. "*My* Company Commander?! I don't even know what that means. Coleman was right; when he filled out his application for Graham—women were already here. We weren't going to go away. He needs to live with that. I know he's just trying to win favors with upperclassmen, but he just fucking drives me —."

Max's glazed look stops me.

I wasn't really having a conversation with Max but rather with myself. And it wasn't even a conversation. It was a rant. Max has just been standing there, smiling. Listening. Hot glue gun in one hand. Construction paper in the other. Feather stuck to his right calf.

"You're cute when you go off on a tangent." His ears glow red in an instant. "I mean… I mean, your tangent was cute. It was interesting. Unique. You know what I mean." He sits back down to work on his headdress, avoiding eye contact. Ash and Reagan always teased me about Max liking me. Were they right for once? But I am not here to date. And if things already went bad for him for being in my room during ESP, I can't imagine what the upperclassmen in his Company would do to him if they found out that he was dating a another cadet.

I need to change the topic. Quickly. This is awkward for both of us.

I proceed to tell him everything I overheard Ward telling Coleman yesterday before parade, hoping to create an equilibrium between us again. I'm leaving out the part where Ward pretty much threatened me if I told anyone else. Max doesn't need to know that I'm taking a risk for him. He might get the wrong idea.

He pulls out his dark blue notebook. "Hmmm…that's pretty much what Caroline printed in her column today." He scribbles something down feverishly.

"What do you think it means? That Malone is President of the LAMC and now will have a position at Graham?" More of a rhetorical question, since Max is as clueless as I am. We are just two knobs thinking they can solve some sort of perceived mystery. If there's even one to solve. A sickening thought sprouts.

"Max...." He leans over to hear my whispered words. "What if...
what if...this is the beginning of the end? What if—as of right now, the
Foundation already raised enough money to privatize Graham? And the
school just doesn't want to tell us 'cause they know a bunch of us
probably wouldn't come back after Thanksgiving. And definitely not after
Christmas Furlough."

Max notebook slides down his leg into the sea of art supplies, as he
shakes his head and grabs me by the shoulders. "That's fucking crazy, K. I
see where you might think that, but it's completely irrational. Look....I
don't disagree that there's a conflict of interest for Malone. But after five
years, the school has *way* too much to lose. Maybe bringing him in as head
of diversity is a way to appease the LAMC Foundation. A concession of
sorts, y'know? Build bridges. It's not like he's going to replace anyone."

The logical side of my brain wants to believe him. Wants to trust in
the system outside of Graham. But the other side can't help but see
everything we've uncovered so far - the editorials, the donations, Malone
now working at the school. And what would happen to *me* if Graham
wasn't an option for me next year? I don't know what other college I
would even go to. What would Dad accept? What would he want me to
do?

"I feel sick, Max," I confess with my head in my hands.

"I can't begin to understand what it must be like being a girl at
Graham. Everyone knows your name because there's only like five of you
—or whatever. Everything you do is watched. Somewhere, someone wants
you to fail. Then there's that whole Field House thing...." Max pauses, his
index finger playing with the trigger of the glue gun. "But we only know
what we know. And even if what we do know doesn't look that great right
now, there's plenty we don't know that could explain it all."

Right. The Field House incident. Timing on that was pretty bad but
how could anyone have predicted the Foundation's influx of donations, or

Malone's new position within the administration? At least Chris hasn't made any headway on the investigation. For once I'm glad that the gossip incubator remains air tight.

"It's ...*okay,* Max." I smile more for me than for him. "Thank you. Thanks for knowing what to say and for understanding. For being a ... .*friend.*"

"Of course, K." He picks up his headdress again. "Now...you wanna finish this and then get lunch with Stacey and Dean?"

I couldn't think of a better idea myself.

After a quick lunch, we venture back into art class on the patio.

With the glue dry on both of our skeletal wooden frames, we can now move on to the actual decorating. We work through most of the afternoon with only idle conversation, the low drone of the television as white noise.

Gluing, cursing, cutting, taping. Re-gluing. Cursing again.

"You guys do realize you're taking this headdress thing way too fucking seriously, right?" Stacey's voice interrupts us unexpectedly. "I did the same thing, so I recognize and kind of appreciate, the effort."

Max looks up at her with a blank expression. "Okay. Well... then you know it's serious in the moment, Stace." Max quickly moves beyond the moment. "What're we doing for dinner?" Max asks with a grin to soften his harsh comment. We may be at our host family's house but Stacey is still an upperclassman.

When the final feather is glued, we stand back to admire our work in the overhead light. (The sun set long ago.)

Both of our headdresses come in at nearly six feet tall. Malone's is covered with dark feathers and random items that he apparently likes. Max even went so far as to pin on the rank of Regimental Commander, symbolized by three diamonds. It's a ballsy move, but we all do what we need to survive and fit in.

Coleman's, on the other hand, is an explosion of pinks and purples, glitter, and even an array of fake gemstones that blink when the light hits them just right.

I pet the elephant in the room. "Pretty bold on that rank thing there…"

"Don't read anything into it, K." Max avoids my face and pretends to clean up. "I've always been honest with you. If I didn't think you should be here… I would tell you. I meant what I said earlier about the Foundation. Plus, if I really thought women didn't belong at Graham, I wouldn't be friends with you - openly."

A point I never considered.

Uncomfortable at my silence, Max deflects. "I like the boldness you took in making Coleman's headdress more girly than it should be. You might be starting a new tradition."

"Let's just say I felt inspired to make a change." A wicked smile punctuates my response.

Gwendolyn drives us—Max, me and our six-foot-tall headdresses—back to Graham. I don't think we would've managed to walk back with these creations.

Before I go to sleep, I check my IMs. My weekend starts and ends with a note from Chris.

Happy Sunday night! How was your weekend? I didn't write much this weekend because I didn't want to distract you. Productive? Did you finish that headdress you wanted to work on? I bet it looks great. I obviously didn't have to work on a headdress. LOL I was productive though—did some studying for finals already. It'll ease the load after Thanksgiving. Have a good Monday!

Chapter Eleven: *I would always try to seize that moment and to accept its challenge.*

"*That's* Coleman's fucking headdress? It looks like My Little Pony took a shit on Barbie," Callahan spews at me as I enter the squad room Tuesday evening, headdress in hand.

"That doesn't even make sense, Clint," I fire back, squeezing into the already-crowded squad room. All of us, plus our headdresses, plus the weight of the muggy November air, makes the room even more stifling than usual.

"Kind of like your headdress, Bennett." Bates snickers at his own lame joke. "What in the world is it supposed to be? We're celebrating Thanksgiving...not the coronation of the Queen of England."

"There's no way I want anything to do with it. Nothing. I'd rather upperclassmen think I didn't help at all, than have them think I helped with *that* shit." Callahan crosses his arms in protest. "Seriously, Bennett. Did you think at all about the messaging you're sending? We all know Coleman is a fucking female. There was no reason for you to be so... so fucking gaudy about it." The tone of his voice casts an even harsher frost on his words.

"Yeah...um, I don't want any part of it either," Tillman says sheepishly, avoiding my gaze—pretty much like everyone else in the squad room, to include Ash and Reagan.

"Fine. If that's how guys want it. I have no problem excluding you. But don't come whining to me when you get dropped for push-ups or have to run the stairs." I'm not sure any of that would happen but it sounds good. Plus, the specter of Callahan's words from our last interaction still lingers in the corner.

Callahan lets out a sarcastic laugh. "Give me a fucking break!"

"Happy Thanksgiving, knobbies," Trevino bellows, bounding through the door - a welcome interruption. "I know for many of you this'll be ya'lls first time away from home—and mommy and dad—for Thanksgiving, but don't ya'll worry—we're *alllllll* family tonight. We're going to go have a nice family meal now. You don't have to brace at mess tonight, but ya'll still have to be polite and such. Then we'll smoke a cigar after dinner in the battalion. Callahan, did you buy cigars from that store we told you about downtown?"

"Sir, yes, sir." Callahan's voice is proud as he hands Trevino the brown paper bag resting on the top bunk. Tool. I really wish I could roll my eyes right now.

"Excellent. Here's fifty bucks. I don't want the administration claiming that we're using you little knobbies for personal favors," he says, extending several folded bills in Callahan's direction.

"Sir, no, sir. Sir, permission to speak freely, sir?" What is he up to now?

With an intrigued expression, Trevino gestures him to speak.

"Sir, the cigars are a gift from these cadet privates, sir." Normally I would say he's being a kiss ass, but that was expected. Paying for incidentals like this out of our own pockets gets paid forward when we're upperclassmen. Of course, that's assuming all of us are around to even *be* upperclassmen.

Okay, Trevino… time for you to feign surprise.

"Oh…now that's *sooooo* unexpected, knobbies. Really appreciate that. Guess you new corps knobbies still *can* have a system. And respect." All upperclassmen, and some alumni—okay, *most*, like to refer to the classes that entered Graham after assimilation as "new corps." It's yet another way of drawing a line in the sand to let everyone know that after 1996, the system for knobs changed because of our presence. That standards have slipped. That it's no longer the Graham of your father, uncle, brother. It's total bullshit. Which is why I take every opportunity, to ensure they don't. It's hard sometimes though. Some upperclassmen are afraid we'll report them. And sometimes...*sometimes*, other women block the entry through the door. Born out of jealousy because they aren't liked or as good as of a cadet or no one wanted them to be part of the old corps.

"Durham, let's see that headdress you made for me," Trevino demands jovially.

"Sir, yes, sir."

"Oooh...this is *nice*, Durham," Trevino exclaims. The words wrapped tightly in his Texas drawl. "*Real* nice!"

It is nice. Silas went completely outside tradition and made his headdress in the form of a cowboy hat. Damn. Why didn't I think of something like that? Silas used a helmet as the base and then somehow figured out a way to build a two-foot-wide, two-foot-high cowboy hat around it. Wearable and creative.

The lone bugle note echos throughout the battalion.

"Alright, put your little one-feathered hats on and roll out." Trevino strolls out the door wearing his temporary prized possession. As we stand on line, other mess carvers and upperclassmen scramble to find the knobs on their mess. Eager. Giddy.

Coleman appears in front of me. "Well now. This *is* unexpected, Bennett." She takes the headdress from me and holds it up against the light. "I admire the gaudiness." A grin fills her face. "Glitter *and* jewels isn't something you see here everyday."

"Ma'am, yes, ma'am." I hate myself for saying something so lame.

She walks across the quad, away from 15th Company. My eyes follow her. A brief break in the festive gaggle of grey uniforms and colorful headdresses reveals Ward walking towards Coleman. I watch as they admire each other's headdresses. Excellent. I managed to make Coleman's bigger than Ward's. They pose for a quick photo to memorialize the occasion. Another momento, perhaps, to be stashed away in a cardboard box stored under a bed or closet. Almost forgotten yet always carefully inventoried for each move. Pulled out when hairlines have rescinded, belts have shrunken, and the bad memories faded.

I suddenly remember the box mom kept in the basement. The tattered, water-stained box of all of my crafts from elementary school—blue construction paper with half the elbow macaroni already missing; a clay handprint from first grade; my sixth grade winning spelling bee award, dusty and faded. I swallow the tears percolating from the memories.

"Form up, knobs," a voice commands bringing me back to the now. Back to Graham. Instead of running to our usual places in formation, we—even knobs, leisurely saunter to our spots. It feels a bit wrong, but nice at the same time. I guess even Graham isn't immune to the holiday spirit. When it comes down to it, no matter how different we are, where we come from, or what year we're in—maybe we really have grown into a family.

At least on Thanksgiving.

The mood in the mess hall is equally festive and relaxed. The smell of turkey, pumpkin pie and gravy mask the usual smells of stale food and bleach. Instead of Buchanan directing us to sit and eat as usual once all of the companies are present in the mess hall, Steele, the Regimental Religious Officer, gives a short benediction of thanks. Trevino wasn't kidding. The normally semi-quiet mess hall is filled with a low roar usually reserved for stadiums. We spend our meal in a position that can almost be called "relaxed." It feels awkward. Abnormal even. My body tense with the anticipation of what *may* happen. We still have to tend to the upperclassmen, of course. Everywhere I look, there are upperclassmen posing for pictures with each other and their headdresses. Some even pose with knobs. There's Callahan posing with a group of upperclassmen. Sigh.

"Knobs," Coleman calls from the head of the table.

"Ma'am, yes, ma'am," Tillman, Callahan, and I say in unison, turning our heads towards her mechanically.

"Nice work on my headdress. The glitter might have been a little over the top since it's now all over my uniform," she says, brushing a bit off her shoulders for emphasis. "But I'm really impressed."

Before I can get a word out, Callahan beams, "Ma'am, thank you, ma'am."

What a fucking tool. My right foot makes contact with his left shin under the table. Hard. He winces every so slightly, his face held taught from keeping in the pain. I hope it leaves a mark. He mouths something but I just shrug.

Coleman waves me over. "Bennett, let's take a photo together."

"Ma'am, yes, ma'am. I make sure to purposely bump into Tillman sitting next to me as I get up from my chair. He shoots me a dirty look.

Uncertain of where to stand or what to do, I stand awkwardly in the aisle between the tables. As usual, waiting for direction.

"Hey Chris... come take a photo of me and my knob," she yells as she waves him over.

He turns to look at us, "One sec, Ave.:

Forgetting where I am and my knob status, I smile at him as he comes over.

He looks straight through me. Almost entirely expressionless. What the fuck?

I know he said not to talk in public for a reason yet this is Thanksgiving mess. Looking around, aside from the uniforms, you'd never know we were at a military college. Even Ash and Reagan are chatting with Royce at their table.

"How do you want this - horizontal or vertical?" Chris asks fumbling with the camera.

Coleman walks over to help him. "It's not brain surgery, Chris. The camera will focus itself when you push on the green button on the top right. Here. And one of each."

"Hold your horses. It's different than my camera. I need a sec. Not like the knob is going anywhere." So he does know I am here.

"Alright. You ready, Ave? One… two… *three*."

"Make sure you fully get the headdress in," she yells just as his finger makes contact with the green button. The near blinding flash records the event on film. I'm officially part of Coleman's scrapbook.

"Did you get it? Lemme see," Coleman reviews the footage on her digital camera. "Awesome, Chris! Thanks. You want me to take any photos for you? I can email them to you."

Chris shakes his head. "I'm good, thanks. Already took some. Besides, I've got enough pics from the last three years."

I return to my seat, feeling heavy with disappointment. He could've at least acknowledged me. Friends do that.

After mess, we walk back to the battalion in a gaggle, knobs still in single file and upperclassmen in small clusters engaged in conversation. Aside from the headdress and the relaxed atmosphere at mess, another tradition is for knobs to smoke a cigar with the upperclassmen after dinner. I've only ever smoked a cigarette. Once. It was sophomore year, in New York. I started to hang with this group of girls yet I wouldn't say we were friends; I just didn't want to sit in awkward silence at lunch anymore. This one girl, Desiree, bought a pack of cigarettes with her fake ID at a bodega near her house in Brooklyn. We took the PATH into Jersey City, then walked along the Hudson to Liberty State Park so I was certain Dad - or anyone else I knew, wouldn't see me. We sat on a random bench, and Desiree lit the cigarette for me. I took one puff before erupting into violent coughing and then spent hours scrubbing my hands in the bathroom at the coffee shop near the Exchange Place PATH station, hoping Dad wouldn't smell it on me. It was *so* cliché. I've never smoked a cigar before though. I've seen Dad and his Graham friends do it, and I think it's supposed to be easier than cigarette smoking because you're not supposed to inhale. *I think.* I'll just do what everyone else is doing.

Naturally, Callahan's in charge of passing out smaller cigars to the knobs, while Malcolm passes around the lighter. Predictably, Callahan walks right by me.

"Hey, dude. You forgot to give Kensley a cigar," Malcolm loudly whispers after him.

"I didn't forget." Callahan walks on without looking at either of us.

Dumbfounded and unaware of what transpired at mess tonight yet more than likely oblivious to the magnitude of the incident in the squad room, Malcolm shrugs. After a few seconds, he reaches into his pocket and hands me his cigar. Lights it for me. He walks on before I can thank him, leaving me alone again on the quad while the others group together.

I look around for someone to stand with.

Anyone.

Yet I am unsure. Uncertain of where I fit in.

Clusters of cadets are spattered around the company area, but it takes a second for my brain to catch up to what my eyes are seeing. I don't believe it. Knobs are with *upperclassmen*. Phil Doss and Wade are talking to Sherman in one area of the quad. Karl, Darron, and Reagan (of all people) are laughing with Gibson in another. How did this happen? *When* did this happen?

Loneliness permeates me from the outside in. Or maybe …*maybe* it has always been there. Waiting for the moment to step out from the recesses of my subconscious.

My eyes nearly break from the heaviness. I swallow the tears, hard.

"Hey Bennett," a familiar voice says from behind.

Before turning around, I blink quickly, hoping my lashes fan away the tears.

"Smoke bothering your eyes?"

Oh, it's you. Now you know my name?

I offer Chris a polite smile, "Sir, yes, sir."

"Cut the sir sandwich shit for a sec, Bennett. Smoke is worse if you wear contacts."

I nod in agreement even though I don't wear contacts.

"Is this your first time smoking a cigar?"

I nod again confused by Mr. Congeniality.

"It's not for everyone. Don't feel pressured to smoke it if you don't want to. I clearly don't, as you can see," he says, holding up his empty hands.

"Sir, thank you, sir."

"What did I say?!" He laughs. "Here, let me take it from you though. If anyone asks where yours is, just say you already smoked it." He smiles at me conspiratorially.

"Thanks, sir." He reaches for the cigar in my hand. "I've seen—." I stop mid-sentence as his fingers wrap around mine. I stare at him, unsure of what to say or do or think. The cigar falls onto the red square we're standing on without a sound. The soft glow of the ember twinkles up at us.

"Way to spaz, Bennett." Ward's southern twang is like a bucket of cold water as she approaches. She just can't stay away. I know this is her company but the Homecoming banner should have reminded her that she's not welcomed here.

"Nah. It ain't her fault, Cathy." Chris bends over to pick up the half-dead cigar off the quad. "I was trying to take the thing from her."

"Whatever." Ward turns all of her attention to Chris. "Can we chat later about the investigation?"

I have become invisible again. Uncertain of how to eject myself, I remain frozen in the stuffy November night. At least I am not standing alone.

"Sure. What time? Where?"

Ward pulls out a black index card-sized pleather notebook and leafs through the pages. "Um, 2000. My room?"

"Sounds good. I'll bring what I have so far."

The single bugle note ushering the start of ESP sounds downright merciful from the loudspeakers. My easy escape.

The overhead lights in our room are off as I enter.

Before I can flip the switch, Ash moans, "Don't turn on the light. Please. We got sick from the cigars." Perhaps I dodged a bullet, thanks to Chris.

"Okay. Um, do you guys need anything?" It's still Thanksgiving and Trevino said we are family.

"No. Thanks. Just silence." Her plea whimpers from the darkness.

"And darkness," adds Reagan.

Chapter Twelve. *What has happened to me and will I ever be the same?*

I'm standing in my room at Graham Military College.

In Delta Battalion.

On third division.

Again.

I can't believe how fast the last five days of Thanksgiving furlough flew by. I was mainly just me at Tad's, so I managed to do lots of reading to prep for finals next week in between bouts of television. I did get out to get some "air," as Stacey called it, so I wasn't a complete recluse. Max came back yesterday and we decided to kill time by going to the mall in North Charleston. Actually, Stacey insisted we go. She felt Max and I need to have some fun—even as knobs. It felt exhilarating, rebellious even, to wear civvies out in town. She said when she was a knob, they'd do it all the time. They never got caught because they went to places cadets don't normally go. Apparently, only knobs hang out downtown or in public at all. Upperclassmen hang out at friend's houses or splurge on a hotel or even drive home entirely, if they live close enough.

I bought a new copy of *The Lords of Discipline,* too. I had to. I couldn't bring myself to mark up the copy Mom gave me. But I have yet to start on the assignment.

I just can't.

Breaking the crisp paperback spine means letting loose the caged memories of my youth, filled with smiles, loving looks, and admiration from Dad. Family trips.

But it will never be that way again.

It will never be three of us again. Shit…let's be honest, it will never even be two of us.

My future changed course when the semi truck ran the red light, its oversized halogen haloes barreling towards us through the rain-soaked glass of our sedan. The sound of screeching tires on wet cement; my book bag suspended in midair between mom and me; the feel of thick grey nylon strap tight across my chest and lap as metal forced against metal in a violent, unnatural clash.

Me in the driver's seat.

It was over as soon as it began, leaving in its wake nothing but caustic silence and the swish-swish of our car's windshield wipers. The smell of spilled gasoline will forever make me nauseous.

That was the end of Mom's life, and my life as I knew it. And it was also the start of my path to Graham.

***

I turn on my desk lamp and take in the soft glow of the empty room.

I feed the silence with Charleston's top 40 station. Lip-synching along as I place my neatly folded laundry in my half press, iron three duty uniform shirts—taking care to get the creases perfectly centered and straight, shine my brass and two pairs of shoes, and unpack my books, carefully lining them up in descending height order on the shelf above my desk.

I look around the room hoping to find something else to do. Anything. Shit, I came back too early.

Thank goodness.

"Decent," I shout at the knock on the door.

"Hi," Chris says as he enters. "Is this a bad time?"

"Oh, um…hello, sir" I try to say in a neutral yet still formal tone. "Nope. Not a bad time. Reagan and Ash aren't back yet."

The door clicks shut as he steps further into the room - the sound more definitive as if it knows that it's against the rules for the door to be shut. I stifle a gulp

"Back early, too, huh? Here, I brought you some of my mom's famous carrot cake." He places a semi-clear plastic container on my half press. "I thought maybe…well, I hope it doesn't, um…" His voice trails off to a whisper as he fails to find the words he's grappling for.

What's he up to? "Thank you." It takes all my will to suppress the sir. "That was very thoughtful. It's okay. Really." I offer him a smile.

He fidgets with the strings on his grey Graham issued hoodie.

I'm just as lost as he is. Words and wit are still on furlough.

After a few more seconds, he clears his throat and lets out a sigh. "You know, this is gonna sound weird but…it'd be easier if you weren't a cadet here."

I throw my head back and let out a laugh. "*Everything* would be easier if we both weren't cadets here. But here we are."

"Yes, yes…that's certainly true. What I meant was—." He stops mid-sentence and purses his lips in frustration. He's being really respectful and considerate, trying not to cross a line. I mean, we could both get into serious trouble. Tours would most certainly be awarded. Graham has a strict no fraternization rule between upperclassmen and knobs - even as friends. That is why we constantly refer to ourselves in third person and why Recognition Day is such a big deal. It is the day upperclassmen call us by our first names - maybe.

Yet *are* we friends? Do I even want to be friends with him? I don't know anything about him. One minute he is an asshole and he ignores me and the next, he's IMing me and bringing me his mom's *fucking* carrot cake. Fuck him. I am not here to make him feel good about himself. For him to talk to when he wants female attention. That's not the normalcy I want.

Or deserve.

"Listen…," gleaning strength from my anger, I decide to be direct. "uhm, I think there's…"

"See? I told you she would be back before us," Reagan flaunts as she and Ash enter the room giggling yet immediately freeze in place.

I brace as Reagan's brown eyes lock onto mine.

Chris takes command of the room as. "Alright. Thanks, Bennett, for the clarification." He moves towards the door. "If I need anything else, I'll let you know."

"Sir, yes, sir." Guess I'll be direct some other day.

"Oh my god. Oh. My. God," Ash blurts out the second the door clicks shut. "Still waters certainly *do* run deep, Cadet Bennett."

"What the fuck are you talking about? He just needed me to clarify one of my responses from the interview." I turn away from them and mindlessly stack and re-stack the folders on my desk. "He met with Ward before furlough, who I guess wanted more info about some shit." I ramble on, "I don't know. He was here for like five minutes. And then I...."

"Figures!" Ash cuts in. "Should've known a tool like you ... always thinking you're better than everyone, would be in here with a boy for anything other than school shit. Get a fucking ..."

"Give her a break, Ash," Reagan interrupts quickly attempting to ensure the prelude to tension remains a prelude. "What else did he ask in regards to the interview? And why weren't we asked? All the girls were interviewed so it'd only be fair?"

I roll my eyes. "It's not always about *you*. And if he wants to ask you anything, I'm sure he'll let you know."

Ash doesn't want to leave it at just a prelude, "I am *sure* he will. But will he come to our room during ESP to ask about an official investigation—"

"Don't be fucking dramatic, Ash!" Still feeling like being direct, I turn to squarely face her, "I know this plays perfectly into your narrative and into your...*perception*. He was here for the damn Field House investigation. The same one you were interviewed for." I slam the stack of folders down hard on the metal desk. Ash recoils slightly. "I don't question the status of your relationship with every guy you talk to. And there are a lot!" My jaw tightens. They're ridiculous. "And technically this isn't ESP which you'd know if you bothered to pay a bit more attention to being a cadet than what girl is talking to what boy!" I take a breath to reload," I don't even know why you came to Graham. You have zero interest in its history or being shined up or assimilating into the Corps. You're always fucking complaining about—"

"Save it, Kensley." Reagan cuts me off hard. "We're all here for different reasons. I'll give you that. But ...but just because we aren't bending over backwards to please Callahan - no matter how much of a dick he is, or using certain words like - *douche detail*, doesn't mean we don't want to be part of this school. To one day wear the ring. I gave up a full scholarship to come here. So I sure as shit am not going to sell myself out or what I believe in for the hopes that our classmates, or the upperclassmen who don't want us here anyway, will maybe...*maybe* one day accept me." Reagan takes a measured breath. "So fuck them *and* fuck you, too."

Reagan clamps her mouth shut. Her eyes cut cold and hard.

It's my move.

This could be the end or it could be the beginning. All we have to do is survive together for six more months. Yet six more months in this room - *together,* could feel like an eternity under the wrong circumstances.

"Fine," I declare and walk to my desk. She has to know she didn't win after all. I pretend to leaf through the magazine stacked in the right-hand corner. And Ash and Reagan begin to unpack their bags and bags of stuff they brought back from Thanksgiving furlough.

The pink and white striped bags seem to contain scented candles. A plus in these old rooms while at the same time a fire hazard. And are they even allowed per the blue book? I see various packages of granola bars. I've got those too. Plastic bins with what looks like homemade cookies.

Wonder if they'll share with Wade? Aside from the normal white v-neck undershirts and black socks, the laundry bag did reveal pink flannel pajama pants and hoodie.

"Nice PJs." Hoping six months passes under the right circumstances.

"Thanks. We got them on sale at the mall during Black Friday. They're going to be sooooo much more comfortable than sleeping in those scratchy blue shorts and shirt that were issued to us." Ash squeals, hugging them tightly, making them her most prized possession at the moment.

Stacey's words run through my head. "Not to be a tool—."

"But you're *obviously* going to be one anyway," Reagan interrupts without looking up from her laundry bag, her voice still charged. "Cause you can't fucking help yourself. So go ahead…."

"I'm trying to keep you out of trouble, Reagan. Anyway…you can't wear those out onto the galleries. You're going to have to change into some sort of uniform *every time* you want to go to the bathroom. So you might as well not even bother," I say to her matter-of-factly. "Plus, those are still considered civvies. Where are you going to hide those during Morning Room Inspections, for example?"

"Kensley, cut the crap. Don't pretend like you care about Ash or me. You'd *looove* for us to get in trouble. Get tours so we'd have to walk back and forth on the quad for all to see. So they'd say 'See, only a matter of time before those two girls got in trouble. They were never right for Graham - as you yourself just shared." She spits my earlier words at me. "Get transferred out of the company even. Or better yet, just not come back after Christmas furlough." Reagan stops digging in her bags and faces me, hands on her hips.

Ash blurts, "We've already figured that out, K. We don't need you. We're going to put the PJs with the rest of our civvies, in the—."

"Ashley!" Reagan cuts her off. Fast.

A confused look befalls Ash. And me. Please tell me they don't. They've had civvies this whole time. In this room? And I didn't know. We may not have chosen one another as roommates, but we're all responsible for the condition of this room—and the contraband it hides.

"What do you mean *with the rest of the fucking civvies*?"

Neither one of them answers. Ash shoots Reagan a desperate look.

"Seriously! I want an answer. I *demand* an answer."

"You mean, she... she didn't know, Reagan?" Ash whispers as if I'm not in the room.

Reagan lets out a sigh of frustration. "No, Ash. Kensley didn't know we've had civvies in the room all semester."

This is too good. "Oh...what happened to all that shit you just said 30 minutes ago? That you're all about assimilating yet not wanting to sell out your precious morales." I gesture with my army wide. "You may not use certain words, Reagan but you certainly are trying your damndest." I tap my left foot on the hardwood floor. The rhythmic tapping like a metronome. "Where are they? I want to see them. I have a fucking right to know where they are." Their mere presence in the room is going to get *me* tours too. Subvert my goals. An upperclassman isn't going to know or care whose pink pants are whose. Tarnish *my* reputation. Lump me in with them like Coleman gets lumped in with Ward.

Reagan lets out an overweight sigh and jumps up on top of her half press and begins to count the ceiling tiles from the window. With her left hand she pushes a ceiling tile up and over, revealing a black hole. What I thought was just cosmetic covering for wires and such, cadets turned into a place to hide contraband. An open secret to all except me it seems. Her right hand reaches in and after a few seconds pulls out a green mesh laundry bag and throws it onto the floor. It lands with a solid thud on the hardwood.

We each stare at the bag for a few minutes in silence. I wonder if this is what looking at a dead body would be like.

"Thank you." I break the silence. "Why do you even have them?"

Reagan takes a deep breath and runs her hands through her short knobby haircut as she lets it out. "You know we stand out so much here, no matter where we are on campus. I know you think that stuff doesn't bother us - especially after what I ....uhm said earlier but, but it does. Constantly being watched. Every move critiqued. Reported on to our company commander. Or anyone who will listen. Gossiped about." The confession is like a weight she carries, and she leans against her metal rack. "We just wanted a break from all of that when we go out shopping. Fade into the crowd."

Ash adds softly, "Like normal college students."

I'm speechless. Not because I disagree with anything Reagan said… but because it's exactly how I feel. This whole time, I thought it was so much easier for them to be here. They have each other, and something that almost looks like friendship with our male classmates. And yet they're still struggling. Just like me. Instead of seeing our similarities, we are at each other's throats.

Judging.

"I don't understand. So… just the two of you go out in civvies? Where?"

"Um, no. We know cadets in other companies, Kensley," Reagan clarifies with an eye roll. "It's been with people from the company, too. Not naming names though. I don't fucking trust you. You'd turn us in to score points. And I'm *certainly* not telling you where we go."

She wedges the distances between us firmly in place once again.

"Fine."

Reagan wants to make this about trust when she's blatantly violating the Blue Book on so many levels. And they've implicated me now by keeping the civvies in the room. Like anyone would believe that I didn't know anything about it if they were found out. The nerve of them.

"I don't give a shit where you wear them or who with.," I say flatly. "I still want them outta here."

With nothing but a huff, Reagan picks up the bag and returns it to its temporary resting spot in the ceiling. I don't like it, but they'll have to stay there until general leave on Friday. I hope they get caught sneaking them out of the battalion.

The bugle sounds. The three of us stare at each other in solitary terror.

Fuck. Accountability formation. We completely lost track of time.

The three of us grab our covers and rush to the squad room, the two of them moving to the far rear corner as we enter.

The second after we enter, the screen door screeches and in pops Trevino. "Good evening, little knobbies."

"Sir, good evening, sir," we answer, bracing. That was close. Too close.

"I'm sure ya'll had fun over Thanksgiving, seeing your families and all of that stuff. Any weight ya'll put on will be PT'd right outta you Tuesday morning." He pauses to laugh at his own joke. "So don't ya—."

Trevino stops talking mid-sentence. He bolts out of the room in a single step.

"What the hell just happened?" someone asks from among the room.

Callahan answers. "No clue, man. I was trying to figure out what he was looking at. But with his height, it could be anything."

The door screeches again. This time, Trevino is accompanied by Johnson and Kenny Daniel, one of the three platoon leaders.

"Tell me my eyes didn't go fucking blind from the Texas sun, Tim."

"Holy fucking shit! You weren't kidding, Jose."

"Pitchford, Allen," Trevino commands.

Great. What am I going to be blamed for?

From the near-back of the room two voices chime, "Sir, yes, sir?"

"Don't sir, yes, sir me! Get your fucking asses up here. NOW!" Trevino's voice breaks with anger. "You have 3 seconds."

It takes a few seconds - definitely more than three, for Ash and Reagan to weave through the tightly packed squad room. Each of them trying not to step on another classmate's shoes.

"What. In. The. Actual. Fuck. Where. You. Thinking?" Trevino's hand is a blade, pointing at their heads. "You think—."

"Wipe that fucking smile off your face, Allen! You think this is funny?" Johnson steps next to Trevino. "You think this is a *game*?"

And now, with the brightness of the overhead lights, I realize what caught Trevino's eye. Aside from coming back with cookies and candles and pink PJs, Ash and Reagan decided to adorn their chestnut brown hair with blonde highlights. Idiots. It probably would've gone unnoticed if it wasn't for their knobby haircuts—where the bulk of the hair is concentrated on top.

Civvies, and now this. Assimilate my ass. *Your days are numbered, ladies*, I think uncharitably. It's only a matter of time. I just know it.

"Sir, no, sir," Ash replies, as loud as she can. A drop of sweat rolls down her right temple.

Johnson steps closer. I'm fairly certain Ash can feel his warm breath on her ear. "Is Graham some sort of fucking joke to you? Like…*oh, you just woke up one day and decided to show up? This isn't camp cupcake."

Ash swallows but is stunned into silence.

The bugle call to formation saves them.

"Roll out, knobs," Trevino commands. "Fucking new Corps."

"This isn't over," Johnson calls out after them. "In fact, it's just beginning."

We head back to our room after accountability formation. None of us says a word.

Before we can put our covers down, the door opens and in walks Coleman.

"Ma'am, good evening, ma'am." She walks right past me.

"Highlights? *Really*? Bold choice. Whose idea was it?" Coleman demands. "And why the fuck would you think it's a good idea?"

"Ma'am, no excuse, ma'am," they respond in operatic unison.

"*No.* I want an *actual* answer. No knob responses."

After a few seconds of hesitation, Ash says, "Ma'am, these cadets privates didn't think they would be so visible. Plus we used semi-permanent color. So... so, it was supposed to have washed out already."

"Well, if you only used *semi-permanent color* then it should be fine," Coleman says sarcastically and turns to me. "Why didn't you stop them from coming downstairs?"

"Ma'am, no excuse, ma'am." How could this possibly be *my* fault? I didn't buy the color. Or put it on their heads. And what could I have done to stop them? The light was low while we were unpacking and arguing. (Besides I'm pretty sure someone would've missed them at formation.)

"Now I have to deal with idiots like Johnson. He'll turn this into a big deal and whine about how this is yet another example of 'how women ruined his school.'" The undercurrent of defeat in her voice is audible through the theatrics. "He's probably already fired off an email to his brother, a proud member of the LAMC Foundation."

She turns to walk towards the door yet stops after a few steps. She lets out a frustrated sigh. *Oh hell no.* Her intention is as clear as the night sky.

Their highlights aren't a Blue Book violation, so they can't be written up and serve punishments. Yet they can't not be punished. Yet there's no way I'm going to allow Ash and Reagan their right of passage. Least of all with Coleman. I'm the one who gets PT for punishment, not them.

I deserve a system more than they do. This is my door. I've got to stop her. "Ma'am, Ms. Coleman, ma'am."

She turns to look at me. Surprised. Or maybe annoyed. I can practically see her intentions crackling like lightning around her eyes.

"Ma'am, this cadet private could get her host family to bring a box of color tomorrow, ma'am." Take the bait, damn it.

Coleman considers me for a moment. Turning to Ash and Reagan, she says, "Fine. You've got twenty-four hours to fix that shit."

"Ma'am, yes, ma'am," the three of us reply.

The door closes. The shower of gratitude from Ash and Reagan is nearly unbearable.

Nearly sickening. "Thanks for proving my point," I say to them indirectly.

But I had to do it. Because I'm the only one who deserves to feel her arms burn with pain from too many push-ups, to have her legs go numb from too many air chairs. I'm the one who deserves the treatment that will prove, once and for all, that women can hack it at Graham.

That we belong here.

That *I* belong here.

Chapter Thirteen. *In the barracks, I learned must of what there was to know about my times, my unconscionable century.*

"Hey knobs. Don't forget to buy Christmas decorations this weekend," Coleman reminds us during lunch mess on Friday, four week before finals and Christmas furlough.

The only reminder of Ash and Reagan's highlights is the scowl Johnson throws at them whenever he sees them—whenever he sees *us*. I wonder if Coleman said something to him because he pretty much stays clear of us at all times.

"Good reminder, Ave. Be sure to get lights, a tree....and those long strings of greenery," Corey yells across the table at her from his mess carver position.

"You mean—*garland*, Alex?"

"Yea. That stuff. My grandparents always had that wrapped around their banister at home. I want that wrapped around the railings on *all* divisions," Corey says with wide eyes.   Knobs within ear shot respond. "Sir, yes, sir."

"Make sure it doesn't look tacky or *cheap,*" the word heavy with implication. "Put some thought into it. I don't want it to look like Christmas vomited in our company," Coleman adds.

I pass the news to my classmates when we're in the squad room again prior to evening formation and mess.

"No shit, Bennett!" Callahan says sarcastically. "You aren't the only ones who upperclassmen talk to." Turning towards the larger group in the room, he says, "We're keeping it simple. There's a list of supplies to get on the half press. Sign your name next to what you're getting."

"Let's plan on having everything purchased by noon on Sunday." Darron is such a kiss-ass.

"Thanks, D. Almost forgot that part. I know it'll cut into general leave but I'm sure we would all rather not spend our valuable study time putting up decorations when we can knock it out on a Sunday afternoon," Callahan says. "Our normal weekend sweep detail schedule still stands, of course. We're free to go today after we do a quick douche detail." His mouth bends in a devilish grin as his eyes meet mine.

***

Max greats me in the foyer at Tad's after parade. "About time you got here, K! I've been dying to talk to you all week."

"If only you had an IM log." He rolls his eyes at this familiar point of contention.

"Whatever. I don't want to be one of those people who forgets how to interact face-to-face. That's for another—."

"Is Stacey here?" I interrupt.

"No….but she said she would be over around six or so." Max frowns at the interruption and stomps off to the den. "Are you thinking of dinner already?"

Someone seems sensitive tonight. "I wasn't until now. I need to get some Christmas decorations before Sunday." I follow him, hoping to ease his mood. "What was so urgent earlier?"

"Good planning. I'll go with you….Right, so tell me about Ash and Reagan's highlights?"

Leave it to the Corps gossip circuit.

I tell him exactly what happened: Trevino bolting out of the room, coming back with Johnson and Daniel, and of course Ash laughing. *Laughing.*

"Coleman came to our room after formation and pretty much blamed me. Like I was at their house. Or better yet, like I have any control over those two. Gwendolyn brought by some new color for them the next day."

"Were the highlights… *bad*? Not sure if that's the correct term…"

"Ummm…no. They didn't look skunk-like, if that's what you mean. They were just little strands of blonde hair inside their brown hair." I pause. "I'll deny I said this, but…they looked nice. Why the question? Are you thinking of getting some?" I tease, rubbing his nearly shaven head. "Might be tough with the boy knobby haircut."

Max pushes my hand away playfully. "I wanted to get the facts from you. I mean, obviously it was all over the Corps. Malone had a field day. He made us take our covers off during *each* formation every day this week to look at our hair."

"What an idiot. You don't even have women in 9th Company."

"You know he gets to do what he wants. Even more so now that his dad will be in that diversity position. And the LAMC Foundation started a blog or whatever this week too."

Max's face freezes. I get the distinct impression that cat was supposed to stay in the bag.

"What?" I sit up straight, ready for whatever is next.

"Ooops. I didn't want to tell you this way," Max says with downcast eyes. "So, so you haven't been on their website?"

"Nope. The LAMC Foundation isn't bookmarked as one of my favorites. Besides, everything I need to know about them, I've learned from you." Get to the point already.

Max feigns a laugh. "Okay…Makes sense. You want to go—."

"Umm…not so fast. Why the change of topic all of a sudden? Something's up?"

Max ignores me and begins to get up from the couch to make his exit.

"Max."

Max turns to face me with a look normally reserved for bad television shows. You know the scene where the police officer knocks on the door and the bad news is written all over his face? That's kind of look plastered on Max's face. But for the life of me, I can't figure out what bad news Max would be keeping from me. I know all about Malone in his company. For goodness sake, there are a ton of guys like him at Graham.

"Well…" Max searches for the right words. "It's not like you weren't going to find out anyway. The blog is more like an online yearbook. If that's a good term for it. It's organized by class year… but… it only tracks the femal—I mean women, in the Corps."

"WHAT?!" I shriek, sitting straight up. "Track? What the *fuck* does that mean?"

"I'm sorry," he whispers. "I just saw it pop up this week. I don't remember who told me. Maybe Preston. It has a yearbook photo of each of you and then basic stuff like company, major…let me see, oh if you're Corps Squad or not, what rank you've held. You know, bio stuff."

"Bio stuff?! What. Else," I request, arms crossed tightly against me.

"Umm…if you click on the picture, it opens up to a longer profile. There's a place for Blue Book violations… but mainly just gossip stuff." This might be more painful for Max than me.

"Um, hello, *1984* called."

Max tries to smile. "I-I-I…um, clicked on yours." He averts his eyes. "But…but there wasn't anything. Ash and Reagan had the whole thing about their highlights, aside from their Corps-Squad stuff. And… some other little stuff that I can't remember right now." The words fire out of his mouth in rapid succession.

I want to be mad. Furious even. But maybe this isn't surprising after all. Reagan pretty much said it herself last week—we're always under a watchful eye. Now with this big brother website, every little word or move can not only be taken out of context, but can be shared with people who aren't even in the same state. People that have never met me, or any of us—the women of Graham. I stare into the ceiling lights in the den. I don't want to cry over this, even if they're just tears of frustration. The LAMC Foundation doesn't deserve my tears. Ever.

The fan whirls monotonously overhead.

"Hey…" Max says softly, reaching down to touch my shoulder.

I don't look at him, or answer. I know that if I open my mouth ever so slightly, there would be waterfalls.

"They're jerks. Bullies. I bet… I bet they got beat up a lot when they were younger," he adds, trying to make me laugh. "Don't worry about what's on the website. You and I know the truth. You're a good cadet. You deserve to be here just as much as I do. Maybe even more."

I swallow hard. "Thanks, Max. Thanks for being a good friend. And um… classmate."

"Anytime," he says shyly, almost uncomfortably embarrassed.

"It's hard sometimes, you know. Being a knob *and* a girl. It would be nice to be able to fade into the grey. Disappear. Just to be a …*cadet*." Lately I've felt like something isn't right. I know being at Graham is where I need to be for myself, and for Dad. But sometimes… sometimes during moments like this, the emptiness feels so much more vast. Almost as if it'll never be filled. Like I'll always be lost.

I finally look at Max, uncertainty and confusion reflecting in the golden specs of his brown eyes.

The front door opens and closes. The smell of melted cheese and marina wafts into the room like a welcomed intruder.

"Maaax….Kensley," Stacey yells from the kitchen. "I brought pizza. I think we just had pizza last weekend, but I was in no mood to stand in yet another line at the grocery store."

"Hey, Stace. Will you be around tomorrow?" I ask as she walked into the den.

"You kids need a ride someplace?" she asks with a smile. "Let me think....oh, it's Christmas decoration time."

I shrug and shoot her a "you got me" grin.

"Let's make it more fun though. How about dinner and a movie? We can head to Mount Pleasant." Her eyes widen. "It'll be way more fun than just staying here."

Max and I both nod. A change of scenery might be good for us. I can't remember the last time I saw a movie.

"Would you guys be cool if two of my friends came along? They're cadets. But totally laid back. It won't be weird," she says gingerly. "Promise."

Chapter Fourteen. *A plebe could never fully trust an upperclassman…*

We decide to leave for Mount Pleasant around five o'clock on Saturday.

"Are you guys almost ready?" Stacey calls from the bottom of the stairs. The rhythmic clank of her shoes on the wooden stairs follows. My mind falls into confusion as she enters the room. Instead of her Graham leave uniform, she's wearing brown Chelsea boots, dark brown tights, a red knee-length flute skirt, and a leopard print blouse.

She laughs at my expression. "Kensley, you look like you've never seen anyone in civilian clothes before."

"You look nice, Stace," Max says to her as he walks out the room. "Thanks, kid."

"So… so, uhm you're wearing civvies out." I search for the words in my dry throat. *Don't be a tool.*

"Um…yeah. You're not comfortable with that?" She asks casually. "Everyone does it. It's not a big deal." I feel like I'm in a bad after school special. So this is what peer pressure is. "Plus we're going all the way out to the far end of Mount Pleasant."

Max returns to the room. "I'm ready."

Thank goodness I am already sitting as I almost don't recognize him. He isn't wearing the normal general leave uniform either. Rather, Max is dressed in dark jeans and a red button-down. His outfit is topped off with a black baseball hat to hide his unmistakable knobby haircut. Guess I am the only one who didn't get the memo about civvies.

I pick at the invisible fuzz on the carpet while they stare at me. Waiting for me to make a decision. Any decision.

"We're crossing at least *one* bridge, if that's what you're worried about." Max is clearly trying to console me. And maybe encourage me a little. "You said yourself yesterday… sometimes you just want to fade into the crowd." Subtle, Max.

A reluctant sigh passes from me. "Okay. But just this *once*."

I change quickly out of my flannel pajama pants and into the wrap dress. Guess this is that "just in case" moment. The soft silk-like fabric feels foreign against my skin. Much like my reflection staring back at me. I freeze. I can't believe I am doing this. Am I really doing this? I can't do this. Maybe…*maybe* I have to do this. My mind races without a clear direction.

"Keeeeeensley," Stacey yells from downstairs.

Fuck it. I'll try Ash and Reagan's way of assimilation. I mean, the didn't get tour or cons or get PT'd. And if everyone's out wearing civvies already anyway…

"Hurry up!" Another yell.

I smooth the soft wrinkles of the dress and sigh. "Okay, I'm ready."

No regerets.

"Oh…uhm, wow," Max murmurs softly as I join them downstairs, his crimson cheeks visible even under the baseball hat.

Stacey gives me two thumbs up. "You clean up nice, kid."

Once in her car, I slump down in the back seat, as if on the run from the law. Well, technically, *I am* on the run from the law. The law of the Blue Book.

After we pick up supplies in a large box store in Mount Pleasant, we head to the restaurant where we meet Beth and Forrest. Beth and Stacey are roommates, both in 5th Company. Forrest is a junior in 6th Company. From the looks of it, Beth and Forrest seem to be dating, which explains Stacey's eagerness to have us tag along. She was probably tired of being the third wheel. And they were tired of her being alone.

We rush through dinner due to Stacey's misremembering the movie times.

"Are you alright, K?" Max asks while we wait for Stacey to return with our tickets.

"Yeah…it's fine," I lie.

"You don't seem fine. You've been tense all evening. Stiff even."

"There's obviously no fooling you." A half-smile for his concern, but the bitterness still shines through as he turns away. "Look….I'll be better once we're in that nice, dark theater."

And I am. Once the lights go down and we're ensconced in the shadows like everyone else, I feel my shoulders drop away from my ears. My jaw relax. If it's practically impossible to fade into the grey, I can at least disappear into this crowd. Even if just for a few hours.

I didn't think two and half hours could fly by so quickly. It was a run-of-the-mill action movie with just enough drama to make you forget where you are. Maybe even who you are. And it was definitely more comfortable watching a movie in a dress then that itchy wool blouse, with its collar always tight and claustrophobic. Maybe this wasn't such a bad idea after all.

We follow the sea of people towards the exit and head towards the parking lot. Still euphoric from this normal evening, I skip ahead a few feet and shout back at them, "I'm not ready to go back yet. You guys want to go and get some—."

I don't finish the sentence, the word "coffee" stuck and burning in my throat.

There, walking almost directly behind Beth, Stacey, Forrest, and Max, is… *Chris*.

My stomach drops.

"Cadet Bennett." My name venom in his mouth.

There's no place to hide. There's *absolutely* no way out of this. Why didn't he just pretend to not see me?

"Well, well, well…she's in 15th Company with Avery, right?" Burk joins Chris on his way to me. Suddenly the horror of the whole situation comes clear. Chris is surrounded by other upperclassmen. He can't not do what he's about to do, even if he doesn't want to do it. Part of my brain hangs on to that idea like a life raft: *He doesn't want to do this. He doesn't want to do this.* He has to do this because he's with other upperclassmen, I just know it.

Chris doesn't answer Burk. He's locked on his target. Me.

Chris grabs me by the upper arm and pulls me across the street. Maybe he *is* going to give me a pass.

"You've got some nerve, Bennett!" At least I won't be confused as to which Chris is talking to me. "Are those people you're with cadets, too?"

I stare at him blankly. No words catch in my mouth.

The vehemence of each passing stare from those around me warming the December air.

He shakes me by the arm and jolts me to the present.

What have I done?

"This isn't the time for fucking games, Bennett. You don't want me to pull you for an honor violation, too. Do you?" *A cadet will not lie, cheat, or steal, nor tolerate anyone that does.* An ethos etched into our souls from day one until forever, memorialized on a brass plaque at each front sally port. An honor violation spells an automatic expulsion.

All I can think of is that everyone is staring at me and thinking to themselves, *Look at that girl cadet. She couldn't follow a simple rule to not wear civilian clothing. This is why they shouldn't have let women in. She should never wear the ring!* Be serious, Kensley. No one is paying attention to you. No one cares about you. There's no spotlight, no police lights…just a guy in a Graham blazer uniform talking to a girl with a 12-year-old boy's haircut in a wrap dress in the parking lot of a movie theater, trying so desperately to fit in.

Chris points his chin towards the others. "I know that one kid with the knobby haircut is in 9th Company. So I assume the other four are also cadets....."

Unable to form words. I nod.

I want to explain to him so badly that we just wanted to have a little fun. I just wanted to feel normal. Fade into the crowd. I wasn't hurting anyone. Cadets wear civvies all of the time. It's a stupid rule in the first place.

"About time you give me some sort of response." There's a coldness to his voice that I hadn't heard before. "Marc," he says over his shoulder, "can you get the names of those cadets?" Across the street, Marc Harris, the Delta Battalion Academic Officer, pulls out a pen and paper.

"Will do, bro."

Chris turns back to me, his eyes narrow, dark, unfeeling. "Here's what's going to happen. I'm going to write all five of you up for wearing civvies when I get back to campus on Sunday. You know what happens after that…" It wasn't a question.

The white slip will be logged in the Commandant's Office. Gibson, the 15th Company clerk - the position that is now lost to me, will pick it up with the rest of the company mail from Barton Hall and give it to Coleman, and then it'll be delivered to me. I'll have a chance to write a statement explaining the infraction from my perspective. All cadets have the opportunity. Maybe I won't even get tours. It's my first offense at Graham—*ever.* I've got good grades and out-perform my classmates at all levels.

Maybe I can explain to him that everyone else is doing it. That it's no big deal. That …that really I was just trying to be like everyone else.

Yet before I can utter a syllable, Chris just turns and walks away. He and the others disappearing into the evening crowd.

Anger simmers within me.

"Kensley...*Kensley*." Max waves me over from across the street.

Reluctantly I join them. This is all their fault anyway.

"What did Harvatin say to you?" Max asks. Surprisingly, there's no anger in his voice. No resentment. It's like he's talking to me about what he had for lunch today. "Harris just took our names and socials." A small part of me envies his coolness. Why isn't he furious? Just use one word of profanity, Max, please. We're about to end our first semester at Graham with tours. Big fat tours. Tours I'll have to walk on the quad for all to see. For all to judge. Bye-bye general leave. Bye-bye freedom.

Stacey interrupts before I can answer. "Hey guys...we should get back to campus." She taps her watch at us." It's already 10:30 and you guys don't have an overnight."

We follow her in silence and spend the twenty-minute drive to Tad's house drowning in it. I stare mindlessly out the window, watching nothing at all. Seeing only the faintness of my reflection in the window like a ghost. But not the ghost of the girl I was rather of the girl I wanted to be so desperately. Toxic particles of anger, frustration, trepidation, and disappointment float in the atmosphere around us. I'm the only one who really has a right to be angry—at Chris for recognizing me, for not giving me a pass, and at Stacey and Max for pressuring me into this. The weight of our evening accompanies us like a stray dog into the house. You don't want it to follow you but you already fed it.

Stacey changes downstairs while Max and I go into separate rooms on the second floor.

I steal one last glance at my reflection in the mirror by the door. For the ghost.

I quickly step out of view of the mirror, away from my vulnerable reflection. Away from a whole different layer of emotions.

A few hours ago everything made sense. Now nothing does.

I've got to deal with tours. The humiliation.

I've got to deal with Ash and Reagan. And Coleman. And Ward.

I've got to deal with all of their "I told you so's" and all of their pointed fingers.

I sit down on the bed to take off my shoes, yet my arms don't obey.

My tears are the only thing not frozen. So many tears. So much emotion.

I let my setback drop to the hardwood floor in a colorful heap of polyester fabric. I give it a little kick and instantly bury it under the bed. From there it most certainly won't be able to entice me again. *Ever.*

A low murmur of "Kensley" accompanied by a soft knock, pops up on the other side of the door.

Go away, Max. There's nothing to talk about.

"Yeah, you can—," I start to say before realizing I'm still naked. "Wait… nevermind. I need one second." I hurriedly put on my white starched cotton dress pants and my white v-neck undershirt. Three-fourths of my mandatory uniform.

"Okay…I'm all set," I inform him as I wipe the last of my tears from my blotchy cheeks.

Max stands in the doorway, fully dressed in his leave uniform. Unsure of what to say.

I hurry time along. "Look, Max…I appreciate you coming in here to see if I'm okay. But I'm fine. It is and isn't a big deal—."

His expression startled. "Um, I didn't come in here to talk to you."

"I think I, uhm….left my shoes in here."

"Oh." My face flushes with embarrassment as I avert his eyes.

Without another word between us, Max retrieves his shoes from under the chair in the corner and walks out.

A few seconds later, the thunder of the front door conveys what words couldn't.

Guess I am walking back on my own, too.

I grab my cover off the table in the foyer and nearly trip over a large plastic bag nearly blocking the door. "What the fuck?!" My anger is matched by robotic yet jolly chants of "Ho, ho, ho. Meeeerry Christmas! Ho, ho, ho. Meeeerry Christmas!"

Right. The decorations. At least I got that right.

I gather up the bag with Santa and make my way back to campus on foot. The plastic Santa feels awkward in my arms. There's no way to get a perfect grip on him. My humid palms slip on the cheap white plastic bag every few steps.

I pass through the sally port unscathed by the cadet guard on duty and make it all the way to my room on third division.

Here goes nothing.

Reagan and Ash are each sitting at their respective desks as I enter.

"Oh *hello*, Kensley." Reagan's voice is saturated with an ulterior motive. "How was your evening?"

If only the Internet in our rooms worked as fast as the cadet rumor mill.

"It was fine, Reagan. Got some decorations for the company. " I hold up the plastic Santa as if displaying Exhibit A in a court of law. Eager to prove my case. And hoping she doesn't know.

"Oh, I see. We got our stuff too. But we already put it in the squad room." She considers me for a moment. "Do anything *fun* tonight, Kensley?"

At the word "fun," Ash, who'd been flipping through a magazine, focuses all of her attention on me, still standing with Santa in hand.

I don't want to tell them anything. It's none of their business. It's my life. My tours. But I know I won't get off that easy. Not in this fish bowl. And not after I gave them shit for civvies. It's clear Reagan isn't going to give up anyway—not until I give her some juicy morsel of information. Something she can chew on for weeks on end until the information's stale and boring. I don't know what she knows exactly. My best bet is to feed her what she wants, piece by piece. Hopefully she's satiated before I have to feed her the juiciest morsel of all.

Ready. Catch.

"I went to dinner and a movie in Mount Pleasant."

"Oh. That's a bit out of character for you, right?" Reagan crosses her legs, settling into her questioning. "Who did you go with?"

The interrogation begins.

"Max and Stacey. And two of Stacey's classmates."

"Ooooooh… were you and Max on a date?" Ash coos from her perch. Maybe they don't know anything. At least Ash doesn't.

"Of course they weren't on a date, Ash," Reagan corrects her. "Kensley is too busy being a cadet. Learning all of the rules of Graham, remember." Reagan turns back to me. "Anyway, did you have a good time?"

I toss her another morsel. "Yeah…it was cool. Nice to change it up sometimes."

"That's great, Kensley." Her voice is bubbling with slow-simmering sarcasm. "Glad you had a chance to get out and enjoy life before…"

Reagan 's voice deliberately trails off as if she's searching for the right words. The right weapon.

Action beats reaction.

I toss her my last morsel. "Yep. You're right, Reagan. It's good to get out and enjoy life before Christmas furlough."

"If that's what you want to call it." She smiles smugly and turns back to her desk.

Chapter Fifteen. *But the man without honor cannot be the Whole Man.*

No one is innocent at Graham.

No one is a perfect cadet.

Maybe I won't get tours? Maybe Chris is going to let it go.

Nothing seems unusual as I enter the squad room before our Sunday sweep detail.

No odd looks.

Yet I still have to protect myself against what might come.

Maybe news of my tours hasn't made it around the Company yet. (One can only hope.) I hold my head a little higher and look everyone in the eye. I've got to project confidence. Fake it till you make it, right? My tours exist only on a white slip right now. A three-by-five-inch piece of white paper. Or maybe still just on a scrap piece of crumbled paper stuffed in Harris's Graham blazer.

But if it is real then soon—tomorrow, maybe tonight—someone in the Commandant's Office will enter the white slip into the database. And Gibson, the 15th Company Clerk, will pick it up with the mail and bring it to Trevino or Coleman. And soon after that, everyone will know about it.

Everyone will know that I fucked up.

Everyone will think that women really don't belong here.

I'll be just like everyone else.

"If you haven't already….put whatever you bought in the corner with the rest of the decorations." Darron's voice startles me back into the squad room. I look over to the corner he is pointing at. I wonder if there are any Christmas decorations left in the city of Charleston. There's a red nose peeking out from behind a plastic 12-foot-high tree. A kaleidoscope of colored lights in boxes waiting to be brought to life. A corn cob pipe and button nose. Strands and strands of silver metallic garland. A few wayward metallic silver strands already adorn the floor around it. Too weak to stay on the garland. This will take hours to put up.

"I assume everyone kept their schedule clear this afternoon. I think we should be able to put everything up in no more than two hours," Callahan booms authoritatively. "That way, you can still—."

"Why we don't just do the decorating today?" Dane asks. "I just think it makes more sense. We could be done by noon at the latest, giving us a solid …..six hours of general leave versus like, three under your plan."

A low rustling of agreement blows through the squad room.

Callahan, not used to disagreement, strings his words together carefully. "If that's what you guys want to do, fine by me. Makes more sense to me to knock out personal errands first. But whatever—."

The screeching of the squad room screen door stops Callahan.

Coleman steps into the squad room, dressed in her leave uniform. "Good morning, knobs."

"Ma'am, good morning, ma'am," the room responds in chorus.

"This won't take long." She glances at the decorations and smiles. "Nice work. Just be sure it doesn't look tacky."

"Ma'am, yes, ma'am." A few knob voices respond. It's always been like that. Sometimes knobs will just utter one of the three knob responses—just because. Maybe to feel normal, as if part of a dialogue. Or because silence is awkward. Or because we just dont' know what to do.

"Bennett!"

My stomach drops. Please, please, please, call Ash and Reagan's name next. For once I want there to be an all-female meeting.

"Ma'am, yes, ma'am."

"Move the fuck out."

A low hiss emanates from my classmates as I grab by cover,

Coleman stands waiting on the galleries, wearing a dour expression. Hands on her hips.

"We're both due in Dehenre's office no later than 0830 hours." On a Sunday?

Now's not the time for back talk or questions. "Ma'am, yes, ma'am."

"You know how to get there." It isn't a question.

"Ma'am, yes, ma'am."

Dehenre's office is on the second floor of Barton Hall. Thank goodness I beat Coleman.

I take a seat on the bench in the hallway. The cadet weathered wood against my palms feels smooth and familiar. It's the same bench I sat on a few months ago waiting to be interviewed by Chris. I run my hand along the grains nervously when instead of summoning calm, I summoned a ghost instead. *Dad avoids my gaze, standing at the front of the pew. While I sitting in the front row, can't seem to get the wrinkles out of my black dress, no matter how much I swipe my hand against the cotton.* "It was an accident. It was raining. It wasn't your fault." The hushed tones of condolences ring in my ears even now, three years later.

"We've got a few minutes." Coleman is suddenly standing in front of me. Startled, I look up at her from the bench in silence. "Um…you should probably go to the bathroom before the meeting." Her tone empathetic and confusing to me.

"Ma'am, yes, ma'am."

The face reflected in the bathroom mirror is blotchy, red and raw. The unmistakable signs of tears mark my face. Tears evoked by the ghost? Or were they tears of the present? I splash some water on my face and attempt to dry it with the rough, brown paper towels from the dispenser.

I walk out of the bathroom rubbing my hands on my grey duty pants in a last-ditch effort at composure.

"Dehenre's ready for us, knob." Her tone cloaked in authority again.

Dehenre's office is fairly small. I would've expected something larger for a Lieutenant Colonel. Maybe they're already preparing to let her go once Malone starts? There are no windows, only white walls poorly decorated with stock photos of the civil war—I mean, *The War of Northern Aggression*. There's a desk, a file cabinet adorned with some sort of plant—more than likely plastic, and two chairs across from her desk.

Dehenre is at first unrecognizable in her civilian clothes. This could be a good sign. It's not an official meeting. But then again it is a Sunday and she lives on campus.

"Good morning, ma'am." Coleman takes a seat in the government issued green chair closest to the wall.

"Ma'am, good morning, ma'am."

"Hello, ladies. You can sit down as well, Kensley." Dehenre points to the other chair. "I apologize for not being in uniform but I have some errands to run after this meeting. And not having to change in and out of uniform saves a bit of time."

"It's not a problem at all." Coleman crosses her legs comfortably. "Besides, I don't think this will take long. It's pretty cut and dry from my understanding."

"Yes, that it is." Dehenre looks at me almost mournfully. "Kensley, I assume you know you were written up for wearing civilian clothes in Mount Pleasant last night?"

"Ma'am, yes, ma'am."

"I assume there were no mitigating circumstances impacting your decision to wear civilian clothes so close to Christmas furlough…?" My mind searches for an answer. I can't tell if Dehenre is looking for me to have an excuse. Would that make it better? Or worse? Chris wasn't the only upperclassman there. Burk and Harris were there, too. I don't think she can sweep this under the rug.

I stare at her stone-faced and take accountability. "Ma'am, no, ma'am."

"That's what I thought. You're probably wondering why you're here since the facts are pretty straightforward and in the grand scheme of things, you're only getting twenty tours."

I nod. The lowest punishment required per the Blue Book.

"Knob Bennett," I note the sudden turn in formality from Dehenre. "You were one of our rising female cadets. You're in the top five percent of your class academically. You've done very well during all physical fitness iterations, and from what Avery told me, you were at the top of your knob class militarily, too."

Were? Past tense? I want to scream at her and plead my case. It was the siren call of normalcy. She made me do it. She pulled me to her rocky shores. Yet it's the *one* call we aren't supposed to answer when we decide to sojourn through the sallyports at Graham. A temporary barter in exchange for the history….the leadership laboratory that is the Corps….the friendships…the ring…the Long Grey Line. I broke my contract in less than a semester.

"There's a lot of pressure put on you as cadets in a military school. Period. Then add in the assimilation factor, and well…" Dehenre looks down at her folded hands. "I know you might think this is the end of the world for you, but it's not. Plenty of my classmates got in trouble at some point, yet they still went on to lead very successful lives and careers post-graduation. Both the Air Force and beyond."

I keep a neutral and flat tone and expression. "Ma'am, yes, ma'am."

"Good. I knew you were mature enough to understand, Kensley." The once again friendly tone breathed into the meeting. "Being able to see beyond the front gate of Graham—or any college, is important. While Graham is a microcosm for the rest of the world, it's not forever. We grow and evolve and learn from each situation. From each environment." Dehenre lets out a sigh. Her voice almost a whisper. "I think you still have tremendous potential, Kensley. Don't let this get you down. Take some time to reflect on how you got here. There is a lot to learn from this."

"Ma'am, yes, ma'am." I mutter to keep my tears in line.

"I think we should get Bennett's white slip logged into the system so she can start her tours before Christmas furlough," Coleman suggests abruptly and matter-of-factly.

"Right. Thanks for the reminder, Avery." Dehenre digs through the stack of manila folders and papers on her desk.

She plucks the indeed white slip from heap. My eyes linger on Chris's signature at the bottom. All caps. Asshole.

I sign on the back in acknowledgement and hand it back.

"Thank you, Kensley. I know this has been a difficult twelve hours for you. I don't want to keep you since this is your last day of general leave for a while, but remember, my door is always open."

"Ma'am, yes, ma'am."

Coleman and I stand in unrehearsed unison.

"Did you need anything else from me?"

"No….no, thank you, Avery."

Coleman stops me at the top of the stairs. "Bennett—I don't need to know why you decided to wear civvies. But you should've known you weren't going to be able to get away with it. It was a stupid fucking idea."

Finally something I can agree with.

"While nearly everyone has worn civvies at one point or another during their cadet career, we—," her hands gesture back and forth "—are held to a higher standard. And because we're held to a higher standard, there are going to be consequences. Sometimes even higher ones than for our male classmates." She pauses for a beat. "Consequences that go beyond the Blue Book." She hangs her head., shaking it slowly back and forth. "You've got to figure out what survival looks like to *you*." Her right index finger pointed directly at me. "Me and Ward and all the other women have. There's no motivational phrase to recite to yourself every morning and night before bed that'll help you get through it. It's different for everyone. It was different for me than it was for Cathy. Hold your head high. Don't try to argue with *anyone* about it—that includes your classmates in the Company." Coleman walks towards the upperclassmen stairwell. "In the grand scheme of things, they have no influence on your life. They don't take your tests. They're only part of your present and future if you allow them to be."

Chapter Sixteen. *I could not tell which faces contained the elements of danger or redemption.*

"West, Durham, and Bennett."

Trevino finishes leafing through the papers on his clipboard. "You three can start serving your punishments today."

The sound of my name explodes in the air like fireworks, tiny little syllables shining brightly overhead in the squad room. It still had the potential to not be real when Chris called my name across the parking lot in Mount Pleasant. Or when Dehenre handed me my white slip last week. But at this moment, it's no longer a potential. It *is* real. If someone didn't know already that I have tours, they surely know now. It's been said outloud. And no doubt I'll hear about it as soon as Trevino leaves the room.

"Sir, yes, sir," the three of us respond.

"Matthis is going to maintain the sign-in log for tours and cons outside of his room. Remember to be in proper uniform or you won't get credit. West and Durham…I can come by your rooms at any time so you better be sitting cons correctly," Trevino threatens.

"Sir, yes, sir."

No need to come by my room, since everyone will see me walking tours on the quad.   Back and forth. Back and forth. Back and forth.

"Any questions?"

"Sir, no, sir," we respond.

"Roll out in like two minutes, knobbies," he adds before allowing the squad room door to shut.

I hold my breath.

Here they come—comments about me getting tours. Can't wait to hear what creative Callahan spits my way. I know he's eating this up because he thinks it means I'm out of the running for clerk. If you only were so lucky. I only got tours for civvies. Not like I hazed anyone or went AWOL or drank alcohol in the barracks.

A few seconds pass. A drop of sweat slides down the center of my back in anticipation.

Still nothing.

Nothing at all.

Of course. They probably decided to talk about me when I'm not here anyway, because they know I wouldn't hesitate to point out their Blue Book violations—bet they think I didn't know about what goes on in the battalion after taps. Besides, I didn't break Graham tradition. *Everyone* wears civvies at some point in their cadet career, Coleman said so.

A realization smacks me in the face.

But what *if…*

What if no one is talking about me?

At all.

Not in front of me. Not behind my back. Not in hushed tones in between classes or in their rooms. As if my tours—as if *I* don't matter. Because they expected me to fuck up. They've been expecting it this whole time, because I'm a girl. Because I don't fit their mold. Because I don't laugh at their jokes. Because I don't act the way they want me to. Because we didn't go to high school together. The irony is that walking tours only makes it easier for them to stare, point, judge. It makes it easier for me to stand out from the grey.

But ….I'm not like the other girls here. I'm *nothing* like them.

I am like them. I am like the boys. I use their terminology. I'm more a part of this school and its traditions than most guys in this room will ever be; it's in my blood three generations back. I carry my weight as a classmate more than most. I've never fallen out of a Company spirit run

—I don't think Lewis or Arnold can say that. And I'm always shined up. *Always*. Certainly not the case for Glass or Barr or Ash or Reagan.

They may not see it now but maybe when the Field House investigation is finally over, they'll understand.

***

"Thirteen-oh-five. *Thirteen-oh-five.*" Professor Gish's voice brings me out of my unfocused haze.

Shit. I thought he gave us independent study. Why is he calling on me.

I look up.

"Would you have a bit of consideration for the rest of your classmates and not tap your highlighter so violently, please," he says with a hint of sarcasm. As always, upon hearing the word "classmates," the room fills with the suffocating sound of hissing. I bite the inside of my cheek to stifle the roar stuck in my throat. I get it. We're not classmates. I'm a knob and ya'll are upperclassmen.

"Yes, sir."

I go back to my book. Well, I pretend to. Because despite my very, very best effort, my eyes meet Chris's in the process.

Dick.

It's easy to fight the temptation to talk to confront him in person. Even if I wasn't a knob, talking to him would be terrifying. Where would I even begin? *Um, hi Chris…thanks for being a douche and giving me tours. Don't deny that you've never worn civvies when you weren't supposed to.*

Yet his vacant expression does all of the talking.

I hastily throw my book, highlighter, and notebook into my knobby bag, as the bell chimes, signaling the end of class. I grab my cover from under my seat and head to the side stairwell reserved for knobs. If I want to start walking tours at 1500 hours today, I have to make it back to the battalion and change into my tour walking uniform—the waist belt I normally wear for parade, paired with my duty uniform—in the next eight minutes.

I'm back in the battalion, changed and in front of Matthis's door to sign in for tours with one minute to spare. Victory for me, I suppose.

"Hey knob," Matthis yells from behind the screen door.

"Sir, yes, sir."

He opens his screen door. "Which one are you?"

Is he serious? *Which fucking one am I?* There are only three women knobs in the company. And we definitely don't look alike. Reagan is at least three inches taller than me with curly brown hair. Ash is at least an inches shorter than me, also with brown hair. I, on the other hand, have blonde hair.

"Sir, cadet private Bennett, sir." Idiot.

"Whatever." He scans the clipboard.

No need for the suspense, buddy. It's not a VIP access list.

"Yep, you're on the list."

No shit.

"Sir, yes, sir."

Durham and West appear to take their places next to me on the galleries in front of Matthis's door.

"Okay…got you checked off, West and Durham." Seriously? How can he remember their names but not mine. Other upperclassmen begin to saunter and congregate around Matthis's room. Those who are going to sit cons in their rooms are just wearing their field jackets and waist plates, while those of us walking tours are wearing our wool overcoats and leather gloves. And of course we're holding rifles.

"Alright, guys. I'm going to leave the clipboard on my door. No need to bother me. Remember to sign in every hour or you won't get credit." Matthis hangs the clipboard on the nail outside his door. "You can walk or sit off three hours of punishments today."

A single bugle note signals the start of my sojourn to atonement.

I begin my tours by walking from one side of the battalion to the other on the quad. Knobs aren't require to brace during tours but we do have to walk at attention—eyes straight forward, no talking, and rifle held at a 45-degree angle. This is like swimming laps in a pool. Once you get to the other side, flip and push off back to the other side.

Easy. Or at least I tell try to tell myself that especially since I don't like to swim.

Yet just five laps later, self doubt - an old acquittance, begins to match my stride. Maybe this is where I deserve to be. Walking tours for all to see. I did violate the Blue Book. It doesn't matter who else has done it. I knew better. I knew what the consequences were going to be - even the ones that aren't outlined in the Blue Book - just like Coleman said. My feet deserve to hurt; to feel pain - a luxury she'll never have again.

The bugle note rings overhead, ending our first hour and the start of a 10 minute break.

The upperclassmen loiter around Matthis's room—some smoking, some drinking water, some munching on a powerbar. West and I go into Durham's room on first division, out of sight of the upperclassmen, where we can sit down. Slouch.

I take off my shoes and massage my aching soles. Black leather shoes are not made for extended walking on concrete this much.

The bugle note signals the start of another hour.

Wow, that was a fast ten minutes.

I nod to Durham and open the door. Like Technicolor greeting Dorothy as she opened the door of her Kansas farmhouse, I'm pelted with tiny ice droplets.

You've got to be fucking kidding me. Snow in Charleston!

"Hurry up and go get your raincoat, knob," Matthis yells from inside his warm, dry room on third division.

"Sir, yes, sir."

I quickly run up to my room on third division. One foot into the room and I'm enveloped by the sweet smell of pumpkin pie. My stomach growls. Oh, right. The candles Ash and Reagan got a few weeks ago.

"Where's the fire?" Ash asks, not realizing the irony.

"Nowhere." I throw my raincoat—correction, the plastic bag that only looks like a rain coat—over my wool coat. On second thought, it might be too hot for both. Plastic on top of wool might be a dangerous combination. The few times I've worn the raincoat, it hasn't so much repelled water as kept my own sweat in. On second thought, it's December. In Charleston. And although I'll deny saying this if asked, it gets damn cold.

Fuck it. I opt for both.

"She's got …you know, tooouurs," Reagan tells Ash, enunciating "tours" as if it were an STD.

You should've tours for keeping civvies in this room, I think but don't say as I hustle back outside.

With each lap, my feet grow more sodden and colder. My past closer. The squish-swash emanating from my shoes is my own personal soundtrack. My face numb from the cold air and freezing rain, while just as I thought, the rest of me is soaked in sweat from being cocooned in wool and plastic.

I don't know if there's a single part of my uniform that's still dry at this point.

I head straight to the bathroom at the next bugle note. I take off my grey cotton duty pants and try to dry them under the hand dryer in the short amount of time. This is pointless. It only works in movies or television shows where the heroine is about to meet with the man of her dreams the moment she walks out the door. But the only thing that awaits me on the other side of this door is one more fifty-minute block of tours.

I put my pants back on and sit on the bench in the bathroom. Hoping to give my legs a brief but needed respite. The hard, dry surface of the wall feels good against my stiff and aching back and shoulders as I prop against it.

My world goes black. Dark.

————

The one note bugle jolts me awake. I can't fall asleep here. Not in the *middle* of tours. My first set of tours. What the fuck.

I hastily put on my wool coat and rain coat and scramble out of the bathroom for the quad.

"'bout fucking time, knob!" Matthis yells down at me from third division. "You were about to not get credit."

Ignoring Matthis, I fall in step silently next to West and Durham for our last hour.

At the end of the last hour of tours, I quickly head to my room to change before dinner formation. There's no way I'm sitting in the mess hall in wet pants. Or wet socks. Or a wet undershirt. Or wet *anything*.

Reagan and Ash greet me with silence as I enter. Typical.

I feel a tap me on my shoulder as I dig through my laundry bag. "Here, I made you some vanilla chai. You know, it being cold and rainy and all." Ash holds a beige ceramic cup towards me, a hesitant smile on her face. "Thought it might help warm you up after being outside."

I'm dumbfounded - speechless even, and avoid her eyes, lest they betray me. Again.

I take the cup from her. "Thanks." The steam from the sickly sweet concoction instantly warms my face.

"Did you make some for all of us?" Reagan calls from across the room. "Where's mine?"

"In the package by the coffee maker, Reagan." Ash and I exchange a friendly smile. "You haven't been walking tours outside like Kensley."

"Whatever." Reagan huffs in annoyance and adds. "Oh, I almost forgot," Reagan says before we head to the squad room. "Coleman came by earlier and said after mess we have to go straight to Barton for some meeting. It's just knobs and Dehenre though."

"What?!"

"Chill out, Kensley. We're just the messengers." She considers me for a long moment as a slow smirk emerges on her face. "Maybe cadet life is too much for you if you can't handle a change in the schedule."

***

Ash, Reagan, and I make our way to Barton Hall the second we're dismissed from evening mess. We enter through the rear entrance as always and head straight to the conference room on the first floor. We aren't the first to arrive, nor are we the last. *Thank goodness.* The room is stuffy as usual despite the December chill. The dark wood furniture always appearing more like a prop than functional.

The girl next to me taps me on the shoulder. "Do you know what this is about?" I stare at her for a few seconds, scanning my memory for her name. I lean forward, pretending to stretch my back so I can read her name tag.

Hunt. Nope. Doesn't ring a bell.

I smile politely and shake my head.

She mouths "thanks" and turns away.

I roll my eyes without her seeing.

"Good evening, ladies." Dehenre's voice chimes from the front of the room, where two boxes of donuts stand out bright and awkward against the room's dark color scheme.

"Good evening, ma'am," the room responds.

"CONGRATS, ladies of the class of 2004, for completing your first semester at Graham!" Dehenre shrieks, pumping her fists in the air (and forgoing all military bearing and decorum) as if we're at a pep rally. Equal screeches of cheering and booms of clapping erupt around me.

This can't be real. Any minute, cameras will appear from behind the blackout curtains. I just know it. I cross my arms in silent protest, yet no one seems to notice. No one seems to feel the way I do about this... this *travesty*. It's only been one fucking semester at Graham. Who knows how many won't come back after Christmas or not come back at all next year.

"This is *sooooo* exciting!" Dehenre adds. "I'll make this quick as I don't want to take away from your study time, ladies. But I did want to take a brief few minutes to tell you how proud I am—how proud *everyone* in the Commandant's Office is...." Her voices catches as her eyes fill with tears. "—on your successful completion of your first semester. There's been a lot of pressure on you, not just as cadets but with these silly editorials from Caroline."

Like morning fog, inaudible murmurs rolls through the room at the mention.

"Now, now...she's allowed to write what she wishes. The key is not to let it affect you or those around you." A motherly smile warms Dehenre's face. "And you've done that so well. With so much courage and strength. Janel...I know you've talked about this enough but I'd really like to applaud you for your ability to hold your head high after the rock was thrown at you last month in—"

Applause from the room cuts off Dehenre.

Some random cadet threw a rock Janel Woodward, junior, before formation in Bravo Battalion last month. It was already dusk so Janel didn't see his face. No one was ever identified so no one ever was punished. She walked around proudly with a black eye for a week while the entire Corps took their field jackets to the tailor shop to have their name tag sewn on the front right breast.

From across the room, Janel cocks her head and points at her unblemished eye in triumph like a superstar.

"Anyway…I said I'd keep this short so I won't give a speech or anything. I'll just say again….congrats ladies! You did it!"

A few of the girls converge on Dehenre like she's some sort of superstar. "Be sure to take a donut on your way out" She shouts from the mob middle. A few hastily stuff a donut into their mouths before leaving through the thick oak doors of the conference room. No knob—male or female—wants to be seen eating a donut. *Ever.*

I squeeze past Dehenre and her groupies.

"Wait a second, Kensley," Dehenre calls out to me as I push open the heavy door.

I roll my eyes before turning around to acknowledge her.

"Yes, ma'am."

"Ladies, I need to speak to Kensley for a second. I'm *really* sorry. Shoot me an email if you want to talk about this more." Dehenre pacifies the fan club gathered around her before turning fully to me. "Let's go to my office upstairs real quick. It's quieter there."

I nod and reluctantly follow her up the stairs.

As she stares at me from across her desk, I realize that the maternal look I thought she wore is a mask is actually genuine. How did I miss that?

"How are *you* doing, Kensley?"

"Fine, ma'am." I reply cautiously. Where is this going?

"You walked your first tours already, right?"

I nod.

Dehenre lets out a sigh as she picks up a copy of the *Low Country Gazette* from her desk.

"I'll get to it, Kensley." Her voice drops to a low whisper. "I wanted to talk you about the recent *Caroline's Corner*. Did you see it?"

I shake my head.

I lie. Of course I saw it. As much as I don't want to.

She frowns and stretches her arm across the desk. "You should read it then."

I already know what the article says. I've memorized every cutting word. Yet I placate Dehenre and allow my eyes to linger over the words naturally hoping my emotions don't betray me. The sides of the paper crinkle violently as my grip tightens reflexively.

It is my duty as a reporter to present you with all of the facts as I know them to be true. Just yesterday, I learned that the class of 2004's star female cadet, Kensley Bennett, was caught in Mount Pleasant wearing civilian clothing. Civilian clothing. The infraction itself isn't the heinous part, since who doesn't like to look nice when going to dinner and a movie with friends. No, it is the mere principle of the matter. Here we have a young cadet - a lady, who comes from a Graham family, has excellent grades - albeit as an English major, does well on all of the physical demands at Graham. She wants to wear the ring. She wants that ring to mean the same thing it has for all of those who came before her. And all those who are to follow her. Yet what does that ring mean when it is earned breaking the rules? Is this the type of whole person Graham wishes to produce these days?

I hope not!

Flowery wrap dresses do not belong at Graham which means Kensley Bennett does not belong at Graham either.

It is a wonder that the administration did not sweep this under the proverbial rug to protect the fragile image of assimilation. I am relieved to know that there are still a few within the administration that adhere to the pillars of Graham and are looking out for its future.

Max…?

It would make sense. Who else would have known exactly what I was wearing? He's probably trying to impress some newspaper reporter for a future internship. Not to mention he's working on that story for the *Commodore.* And he avoided me after we got back from Mount Pleasant. And he's avoided me since.

I place the crumbled paper on the edge of her desk, taking care to smooth out the edges. As if straightening the paper will smooth everything over. Just like my wrinkled black dress.

Dehenre stares at me in marked silence.

Eventually I'll have to look at her. But not for another few more seconds. I continue to stall with the paper. I've run my hands over it so many times, tiny specs of black newsprint are visible on my sweaty palms.

She lets out a sigh. "I'm not going to pretend that I know what it feels like to see your name in the paper. Or on social media. You're a smart and independent young woman, Kensley. Yet seeing this in print…" Her voice trails off as she shakes her head slowly. "…That would have an effect on anyone. And now with your tours on display…" Dehenre's voice trails off again. "I might be out of line here and making an assumption, but I want you to come back after Christmas furlough. We need women like you."

I'm flabbergasted. She think I'm going to fucking *quit* Graham? Me? Kensley Eleanor Bennett? If this weren't a military school, I'd walk right out of this office. And probably slam the door in dramatic fashion. And never speak to her again.

I know what Graham is like. I knew that as early as I could crawl. I've known about the pressures—regardless of gender—way before Caroline was a newspaper reporter. If one can even call her that. And now, some non-Graham grad is trying to give *me* advice on pressures she also knows nothing about. Sure she went to a service academy, but it wasn't Graham. No wonder General Gentry is going to replace her with Malone, a Graham alumnus.

Yet I swallow all of my anger and simply utter, "Yes, ma'am."

"I want you to know that I'm here for you if you need to talk." She rummages in her desk drawer. "Here's my personal email and cell. Don't hesitate to call me over furlough. Really!"

***

The room is surprisingly empty when I return from Barton Hall.

Quiet, in fact. I don't know how I got here. I don't know if I was asked for knob knowledge along the way. All I know is that I wanted to be alone. Needed to be alone. And fast. So at least I got that wish granted.

I open my computer and begin a new mail message. *Dear Max....*

I stop.

I don't know if I'm fueled by indifference or anger or worse, a deadly brew of both, but I log into IM.

Max may have betrayed me to *Caroline's Corner*, but at least he's doing it to get ahead. The person who's really responsible for this mess didn't even do it for personal gain. He just did it to be an asshole. And I'm not afraid to tell him. Fuck it. I got nothing to lose.

I scroll through my contact list a second time, sure I've missed it in my blind rage.

Then a third time.

Just. To. Be. Sure.

I'm sure.

Distinctly missing from the list is *Chris Harvatin.* He removed me from his contact list.

Confusion. Disbelief. Abandonment. Betrayal. Foolishness.

What a fucking coward to just…to just ghost me.

I slam the top of the laptop down. The sound cracks like low thunder across the room.

Chapter Seventeen. *And he was careful.*

The smell of coffee tickles my nose as I enter the dining room. "Good morning, Dad."

Home. Hopefully the next fourteen days won't pass too quickly.

The last week at Graham was a grey blur of formations, mess, sweep details, finals, and pretending nothing bothered me. I've never been more glad to be home after the four months I've had. Ash and Reagan's shit baggery performance as a cadet, Ward and her need to put other women down, the Field House mess, the banner debacle… Chris and my tours.

I could manage all of it well enough, but Max's betrayal is on another level. At first I thought I could forgive him, because I believed he acted out of self-interest and self-preservation—and those are motivations I could understand. But I trusted him—as a friend and *classmate.* I've told him things. (Maybe not everything but enough.) My fears. My worries. I was vulnerable. No telling who else he's talked to in order to make himself part of the guys. Malone? No matter what the damage, it's a good thing I found out now.

"You're up early," Dad says to me without looking up from his morning paper. "Still on the Graham schedule? If so, the trash could use emptying," he adds with a chuckle.

"Sir, yes, sir," I bark sarcastically, though I'm glad to hear the cheer in his voice.

I take a seat at the table. The soft cushion feels foreign under me. I close my eyes, relishing the ability to fully sit back in a chair for a meal. A serene smile crosses my face. My shoulders relaxed.

"I got bagels from your favorite place down the street. Wasn't sure how many you'd eat." He goes back to his paper for a moment. "Do you want some scrambled eggs? I can whip some up real quick…"

My mouth already full with the soft pillowy insides of a bagel, I nod. I take a swig of my earl grey tea latte to wash it down. "Thanks, Dad."

As he goes about the business of making breakfast, a small spark of hope inside me gains a little strength. Here we are, Dad and me, having a leisurely breakfast like a normal family. Like before. If every ounce of suffering at Graham has led to this, it's all worth it. But if homecoming was a prelude, then hope certainly isn't going to light the path of reality. He might never accept me. He might never forgive me. He might never look at me like he did before. Yet I owe to her to try.

"Here ya go. Two freshly scrambled eggs. None of that carton stuff either." He places a ceramic plate in front of me.

We sit in our own cone of silence, only pierced by the occasional rustle of his paper and my chewing.

I take one last hard swallow before I begin.

"Dad…did you ever have a classmate betray you?"

He puts the newspaper down immediately and looks at me with concern. "Of course, kid. Classmates are human. But more importantly, *betrayal* is really a matter of perspective. What you perceive as betrayal, another perceives as doing the right thing. And in an insular world like Graham, the right thing is usually for the good of the Corps. The greater good."

I nod, continuing to chew on the words. *Insular.* I guess that's one way to put it. I went from the frying pan and into the fire when I left home for Graham.

"As a knob, you spend most of your time in your company and going to class. You're completely unaware of what else is going on in the other battalions or in Barton Hall. And thus, you internalize everything. As if it's about you. *And only you.* You assume you got tours for wearing civvies because the upperclassman that pulled you doesn't like you, right?"

And there it is. Disappointment makes its entrance.

My fork is frozen in mid-air, like the words in my throat.

The eggs suddenly bitter. Cold.

"I know it can seem… '*unfair*,'" he continues, using air quotes to emphasize the ridiculousness of the word, "but you got tours for wearing civilian clothes because it was in direct violation of the Blue Book. Rules are more than rules at Graham. They're the back bone of the whole institution, part of its tradition. They're what set Graham apart from other schools, for example."

I feel suddenly hot and uncomfortable. Almost like a stranger in my own house staring across from him.

"Look, kid. I am not disappointed in you. I know cadets violate the Blue Book *every day* without getting caught." A slow smile creeps across his face. "Hell, I know I broke a rule or two. There's a thrill in breaking the rules. You can't deny that. Peer pressure isn't what got you to put on the—what was it? A 'flowery wrap dress'?"

I swallow any response as I bask in his words.

He *isn't* disappointed in me.

He *isn't.*

He continues. "Graham isn't about parades or who had the shiniest brass or even who had the highest rank. It's about being a Whole M— *sorry*, Whole Person. Well balanced. Someone who embodies the four pillars. And in being that person, you'll form life-long friendships with those to your left and to your right. People who knew you when. People you can call up twenty years later for dinner because you happen to be passing through town. *That's* what matters, Kensley." Dad's voice takes on a low tone he uses with juries for effect. "Consider your classmate's perspective before you judge him on what you think is a betrayal. Hear 'em out."

I nod in hesitant agreement still distracted.

"I just wouldn't want you to miss out on a life-long friendship due to a misunderstanding."

He *isn't* disappointed.

Chapter Eighteen. *Try to take it as a big joke.*

After breakfast and still relishing Dad's words, I log onto the computer to check the subway schedule for my trip to Jersey City later that afternoon to meet Desiree. My email account pops up automatically. Spam, spam, spam. There's an email from Professor Gish, with suggested reading and a packing lists for the upcoming Savannah trip in the spring semester, and a reminder of when our first assignment is due. A knot forms in my stomach when I read "civilian clothes are authorized." Maybe I'll just wear my uniform in protest. Not like any of the upperclassmen on the trip will care what I wear.

A scroll through more junk emails and then...

I freeze.

There, stuck in between an email about a forty percent off sale and my book order for next semester is an email from *Chris.*

What the fuck?

He just sent an email, like we're pals. I have tours as I have tours. My name was in the paper. Someone who I thought was my friend betrayed me.

I could never forgive Chris. Never.

My shaking hand moves the cursor over the delete button.

It hovers.

What if...*what if* we can still be friends? His classmates were teasing him because they saw us talking so he had to pull me to show them that he is treating all cadets fairly. But if he wanted to be friends, why did he erase me from his IM contacts?

The cursor continues to hover dangerously over the delete button.

Before I can change my mind again, the email disappears.

Unopened. Unread. Unknown.

"Oh. My. God!" Desiree shrieks at the glimpse of me at the Exchange Place PATH station that afternoon. "I'm *soooo* super excited to see you, Ken."

Ah yes, how quickly I'd forgotten Desiree's nickname for me. From day one of tenth grade in Mrs. Dyer's English class, my grandmother's proud southern name was turned into that of a male plastic doll. There was no changing her mind. No matter how much I ignored her when she called, pleaded with her. But Desiree was the first person who talked to me at my new school, so I accepted it.

We hug in the middle of the platform, earning death stares from other riders who are forced to step around us - no doubt on their way to their home from a busy day.

"Your hair looks awesome," I say in an overly high-pitched tone, normally only heard on reality shows. How I'd forgotten the facade I adopted in order to melt into her world. "And cute," I add as I survey her head from right and left. Some time over the last four months, Desiree cut her long auburn hair to a Hepburn-style pixie cut. It almost seems shorter than mine. But hers looks...*well,* it looks cute and fashionable. What the fuck? Whereas I'm stuck spending my freshman year of college looking like a 12-year-old boy.

"Oh this." She runs her fingers through her perfectly coifed hair. "I did this out of total boredom one day. That's not true. It wasn't boredom. I had just broken up with that guy I wrote you about... damn, I forgot his name now. Whatevs. We started seeing each other right when I got to college. A month later I realize he's a *total* jerk...."

She proceeds to tell me more about the guy she dated after what's-his-name. My mind turns off to the rest of the soap opera. Listening to her now, it's hard to remember what we ever had in common during our two years together in high school. At first she was just socially polite—she was class president after all. One day, it all changed. It wasn't until a year later that Desiree admitted someone had shown her the newspaper article from mom's funeral. From that day on, she'd decided I would be a permanent fixture in her social circle. As good as it was to belong somewhere again, I always felt like she kept me around because she felt sorry for me after my old friends stopped taking my phone calls.

"...so do you think I should text John back?"

I have no idea how long I've *not* been listening to Desiree.

Four months out from under her aura and our differences are as stark as our haircuts.

I stall for time. "Ummm...what do *you* want to do?"

"You're right. I don't want to call him. I mean, if I wanted to get back together with him then I wouldn't be having this long drawn-out conversation about him right now. I just don't want to be a jerk and tell him that. Guys can be sensitive sometimes, and—."

I cut her off. "Oh I know. Imagine living with nearly 2,000 of them for the last four months. Granted I don't interact with *all* of them all the time, but in my company I do. There's this one guy in my company, Callahan—he thinks he's tough but really he's just insecure. He's always —."

"Ugh, guys always *think* they're tough." She returns the favor. "There's this guy on my floor in my dorm who constantly walks around with this scowl on his face and never says hi. To anyone. Yet then when it was time for finals, he wanted to borrow notes from everyone. Joy and I refused to share ours..."

I shift her story to background noise and let her drone on about her life at a *normal* college. It's too exhausting to wrestle her for conversation time about things I can't relate to and vice versa. We continue to walk around the City with no set agenda yet manage to hit all of our old stomping grounds as if on auto-pilot.

We say goodbye after a few hours. I knowing everything about every minute of her last four months. She understanding nothing of mine. We part ways with tentative plans to see each other again before my furlough—*her vacation* ends.

Yet as I board the train and wave back at her on the platform through the smudged subway windows, I know this is the last we'll see each other for a long, long time.

***

I spend my last full day of furlough checking and double checking that I've got what I need for my life back at Graham. Somewhere, somehow, before arriving at the front gate of Graham on Sunday, I've got to change from my *authorized* civvies to my Graham leave uniform. Probably at Tad's, since he already agreed to pick me up.

Max. He'll be there too.

The thought of him rips off the bandage I'd hastily stuck on for the last ten days. But now the wound is exposed again. Fresh. Oozing. Forcing me to tend to it. Reminding me to get myself back on track and to get my shit together for the spring semester.

With my suitcase packed and ready to go, I only have one last thing to do.

I gingerly close the bathroom door, hang an old towel over my shoulders, and pull out a brand new pair of hair clippers. I've never cut hair with clippers before—and really, I've never cut my own hair at all so no telling how this is going to turn out. Maybe I should let a professional do this? But then again, how hard can it be? My hair will never look cute like Desiree's. Cute isn't the goal. So there's no need to be picky.

I take a deep breath.

I plug the cord into the socket and flip the switch.

The clippers come to life in my right hand with a faint buzzing sound.

My hands shake slightly - hopefully from the clippers and not my nerves, as I attempt to fit the plastic guard on top of the metal teeth.

Here goes nothing.

I set the clippers onto the base of my forehead where the hairline begins and slowly drag the clippers to the back of my head. Like the first snow fall, short, tiny pieces of hair land softly on the white vanity.

I take a look at my work in the mirror.

Fuck! What have I done?

Maybe this was a mistake? In its wake, the teeth have left a jarring, one-inch furrow through my hair along the right side of my head. But how would I explain *that*?

There's clearly no going back.

I quickly push through the rest of my hair, eager to get it over with. Maybe it will look better when all of my hair is off.

With the counter now blanketed in a thin layer of dark brown, I inspect the results in the mirror. Well, I was wrong. It doesn't look better with it all off.

But it's the only thing I could think of that'll be an advantage to blend into the grey. To be part of my class, the Company, the Corps.

***

"Hello there, kid." Tad's smiling face greets me at the unusually crowded Charleston airport. I realize quickly that most everyone here is a cadet. If it isn't the haircut that gives them away, it's their gait. Or their posture. Or for some, their already earned band of gold glinting in the fluorescent airport light.

"Hey there." We hug briefly. "Are you picking anyone else up?"

"Nope. It's just you. " A wave of relief passes over me. "Max arrived yesterday." And it quickly washes away. "Now that you're here, maybe you can get him out of the house." Over my dead body. Fuck that guy.

"What's with the hat?" Tad reaches for it. "Are you in the witness protection program now?"

"Cut me some slack." I swat his hand away quickly. "I'm trying not to stand out as a cadet too much.

"Okay, okay…I got it. Don't touch the hat."

After retrieving my luggage at the luggage carrousel, we walk to the car in unusual silence. Tad breaks it first. "Do you need to stop off anywhere before the house? Gwendolyn and I are going to an alumni function tonight, so you guys are on your own for dinner."

"Alumni function? *You*?"

Tad lets out a laugh. "Yea, I know. Very much out of character for me. But with Malone starting his new position this week and the LAMC Foundation's efforts….well, I just felt like I had to do *something*. Anything. To support you girls. To get my voice out there."

Everything rushes back to me all at once - Malone. The Field House Investigation. The LAMC Foundation. The blog. Caroline's Corner. Me in the paper. I slump down into the leather car seat as soon as enter the car. Wishing desperately for the seat to swallow me whole.

Max doesn't greet us when we walk through the door. *Coward.* Of course he's avoiding me. Yet the sitcom laugh track emanating from upstairs gives away his location. I don't have to go up there. With Tad and Gwendolyn gone for dinner, avoiding Max isn't difficult. The house is big enough for the two of us.

"Alright, kid….sorry to just drop you off but I better get moving…." Tad pauses while reading the piece of paper in his hand. "Gwendolyn left a note that she's already gone ahead as there seems to be some sort of mix up with our tickets. Not sure when you want to head back to campus, but I'll gladly take you and Max if you want to wait till we get back."

Thinking of my luggage, I eagerly agree before remembering I'd have to share the car with Max. I almost offer to call a cab, but then I remember that I'm not the one who did anything wrong. I don't have anything to be ashamed of. And I can't avoid Max forever. We've got a class together this semester. Not to mention three and a half more years at Graham.

"That sounds great, Tad." I say reluctantly.

With the clang of the front door, the house becomes eerily still. The low hum of the central heater sounding louder than ever. A small part of me—the part of me who misses my friend—expects Max to thump down the wooden stairs. For him to stand in the doorway of the den. For him to hesitantly call my name. For him to apologize. For him to have *some* explanation. And at the end of the night, we'll be friends again. Laughing.

I walk into the den and settle into the soft sofa to wait out the hours before I head back to Graham. Not heading back early like I did back after Thanksgiving furlough. The tv absorbs me.

Suddenly, a motion registers in my periphery.

It's Max. My heart beats a faster cadence. I ready my thoughts.

Yet instead of stopping in the den's threshold, he creeps past the doorway like a thief avoiding the light.

The freezer door opens. Closes. The microwave beeps.

"Hey Kensley." And he disappears back upstairs before the words even hit my consciousness.

I make it a point to turn up the volume on the television. To even laugh at the scene flickering in front of my eyes. Anything to maintain my facade that I don't need his camaraderie.

Fine. If that's how he wants to be about it. There are other people at Graham aside from Maxwell Brown. I don't need him. And he clearly doesn't need me. Or cares about me. It was all a facade so he could get me to tell him what other women are doing so he could pass information back to Malone and the others in his company.

***

"Helloooo there," Tad calls from the front foyer. "Hope I'm not back too late. Furlough still ends at 2200 hours, right?"

"Oh hi. Yes…no change in the time." I answer still on the sofa in the den. "How was the dinner? Was it good?" A low growl emanates from my stomach at the same time. Shit, I forgot to eat dinner. "I mean…was there *progress*?" My voice bubbles over with nervousness. "Wait, I'm not sure how to phrase this…." What does one ask about a fundraising dinner to keep you in school? To keep you on track to get a degree?

"It was a good dinner. Well, let me correct that: the food was not good but the event was. I don't understand why alumni plan events with nearly the same food we ate as cadets. We hated that stuff then, so why would we like it now?" Tad shakes his head in confusion. "Anyway, we raised about eight thousand dollars at the silent auction. Only thing we won was a weekend hotel stay in Savannah. Gwen really had her heart set on the cruise though."

"What will the money be used for?" I ask, putting on my shoes.

Tad is lost in thought for a moment before replying. "It turns out that the money won't be used to *counter* the LAMC Foundation. Not sure if that's the best way to phrase it. But the school is already co-ed. And from General Gentry's opening remarks, all that stuff in *Caroline's Corner* is utter nonsense. Fear mongering. Speculation. Nothing to worry about."

"Are you sure?" I ask confused. "Don't you think with Malone taking on the new position—?"

"Kid, stop worrying about it. Seriously." Tad's face flashes with anger for a brief second as he cuts me off. "Malone and other grads like him have been beating their chest from the moment the first woman joined the ranks of the Corps in 1995. And they haven't stopped since. Always wanting to turn Graham all-male again. Always complaining about how women ruined their school" - Tad adds air quotes, "...and how there's no system now" - and here again to punctuate an oft repeated refrain just eager to make its appearance on a bumper sticker. "All of that is garbage, Kensley. The addition of women shed light into the dark corners of this school. It forced us to take a strong, hard review of policies and practices." He stands a little straighter. "And you know what we did, we updated what we needed to...got rid of what served no purpose in order to shape and refine the best version of all cadets."

I nod reflexively, not really knowing what the Corps was like *before* assimilation. All I can hope, *no*...all I must do is accept responsibility for my role, for my contributions, for my burden.

"But let's worry about stuff we can do something about." Tad pivots the conversation suddenly, "—like getting you and Max back to campus. Are you guys ready?"

"Hey Tad. Good dinner?" I keep my back to Max as his voice indicates his closeness in the foyer.

"Yeah. I was just telling Kensley that we raised eight thousand dollars but the food was terrible as usual." He laughs as he grabs the car keys and heads out the door.

Max and I pour into the backseat from opposite doors.

Campus is just a few minutes from Tad's yet the weighted silence between us pushes against me like a third backseat passenger. My eyes try to concentrate on the world on the other side of the rear window.

At the sight of the street sign for the college, a rock forms in the pit of my stomach. Terror. Joy. Anticipation. Dread. All solidify in a geological phenomena within a matter of seconds. Does Max feel it too?

Out of the corner of my eye, his hand twitches in the darkness on the seat next to me.

I want to grab it. I want to ask him about starting the spring semester. About the rock in his stomach. About the article. About what he did.

But before I get the chance to decide, he disappears into the glowing sallyport of his battalion.

Chapter Nineteen. *It was not a dilemma of language but of emotion and persona.*

"Hey guys," I say to no one in particular as I cross the threshold of my room, immediately trying to hide my look of disapproval yet taking care to keep my cover on. Visitors already. Couldn't Ash and Reagan get their fill of male entertainment over furlough? My roommates are perched on their beds like queens entertaining their court. The soft light of the desk lamps and their favorite Top 40 station on the radio amplifies the mood. Both are giggling, though I have no clue at what. Themselves, no doubt. Dane, Wade and...*Karl* are scattered around them, draped on the room's chairs like suitors vying for just a scrap of attention. I half expect to step on discarded grapevines. Never thought I'd see Karl in our room. A *girl's* room. Granted our only interaction last semester was while painting the banners so maybe I misjudged where he stood with women at Graham? Or maybe Callahan kicked him out of the Boys Only club.

"Hey, what's up, Kensley? How was your break?" Ash asks.

I get straight to the point. I already had one person betray me this year. And I don't have time for games. "What's with you in here, Karl?" Before he can even process my pro forma question. "I need my fucking chair."

His ears flush. "Oh...um, you know. I saw the door open and thought I'd come in and say hi." Karl lives on second division. Liar. So he couldn't have just walked by. His lie peaks my curiosity about his motives. About *him*, even.

Let's see where this goes.

"Yeah, I could see that. Ash and Reagan are quite the entertainers." I toss a glance at them haphazardly. "Plus they seem to know *everyone* on campus."

"Honestly, Bennett…" He scratches his head and takes a few shuffling steps toward me. Is he nervous? "I'm here because…well, I was waiting for *you* to come back." His voice is low and somber.

Me?

I freeze in front of my full press, crossing my arms in preparation for battle.

I knew something was up. Who sent him?

As if he could read my mind. "Wait—I'm here on my own. Callahan didn't send me. Nor does he know that I'm here. Besides, I'm a grown ass man and can do what I want." He smiles, trying to ease the tension.

I raise an eyebrow, signaling for him to continue. Cautiously.

"Look, over Christmas break my cousin came to me with some boy trouble she was having in high school. I won't bore you with it but… but in talking to her and being away from Graham for even just a bit…" He pauses, wringing his hands. "It made me think back on last semester. And how…maybe… *I* could've been a better classmate." He smiles apprehensively at my masked expression. "I am not saying friends and all. It's just…just that in talking to her that I never considered your perspective…" His voice trails off unable to find the words that would bring meaning to this realization. The kind of words that would make this a pivotal scene in story if this were a television show and I a character. But it's not a fictional scene. It's my life. And one experience with his cousin isn't going to make up for an entire semester. But I need allies right now. I uncross my arms. "Oh," I start lamely. That definitely wasn't what I expected. "Wow, Karl. I'm not sure what to say actually."

I continue to stand there. I'm not really sure what he expects me to say.

"Yeah, I know it's lame but... I guess she just got me thinking. Y'know, about stuff I've seen and heard last semester - especially when you guys aren't around." He lowers his voice and takes a step closer, but looks me straight in the eye when he continues. "You're a locked-on cadet, Bennett. Better than most." He throws a conspiratorial side glance at Ash and Reagan. "I wasn't excited about having girls in my company. I wanted the same system my brother had when he was a cadet. But... you're alright." He lightly punches me in the shoulder signifying the end of his vulnerability in true boy fashion.

My masked facade breaks on contact. They *have* noticed I'm better than the other girls. "Thanks, Karl. I appreciate it."

"Well...I better get back to my room and get shined up. We've got accountability formation in like, thirty minutes. See you around, Bennett." Karl says over his shoulder with a smile before he disappears into the galleries.

––––––––––

"Greetings, knobbies." Trevino's voice booms behind us as soon as we enter the squad room for accountability formation. I kind of missed that Texas drawl.

"Sir, good evening, sir." We announce in unison. My back aches in protest after not having to brace for two weeks.

"Ya'll have a nice little holiday?" He starts to inspect the brass of the those in reaching distance. "Did Santa bring you everything you wanted?" Chucking at his own joke.

"Sir, yes, sir," a few voices reply shakily. I'm certain his question was rhetorical. The mention of Santa should've been the tip-off.

"Some of you should've gotten coal. In fact, some of you *did* get coal, and then used it to shine your buckles from what I can see." He shakes his head dramatically, tossing the friendly tone with it. "This is a fucking disgrace. Did you knobs not look each other over before formation? Did you forget everything during the last two weeks that you fucking learned last semester?!"

Still rhetorical, but we reply anyway, "Sir, no, sir," loudly and hopefully convincingly.

"Really? Could've fooled the shit out of me." He holds up someone's belt buckle. "I mean, it's not hard. You take a cloth, dip it into some brass-o and polish away. You learned this on your first fucking day here." His voice is firm and steadfast. Almost like his speech is rehearsed.

"Sir, yes, sir."

"I know, I know—you guys sat around over the last two weeks watching television, drinking an icy cold beverage or two of your choice, listening to your high school friends talk about their college days. And you thought, *You know what? Fuck it. I don't need to shine up for formation. It'll be dark and those dumb-ass upperclassmen won't notice. My buddy Pat doesn't and he's still going to get a degree like me. So why should I? Fuck that shit!*"

Yep, definitely a rehearsed speech. Maybe even one given to Trevino when he was a knob.

"Sir, no, sir."

"Well, the party's fucking over, knobs!" Trevino roars. "You're back at Graham. And if you don't—." He interrupts himself as our eyes lock. "You've gotta be fucking kidding me."

I roll my shoulders back further. Tuck my chin in tighter. Try to swallow the dryness in my throat. Bracing for impact.

"Bennett! Explain yourself."

What does he want me to say? What could I say? The truth.

Well, you see, Jose…I've had a bit of a tumultuous four months. More than most knobs, trust me. While I do come from a Graham family, I'm here because I was trying to connect with my dad again. Maybe anyone really. I've been trying really hard to fit in

and do all the right things I thought I'm supposed to do as a cadet.
Yet I still can't seem to fit in - at Graham, with my dad. Square peg
round hole kind of thing I guess. Have I mentioned that the LAMC
Foundation wants me gone forever cause my kind apparently
"ruined this school." So I thought to myself - shit Kensley, let's try
a different way. So I wore civvies in Mt. Pleasant just like I am
sure you have, Jose. But that definitely didn't work out. Cause not
only did I get tours but now I got lumped into the same category as
Ash and Reagan. Anyway, Jose, I took matters into my own hands,
and well, here we are. Me, with a male knobby haircut. It's the only
thing I could think to do because I need to be here. I have to be like
you. Like Callahan. Like Johnson.

I swallow my thoughts in one gulp and stand across from him in silence.

Trevino storms out of the squad room with one step.

All eyes are on me.

"Holy shit," Ash screeches. "That certainly tops our highlights."

I roll my eyes. You wish.

"You know you're going to get pulled for that, right?" Callahan informs me flatly. "It's against fucking Blue Book regulations." What made him a sudden expert on female hair standards at Graham?

"It isn't. If it were, then every guy here would get a white slip," I say, keeping my voice as steady as I can. What I can get is some one on one PT time though. Finally.

We wait in silence for Trevino—for *any* upperclassman, to come back.

Without warning, Trevino's face appears on the other side of the screen door. "Roll out, knobs."

As we make our way back to the room after formation, the upperclassmen's words float around me confusingly like thought bubbles in a cartoon.

Fucking Ugly. Appalling. Dyke. Motivating. Disgusting. Disgrace. My room never felt safer.

"You really do think you're fucking special, don't you?" Reagan volleys as soon as I enter the room behind her.

Ash stands nervously, clutching her rack. Like a child feeling the onset of a fight between her parents, wanting desperately for them to just get along.

"It was *my* choice." My voice and words firm and assured. "I didn't need your fucking approval—then or now, Reagan. Certainly not from someone who spends more time flirting with upperclassmen than trying to be knob."

"Oh I know. You tell us all the time about how much we suck! But see, this time, you stepped in it yourself. You're always telling Ash and me to blend in more. *Do this Reagan. No, do that, Ash.* Shine your brass like this. Don't talk to our male classmates. You have to blend in." Her lithe hands wave about intensely. "You've always thought you're better than us. From day one. That you and only *you* are the only female that should be in the Corps. That not even Coleman belongs here. Then you got tours and realized you were *juuuuust* like the fucking rest of us—fallible. Not special. Not unique." She lets out a bitter cackle. "And the best part was, you got in trouble for something so basic. You were —" Her words inaudible from her sudden laughter. "You thought you knew this place better than us. Yet you....you were too stupid to get away with wearing fucking civvies —"

Her laughter takes over the rest of her acquisitions.

Fucking Bitch.

We stare at each other from across the room like two mortal enemies who finally meet in the season finale. My chest heave with anger and frustration, spite and contempt; while hers with laughter and satisfaction. The viewing audience is on the edge of their seats as the cliffhanger plays out.

My body tense with resentment. But not at her rather at the truth she brought into the room. I cross my arms in marked silence hoping if I ignore it then it'll recede just as quickly.

"What-the-fuck-ever. You can play tough, but I know you're not." Reagan lets out a huff. "It's ironic you shaved your head like a guy." The word hisses between her teeth. "Cause you think you'll blend in more, but really...*really* it just makes you stand out more."

She turns and begins to walk to her desk. "And by the way," she says, turning back to me. "You look fucking *ugly*." The word shoots out of her mouth like the fatal shot.

The dam breaks. Hot tears pour down my previously stoic cheeks, onto my shirt.

Her words find their kin uttered earlier by the unknown upperclassman earlier. Together they echo throughout the galleries of my mind.

I quickly wipe the tears from my face lest I give her the satisfaction. I grab my physical fitness uniform and go through my normal pre-bedtime ritual: wash face, brush teeth, shine brass, lay out new duty uniform.

Fuck her. She doesn't know what she's talking about. She just thinks she does.

"All clear," the three of us shout in response to the unexpected knock on the door.

We brace as the door handle turns.

"Hey Bennett..." Dallas Lawson pokes his head into the room. "Coleman wants you to meet her at 0730 hours in front of Dehenre's office tomorrow."

"Sir, yes, sir."

I can feel Reagan's smug, self-righteous stare on the back of my head as I shut my desk light off and climb into bed, hoping the darkness will slow my wayward thoughts seeking permanent agency.

Another meeting with Coleman and Dehenre awaits.

And here I didn't think today could get any worse.

Chapter Twenty. *But from that night on, the year was marked with a curious inevitability, as though we were all engaged in an amazing and irresistible game.*

I practically fly to the second floor of Barton Hall after breakfast. This isn't a meeting I can afford to be late to.

Coleman's voice drifts out of the office as I approach.

Uneasily I continue forward, the leather soles of my shined black shoes making audible contact with the linoleum floor.

"Bennett." Coleman's head pops out of Dehenre's office,

"Ma'am, yes, ma'am."

I walk into Dehenre's office, assuming that no further word from Coleman meant they were ready for me to join them.

"Good morning, ma'am," I say to Dehenre, my tone polite but flat.

"Good morning, Kensley." Dehenre motions me to the empty chair —the same one I sat in when she showed me *Caroline's Corner*. "Please have a seat. I know you have an eight o'clock class so I won't keep you long." She pauses a beat. "But, well, you know why you're here so early."

I nod.

She lets out a long sigh. "I don't really know what to say about your haircut, Kensley." She shakes her head like a disapproving mother. "We've reviewed the Blue Book and... and there's no rule against it. I mean, it's not addressed in the Blue Book because, well because—."

"Because no one thought a girl would shave her head, Bennett," Coleman interrupts. Her voice is sharp with irritation. "Seriously! What the fuck were you thinking? None of my classmates *ever* thought of something so...so *stupid*. Your haircut doesn't make you a good cadet. I don't understand why you thought it was a good idea." She gestures at my head. "In the end, it only alienates you. Even from the guys."

She's wrong.

Can't she see what's happening? Everyone thinks of assimilation as Graham adapting itself to women, but that's backward. Assimilation is about *us* adapting and adjusting to the culture at Graham—the already-existing culture. My shaved head won't make me stand out; in fact, my hair is now one less thing that'll allow the cadets and alumni to pick me out in formation. From afar at parade or in the squad room or during football march-overs, I'll look like just another one of the guys.

"Thank you, Avery." Dehenre's voice is warm but her face is clearly telling Coleman to ease up. "When the school lost the South Caroline District Court ruled in 1995 that the Graham had to establish a timely plan to assimilate women into the Corps, one of the contentious pieces of discussion was the female knob haircut. Our only model was the Service academies, really, given that women had been a part of their fabric since 1976. And we certainly didn't want to begin down a path of becoming like A & M. Yet we didn't want to entirely lose the personality of Graham. " Dehenre takes a sip of her coffee. "Everyone definitely agreed that we weren't going to make the women shave their heads like the men. So we agreed on your current....well…" Her words become inaudible.

"What Lieutenant Colonel Dehenre is trying to say, is that the school put a lot of thought into us coming here, Bennett." Seeking approval to continue, Coleman looks at Dehenre. "They didn't just put shit together in haste. And they *certainly* weren't going to have us walking around with fucking shaved —"

Dehenre signals for Coleman to retreat at the sound of her rekindled irritation. "Kensley, you won't get cons or more tours since you didn't *technically* violate the Blue Book…but I think it's best you keep a low profile until your hair has grown out more. The LAMC Foundation would have a field day with this."

"Yes, ma'am." Fucking Callahan was right.

"Is there anything you want to say?"

I pause for a few seconds to make it seem like I'm taking her question seriously.

"No, ma'am. Thank you."

"That about covers it, I think. Avery…" Dehenre darts a conspiratorial look at Coleman.

"Just one thing. I think it's okay to tell her, *right*?" Dehenre nods. "The school is planning on doing some articles to counter *Caroline's Corner*. The plan is to interview two women from each class year. Your name had come up, but…*well*, given the extreme haircut, we decided that you're just not the best representative of women in your class anymore."

The room goes silent. My body numb. *I'm not the best representative of women in my class anymore.* The words roll around my conciseness like marbles, clanging together as they circle around and around. S*he* didn't think I was the best representative. She's my mentor; she's supposed to guide me. Talk to me. Help me through Graham. I don't understand why I'm suddenly Coleman's enemy. This isn't Coleman, this is Ward.

"Yes, ma'am." I utter softly.

"We just wanted you to hear it from us directly." Dehenre adds in finality.

The three of us remain seated in silence. The tick, tick of the second hand clock on the wall above Coleman keeping us company.

Finally, Dehenre stands. "We don't want to make you late, Kensley."

"Yes, ma'am. Thank you." I grab my cover and knobby bag and am out the door, down the stairs, and out the back door of Barton Hall without being aware of my movements.

I'm not the best representative of women in my class anymore.
Fuck them.

I'm the perfect representation of a female cadet—of a *cadet*. Period. Rage now my companion.

I had a perfect 4.0 grade point average last semester. As a *knob*. With all of the shit we have to do. The school is riding high and mighty because all the women in my class came back after Christmas furlough—a first since assimilation three years ago. They've met their unofficial quota. So they don't think they need women like me. They can't put Ash or Reagan out there and get the same results. The same type of support from Alumni or for recruitment. Clearly Graham doesn't know what it wants women at Graham to look like. To be like. To represent.

The school doesn't want to feature me in the newspaper because my shaved head isn't the right message …or look for Graham. Whatever. This will backfire regardless. Dehenre didn't say anything about the school interviewing male knobs. This *is* just the type of thing the LAMC Foundation will capitalize on, not my male knobby haircut. It's not fair treatment for them. All of which will trickle down into the Companies and we have to bear the consequences of the decisions the staff at Graham make.

I take my seat in Gish's class just as the bell sounds in Harris Hall.

"Ah, Thirteen-oh-five. Just in time," Gish remarks as I slide into my seat.

"I'm making final hotel arrangements this afternoon. Since you can't room with anyone in class, I need to book a separate room for you."

The room turns into a snake pit. It's especially hard not to roll my eyes at their hissing today.

"Today's not a good day to fuck with me, assholes." My thoughts sneer at them.

"I need to room on my own, too," a voice from the front of the room says.

"Oh? Why's that Mr. Bryant?"

"Cause um—."

I smile as Gish cuts him off. "When you come up with a viable excuse that has nothing to do with your girlfriend in Savannah, we can continue this conversation."

The sudden flare-up of laughter in the room takes the attention off of me in an instant.

———

The first parade of the spring semester. And my last weekend of tours. Finally.

I finish putting on my web belt, take one last look at myself in the mirror, and head to Coleman's room.

I knock confidently yet apprehensively on her door.

"Yeah…" I enter without waiting for further instruction or comment.

Instantly, I regret the decision.

There, sitting in Coleman's desk chair, with his feet propped up as if he owns the place, is Chris. *Asshole.*

Coleman, like most upperclass women, tends not to abide by the rule that the door must be open when a male cadet is in the room. I haven't figured out if it's an act of rebellion or just a way to be like one of the guys. Kind of like shaving your head I suppose, but who am I to judge?

It takes a few seconds for the blood to flow through my veins again. It's one thing to see him in class twice a week or occasionally in the battalion; I can be prepared for those sightings because they're expected and the confines of being a knob have kept me from confronting him for pulling me for civvies.

But a moment like this? Quiet, intimate. Relaxed.

No, I'm not ready for a moment like this at all.

"Oh shit. It's almost time for parade. Can you believe this is our last semester?" Coleman says with a smile in her voice.

"Hell no! Seems like only yesterday we were trying to figure out why the butt box is called a butt box. Remember how Walker's always hung on his back like a little black back bag?"

They both laugh at the shared memory.

"Ugh...don't remind me. I think we *all* cut webbing for him at some point."

Coleman takes her grey dress blouse off the hanger in her full press and puts it on. "Okay, Bennett, let's do this." I walk over to her desk to retrieve her maroon sash, three large safety pins, and the name tag she always wears underneath as usual.

Chris and I have yet to acknowledge each other's presence in the room. That's not unusual; I'm a knob and he's an upperclassman. Or is it? When I was in Corey's room earlier this week to drop off his laundry, Sherman was in there and they both acknowledged me. It wasn't a big thing. Just a "Hey, Bennett." Same thing when I dropped off laundry in Trevino's room—he and Gibson both asked me about my Christmas furlough seemingly having forgotten about my hair. My hands clutch the maroon sash. My knuckles turning white from the unspoken anger against Chris.

"Well, I better get back up to my side of battalion. You know, where real important shit happens," Chris says, smiling sarcastically. "Terrence would be none too pleased with me if I were late for parade."

"Terrence is a tool."

They both laugh in agreement.

"Can't argue with you there. He probably would've been just as pouty as Fred if he hadn't gotten Battalion Commander." Chris pauses. "I don't get these guys. It's fucking *fake* rank."

I secure the final safety pin on Coleman's sash. What an asshole. It's only fake if you don't take it seriously. Rank in the Corps is a privilege and an opportunity to truly experience Graham as a leadership laboratory. His fucker should now better with his step-dad being a grad.

"Oh…is Fred talking to you again? You guys were like brothers until…well, until Cathy was selected as RC and he wasn't."

Chris is silent for a few seconds.

"Yeah, I think we're good." His tone and words move cautiously. "I don't know. It hit him a little too hard because he…I don't know, subconsciously felt the pressure from his dad. Pressure to live up to his dad's time here. I get it. One thousand percent." I steal a glance at Chris actually hoping he'll see my eye roll. "But there's no need to be a sore loser about it. I have mixed feelings about Cathy as RC, for reasons we've talked about before, but… that's a moot point now. I think he's finally starting to understand that he could've handled his reaction better. With more dignity. Composure. Like a Graham man."

Coleman shrugs dismissively and looks at my handiwork in the mirror. "I'm glad you two are back on track. Or at least talking. I agree with you that he could've handled it better. Taken the fucking battalion rank." She turns squarely to Chris. "And if Fred had bothered to ask me— or talk to me at all—he would've known we share the same thoughts on Cathy as RC. She's my friend, but—cover your ears, Bennett—I don't think she was the *best* choice either —"

"What the fuck!" Chris interrupts Coleman. "How did I not know this. You are always so chummy and talking nice about her. Every time I see you two are giggling."

"Giggling? Really. The school wanted a win. A good headline after the last few years of bad publicity. So maybe they rushed it. I don't know, really. But in the end, we've got to support each other. - as cadets, classmates, and women."

I hand Coleman her sword.. "Random but not: How's your dad…er step-day"

"It's cool. Same. He's working on a new project that he's really excited about. It's taking up all of his time but he seems to be enjoying it."

"I thought he was retired?"

"From being a judge. Absolutely. But you know… he always needs something to do. Keep him busy. He's doing some non-profit work, I think."

"Yeah? In what field?"

"Um, not really sure." Chris brushes off his grey pants uncomfortably and pivots the conversation. "But it's more fun than the Field House investigation. I'm turning in my final report this week. I'll be glad when that shit is done. So fucking tired of asking the same questions over and over again. All because of some lame-ass anonymous note slid under a door in the Commandant's office. As if cadets are going to narc on each other. There's the honor system, and then there's honor among classmates, y'know?"

Coleman gives a knowing nod as makes final adjustments to her uniform.

"In the end, they're just going to install a new lock and keep the master key in Wright's office. Total waste of fucking time."

"So you found *nothing*?"

"Nope." Chris looks at his watch. "Shit! I really have to go, Avery, or I'm not going to make parade. I still gotta get a sash wrap."

"You should've brought your parade stuff. You know damn well you've always been late for *everything. "* She looks at me. "Bennett could've given you a sash wrap."

I could've *what*? Is she fucking kidding? Thank god that fucker didn't bring his parade stuff. I'd probably choke him with his sash.

Chris laughs uncomfortably. "Uhm…"

"This is interesting." Recognizes the his hesitancy, she considers Chris. "Why are you being weird about this? Would you've been afraid of a girl wrapping your sash? Or Fred or wait… your *daaaaad* finding out? The super alumnus, Mr. Quante." Coleman faces Chris with a sarcastic salute.

Chris eyes Coleman from across the room. The mood in the room just shifted palpably. The friendly facade just an illusion as the undercurrent of years of unspoken words, feelings, toleration, thoughts—perhaps even resentment—seep in through the hardwood.

"Cut the shit." Chris jeers. "That was low and completely *fucking* unnecessary - especially for a hypothetical situation, Avrey!"

Coleman shifts her hands onto her hips, her glare saying all that needs to be said. *We may be friendly and classmates, but I know how your dad really feels about women at Graham.*

"Fuck this." His voice is bitter, strained, exposed as he grabs his cover and stomps out.

Chapter Twenty-One. *I didn't earn their friendship on my own.*

"Hello?" The front door closes behind me. Yet there's no echo.

I inhale deeply, taking in the smell of Tad's. Pledge, stale coffee, and remnants of last night's dinner. *I've missed this place.*

I scavenge through the kitchen like a feral animal who hasn't eaten in weeks, ripping open three different bags of chips unable to decide. Get a fucking grip. It's only been six weeks since furlough and I should be used to the mess hall food by now. When I've settled on the proper sandwich and condiments, I saunter upstairs to the TV room, where mindless distraction awaits.

"Hi!"

Max greets me with a smile. He mutes the television. Sits up.

I nearly drop my plate.

What the fuck. "Oh…hi. I …I didn't know you were here. I can go watch TV downstairs, it's not—."

"Kensley, wait! I'm glad you're here."

It didn't cross my mind *once* that since I finished my tours yesterday, that Max would've finished his as well. And that he, like me, would retreat to Tad's for a lazy Sunday of television, comfy pants, and *not* walking back and forth on the red and white checkered quad for all to see.

For all to *judge.*

A drop of condensation slides down the glass of iced tea in my hand. Its landing onto the hardwood floor makes the silence between us all the more noticeable.

"Don't be difficult, K." His voice cracks with uncomfortable laughter. "If your feet are anything like mine, I know they're hurting." He gestures towards the chair in the corner.

He's not wrong. My blisters have blisters.

I feign a smile and settle into the armchair next to the sofa uneasily. I pull at the sandwich with my fingers - famished and reluctant. The television flickers in the background. I notice the sides of Max's mouth twitch every so often, as if he wants to start talking but doesn't know where to start. He could start with an apology. There's no reason he should've been mad at me after we got back to Tad's that night. I didn't force him into civvies any more than Stacey forced me. I didn't do anything wrong. He's the one who told Caroline all about me and that night.

His posture straightens. "Look, I know we haven't talked in awhile. Seems like forever, actually…" His words trail off as he attempts to pull strength from his nervous laughter. "And I don't know really what I last said to you exactly. If anything. That night was such a blur. It happened so fast. One minute we're like normal college freshmen, laughing having dinner, and the next that *asshole* Harvatin appears out of nowhere and we all go home with twenty tours. Yeah, so I was a little pissed at you for assuming I came into the room to talk to you. I just…I'm a knob here too, Kensely. With the same consequences. I just don't—"

Let's just get to it. "But …that wasn't an excuse to fucking sell me out to Caroline's Corner."

Max stares at me in utter stupor. Guess he never thought I would figure it out.

"What…what the fuck are you talking about?"

"Don't play fucking dumb, Max!" My stifled anger eager with its prey insight. "The latest *Caroline's Corner* had all the details about the night we got tours. Except it only seemed to mention *me*!" The force of my own index finger on my sternum surprises even me. "Granted, I could understand why it didn't mention you or Forrest…but Stacey was there too and last I checked, she's also a girl at Graham, too. But *noooooo*! You wanted to get in good with Malone and who-the-fuck-ever-else and so you __""

"Kensley, I …I really don't know what you're talking about." His voice a bewildered whisper yet firm enough to stop me on my hunt. "You thought…you thought *I* told someone at the Gazette about you wearing civvies…" There's a sadness to him suddenly. "…because you thought I was mad at you?"

I shrug. Maybe. But who else would talk to Caroline?

"Wow. K, that's fucked up. Really fucked up. What, you thought I was just hanging out with you because it seemed like a good idea at the time? Because we were the only knobs at Tad's? That I'd talk shit about you in my *all male* squad room? And we'd have a good laugh about it. About you?" He shakes his head. "I wouldn't stab you in the back like that. I am not a hypocrite."

I force a sip of the iced tea to stall a response. Needing the chill of the sweet liquid more than I though.

Thankfully he continues. "After all this time, K, after *alllllll* the shit I shared with you, you lump me in the same fucking category as every other guy on campus! Is that how you treat *your* friends…."

The bottom drops right out of my stomach.

"I'm sorry." The words low and reflexive. "I do trust you. And I wouldn't do you like that. But sometimes…sometimes it just gets all so confusing here. I don't know who is being genuine or who I can truly rely on. And I don't really fit in with my guys in my company no matter how much I try to be like them or laugh at their stupid-ass jokes. I've been doing the best that I know how, yet lately…" I blink away the standing tears quickly. "…lately, I've just been fucking it all up. And I hate feeling like that. Like….like you know, like I am not in control of it all. Like nothing I do or say or how many pushups I do is every fucking good enough for this fucking place." The anger of the ceramic plate making contact with the opposite wall jolts me into the present. "Shit."

"Uhm…yea. I'd say." Max offers with a light-hearted grim as he plucks a slice of turkey from his atop his shaved head.

"Shit…shit…shit." I say frantically and in shock at the display of my physical emotion. I stand yet quickly plop back down again. "I shouldn't let it get to me like that. I know better. I know this is just part of the system -" air quotes for emphasis —" to make break you down….make you rebuild yourself so you know how strong you are….that you can survive anything…" My thoughts trail off.

Max takes a pause from brushing together the shards of sandwich and ships on the hardwood floor and looks at me. "I get it, K. I truly do. All those things you said just now…I've thought…*felt* those things, too. It's like you said - part of the system. You got this; *we* got this!"

"Max, I'm *really* sorry."

"I know." His smile is reassuring. Honest. For a second, it feels like more than I deserve. "Now, let's talk about the LAMC Foundation." Max pulls out his notebook. "Good. Okay…well, Preston was obviously still cool with my being on staff at the *Commodore* despite the tours. Plus I'm the only one he'd shown that memo to about this being the last year for the Foundation to fund privatization."

"So he's kind of stuck with you then." Hoping humor will quickly rebuild our friendship.

"Yeah. I guess so. Anyway, last we talked, I think…I needed to find out who this big silent donor was, right?"

I nod.

"I haven't found much since then, unfortunately, because the Foundation's financial records aren't easily accessible. Even though they're *technically* a non-profit." Max takes a deep breath. "The best I could do was finding a record of donation amounts and donors. The only identifying notations are initials though. It's like... it's like the LAMC knows it needs to be sneaky about all this. They don't want to implicate anyone, which begs the question: What, or *who*, are they trying to hide?"

I stare at him for a second in genuine astonishment and equal parts chagrin. "There has be like thousands of alumni out there - some with even the same initials. I mean, Graham has been around since 1842." I leaf quickly through the stack of excel spreadsheets he thrusts in front of me proudly.

"I'm an English major, Max. This is all Greek to me."

"Well, to me too. For now." He smiles. "I thought we could divide the stack and highlight significant donation amounts. Remember, the LAMC Foundation had a significant about-face in public relations and fundraising at the start of this school year. My hunch is that it's still just due to a small group of donors and maybe...maybe just one person's influence. So if we can track those dates and amounts, we might be able to corroborate attendance at some of the bigger fundraising events—maybe catch a consistent face in published photos?"

"Yea..that makes sense. Anything I can do to help." I won't have a school to go to next year if Graham privatizes.

After about three hours, we're exhausted. My eyes dry from staring at numbers and letters on an spreadsheet.

Max inputs both of our results into his spreadsheet on his computer. Max creates a pivot table and we instantly spot the trend: once "WQ" started making donations, the LAMC's star began to shine brighter. It's also when Caroline started having more by-lines.

"WQ...WQ," Max whispers to himself like a mad scientist. "You can't hide forever."

"Do you know how you'll find out who the initials belong to?"

Max shakes his head. "The only option is to leaf through yearbooks. Though it could as easily be a company as an individual."

"That could take years, Max. Wait—didn't you say the LAMC Foundation has a web site? We could cross reference the initials with current and active members. Those in the photos, right?"

"Shit. Yeah, that should totally get us closer."

Thankful to have my friend back, I mirror his beaming smile.

Chapter Twenty-Two. *Fear was a citizen of the stomach, a thin man at the knees.*

In two hours I'll be on a van to Savannah.

Just six upperclassmen and me - a lonely knob.

And Chris.

It's been a week since I last saw him in Coleman's room.

Gish divided us into two groups of eight. And of course, Chris and I are in a group together.

It's only a three-day trip, yet when I try to pick up the duffel for the trip I discover a flaw. How the hell am I going to carry this from third division all the way to the sally port while bracing? It nearly weighs fifty pounds. I wouldn't dare use anything that rolls. I'd never, *ever* live that down.

Few cadets are up at 6AM on a Saturday morning. At least not on an SMI day. Sweep details don't start till seven either, per the request of the upperclassmen. Which means there's a chance that I can struggle with this behemoth down three flights of stairs, through fourteenth company, and out the sally port without getting harassed. Maybe. Or worse, be called out for my shitty military bearing. Everything in this bag better be of use in Savannah.

"Good morning, Thirteen-oh-five." Gish is standing by two, white, fifteen-passenger vans. He points to the first one in the caravan, and I hoist my bag in the way-back.

I put one foot on the step into the van and recognize quickly from the glares that I'm not welcome. I move to my *only* other option—the single front passenger seat next to Gish.

"You'll be stuck listening to my latest book on CD, Thirteen-oh-five. Sure you want to sit up here?"

"Yes, sir." What choice do I really have?

I nod off shortly after we leave Charleston.

At the hotel, Gish hands out our room keys and tells us we've got about thirty minutes to freshen up before our first planned activity starts. We're only in Savannah for two and half days. Every second counts. And he's booked a full itinerary.

"Must be nice to room fucking alone," a voice cuts through the air as I grab my mammoth of a bag and head towards the elevator.

"Leave it, Dan," Chris says. Or at least a voice that sounded like his.

My hand squeezes the strap of my bag a little tighter as the lobby disappears behind the elevator's silver doors.

———

It feels like we walked miles and miles of this city today, seeing everything from the low-hanging Spanish moss in *Midnight in the Garden of Good and Evil* to Conrad Aiken's graveside bench. I'm lucky my feet were already broken in from walking tours. And that we were allowed to wear civilian clothes. For real this time.

Gish reviews tomorrow's schedule with us before dismissing us for the night. As soon as he disappears into the elevator, a debate among the upperclassmen begins on what to do with the rest of the night, with their freedom.

I roll my eyes and walk toward the elevators. I already know I'm invited anyway. And even though my stomach is yearning for sustenance, my legs won't corporate.

"Hey, Bennett."

I turn to face the voice. "Yeah? Um, I mean yes, sir." I'm not quite sure what the protocol is here. Yes, I'm still a knob and they're all upperclassmen, but we're not at Graham and we're not wearing uniforms either.

Chris faces me. "You want to join us for dinner?"

My eyes shift nervously among the group. I look around at the other upperclassmen. I don't think he was speaking for the group. Most are avoiding my gaze, whispering instead to each other. About me, no doubt. About Chris asking a knob, and more abhorrently, *a girl* to join them for dinner.

"Seriously, bro?" one laments, confirming my suspicions.

"What the fuck dude. Cut the shit. You're not an ombudsman here. You don't have to be nice to her." And another.

Chris doesn't turn to face them. Is he being brave for me? Is he trying to tell me something with this public gesture? Trying to make up for getting me tours?

"Thank you, sir. It's okay."

"Okay, you did the politically correct ombudsman thing, Chris. Now let's go eat. I'm starving." A hand grabs Chris by the arm and pulls him toward the automatic sliding glass doors of the hotel.

"Don't be a tool." Chris yanks his arm away. "She's in our class just like Tom over there. And she gets better grades than you. Probably than most of us. It's just dinner."

A warm flush creeps up my neck and onto my face. Maybe we can still be friends.

"Maybe so, but that doesn't mean I've gotta spend my fucking free time with *her.*" His retort carries a bitter edge. He never once looks at me. Like maybe if he doesn't, I won't actually exist. "It's enough some court said they had to be here."

"Guys, what's it going to be? Are we going to dinner or not?" Dan calls out impatiently from near the automatic sliding doors of the hotel.

"I am. But I think Chris here wants to earn extra Barton Hall points and take the little knobby out to dinner," the snake spews again. His comment met with laugher from the others.

"You're a dick, Walker." Chris steps away from the sliding glass doors. "Enjoy your dinner."

"Suit yourself."

The group walks out into the night.

Then it's just Chris and me.

"Hey," he says, like this is totally normal. "So what do you feel like eating?" Always confident, always so sure of himself.

Unbelievable. I'm not sure if I should be touched by his bold interactions with his classmates, or offended at being a cheap excuse for him to be cocky.

"Whatever. I don't care. You seem to have all the plans. You really don't have to go to dinner with me, *sir.*"

"What's with the sarcasm. I'm just trying to be friendly."

"I didn't know we were friends."

"Fair. But I could say the same to you. Guess my email got lost...." He raises an eyebrow at me.

"Nope...not lost." I cross my arms in front of me matter of factly. "Just deleted."

"Well played, Bennett." His face breaks into a shit eating grin. "Nice fucking power move. But seriously, why the cold shoulder? Cause I pulled you for civvies..."

I stare at him for a few seconds contemplating lying or telling the truth. "Uhm...yea." A cadet does not lie, cheat or steal.

"Get serious, Bennett! Is that *really* the reason? Tell me you are making that up. Please!"

I avert his eyes.

He inhales and exhales loudly. "Fine. I thought maybe Coleman would've given you some mentoring on this. But I guess not. Since you didn't read my email, I'll explain it to you here. I *had* to do it. Plain and simple. If it had just been me, I would've maybe let it slide. I mean, who hasn't worn civvies as a cadet. But…well, Courtney saw you guys first. And he *certainly* wasn't going to let it go." Chris pauses for a moment before continuing. "I know you have aspirations here. It's not the end of world—or your cadet career for that matter. Lots of my cadets - even those in leadership positions now served cons, or even walked tours."

I lean against the blue standard coach in the lobby. "I just…I just…." My words don't find traction. What was it that hurt me more - thinking that we were friends or that he tarnished my cadet reputation? Maybe both? If it's true what he said - that other cadet leader have had cons or tours, then maybe I too can still recover. And Max and I are friends again so maybe Chris and I can be friends, too. He clearly cares about me since he wanted to go to dinner with *me* over his classmates who were giving him shit.

But I can't just give him a pass. "What was I supposed to think? The IMs, checking in on me, on the quad at Thanksgiving…. Yeah, I was mad at you for pulling me. But I'm more mad at myself for letting my guard down. For telling you about my mom. For you then ignoring me. Deleting me. Like I meant nothing to you. I don't—I didn't understand. And I still don't. But I guess…" I run out of energy.

Chris nods his head slowly. "At the end of the day, I am still an upperclassman and you," his right index finger pointing at me more like an accusation, "are still a *knob*. I don't want people talking. Perception is reality. Maybe if we weren't here, we'd be more like normal people but we're here - at Graham." He pauses for a brief moment. "Look, I got my own shit to worry about. I mean, I graduate in five months. It's been cool to get to know you and chat. Yet I don't want to force anything on you. And if you don't want to go to dinner or have any contact for that matter…that's cool." He shrugs nonchalantly as if it makes no difference to him. Or maybe he's just playing it cool?

A panic simmers within me and speaks. "No...I ...I ...I liked chatting with you, too." The desperation in my voice foreign to me yet it has clearly taken over. "Like you said, I am a knob and you're an upperclassman. Yet in five months it'll be different and easier. No one would care!" I end enthusiastically.

"Maybe." His only offer.

I smile at the possibility.

"So ...we never settled on where you stand with going to dinner with an upperclassman."

"There're a couple of places right outside." I head towards the sliding glass doors eagerly. "I'm sure we can decide on one of them."

"Well then...what're we waiting for?"

Chapter Twenty-Three. *Do you ever think about your place in history?*

I'm awake before the alarm goes off. *Thank you, Graham for the conditioning.*

Darkness peeks through the sliver of space between the brown and red vinyl curtains. It's probably not even 5AM. I take a quick look around the room. Faint outlines of yesterday's clothing litter the floor, leaving an aimless trail.

Most everyone is already downstairs by the time I enter the lobby. I carefully scan the gaggle of upperclassmen for Chris. I've got to act normal. Perception is reality.

There he is.

I take a seat on the blue couch in the lobby, casually leafing through the magazine on the table as I wait for the others to finish their breakfast.

I only hear snippets of the conversation going on among him and his classmates.

I freeze mid page turn.

"So how was your dinner *date* with the knobby?" Punctuated with kissing sounds.

"Oooooo, yea, Chris. Did you give her a system?" His lewd hip thrusting visible in my periphery.

"Ugh, that's gross, Dan. I'd never fuck a knob." Another voice clarifies. "Disgusting."

"What the fuck!" Chris's voice firm but annoyed. "You guys are so out of line right now. Who are you?" The staccato bark of his words continue. "We are in a public setting and not the battalions. Get a *fucking* grip."

"Damn, dude. We were just kidding. No need to jump down our throats about it."

"Yea…we just wanted to know what you did for dinner. We know you didn't sleep with that knob."

"Well…you guys seemed a bit off the rails there." Chris says calmly. "Since you want to know so badly. there's nothing to tell. I went to dinner with Bennett - the *knob*, at some place down the street. Don't give me that look, Pat. It was a quick thirty minutes. Like you said, I'm the ombudsman." He lets out a laugh. "Um, let's see… then I went to some bar off some side street and hung out there for a bit. You know, chatted with the locals about anything other than literature."

"Sure. If you say so." They all laugh in unison, like it's some inside joke. "You're coming with us tonight. I don't care where we go. Dan's choice in drinking establishments is terrible. I mean —"

"Good morning, gentlemen. And Thirteen-oh-five," Gish says from behind me. "Hope everyone can bring that same level of enthusiasm for our adventures today. Remember, once we get back, I expect to see some quality work in your assignments."

———

We get back to campus just as the rest of Corps is marching to lunch. We're excused from mess but not from our afternoon classes. And I certainly am not excused from any knob duties. When I get back to my room, there's a note on my desk telling me to find Coleman after afternoon classes. Wonder what this is about? Can't be that bad because I don't have to go see Dehenre. But the day is still young. I quickly unpack and load my knobby bag for the afternoon—biology and history of pre-revolutionary Russia.

I knock apprehensively on Coleman's door after class.

"Yeah. Ah, good…you got my note."

"Ma'am, yes, ma'am."

"How was your trip? Good, bad, indifferent?"

I'm not sure which question to answer first or if she wants an answer to any of them. "Ma'am, fine, ma'am."

"You were the only knob on the trip, right?"

"Ma'am, yes, ma'am."

"I bet *that* was fun." She flashes me a knowing smile.

"Ma'am, yes, ma'am." Even if I could tell her more, I'm not in the mood to talk.

"You're a pretty good runner, Bennett. So your name came up for the cross country team. My classmate—the team captain—wanted to talk to you about it personally. Let me see if she's free right now…" Coleman picks up the phone in her room—an upperclassman privilege.

Cross country is Corps Squad, so that's a *no* from me right from the start. I can master the pillar of physical fitness without being on an official team sport. Besides, I need to be in the barracks in order to beat Callahan for rank.

A few minutes later, Nicole Craft appears. Tall, lanky, blonde. The quintessential cross country runner. I'd seen her at several of these all-women meetings, but her role within the Corps never registered before.

"Thanks for agreeing to talk to me, Bennett." I can't believe Coleman is tolerating the familiar tone she's taking with me. And I didn't "agree" to talk her. I'm a knob. I do what I'm told.

"Ma'am, yes, ma'am." Yet I'm no hypocrite. I know my place as a knob and within the fourth-class system.

"You probably don't follow women's athletics at Graham much and honestly, we it is very scant as there aren't well…a lot of women at Graham right now anyway." She laughs at her own sarcasm. "Anyway..that brings me to here. We're short two girls this semester on the cross-country team. And, well, we need the full team roster in order to compete in the remainder of the races this year. And to maintain our funding. You won't need to compete per se. Just be there on race day,"

Craft says, nearly pleading. "Avery says you're a *really* strong runner, so maybe this could be like fun for you." Her voice pitches high on the word fun. "Unlike spirit runs."

Is she fucking for real? The answer is still no. I just finished tours. Just got my free time back. And she wants me to commit cadet suicide and join Corps Squad? As a knob, no less. I'd miss practice parades, parades themselves, eat upstairs away from the rest of the Corps—away from anyone that matters. Anyone that has real influence over my role within the Corps as a future rank holder. And I certainly don't want to be accused of not having a system. And for what? To make up for the fact that Graham didn't do a good enough job recruiting women for the team? Thanks, but no thanks.

I let the question linger in the air for a few minutes, as if I'm seriously considering it. "Ma'am, thank you, ma'am. But this cadet private does not think that she will be able to fit in the practice and races into her schedule due to her academic schedule, ma'am." Not the strongest excuse if she were to go so far as to pull my class schedule, but then again, she can't argue against academics. Graham is a college despite outward appearances.

Coleman gives me a pensive look from her desk but says nothing.

Craft hangs her shoulders. "Oh…I understand. It's a lot to ask. I probably should've come to you at the end of last semester. The Registrar's Office could've maybe moved around a class or two. Or you would've had more time to think about it." She doesn't know that wouldn't have made a difference, but there's no harm in her imagining I would have said yes. "Thanks for at least considering it. If you see a change in your academic workload, *please* re-consider. Maybe even next year…"

"Ma'am, yes, ma'am."

I turn to leave but am frozen in place at Coleman's request to "stand by." I knew I wasn't fooling her. I wait for her and Craft to finish some idle talk about spring break in a few weeks. I had completely forgotten that we get a whole week off in early March.

Coleman gets to the point as soon as Craft leaves the room. "Bennett, cut the bullshit. What's your real issue with Corps Squad?"

"Ma'am, no excuse, ma'am."

"Nice try. Explain yourself. Now!"

Here goes nothing. "Ma'am, this cadet private does not want to join Corps Squad. This cadet private wants to devote her time to being a cadet. To being part of the Corps. To not missing parades or spirit runs." There. Pretty simple. If anything, Coleman, being a rank holder, should understand my reasoning. She fought for her rank and earned it. Yet now, she's the same rank as Craft. And she said herself that she didn't think Ward should've been RC, so obviously she puts some weight on earning things around here.

She gets up from her desk and walks slowly towards me, the perfectly spaced out footfalls signaling doom. "You've got some fucking nerve. You really *do* think you're better than other women at this school, don't you?" Her voice is low and cutting. "Cathy told me as much after your run-in during Hell Night. How you were all disappointed things didn't go your way. But I didn't believe her. I told her—Nah, you're just being a hard-ass on the knobs." Coleman takes a deep breath before continuing. "Well guess what, sunshine? You're not. Far from it. You may be a shined up cadet and all, but you're not accepted by your male classmates and your female ones. In fact, I daresay they resent you for it. Allen and Pitchford are more accepted than you. Why? 'Cause they're genuine. But you…you always seem to have some hidden agenda. As if you're here for the wrong reasons."

I stare wide-eyed out the window at the side of Charlie Battalion as she continues this unexpected barrage. I'm not going to let her get to me.

She takes one step closer, her face inches from mine. "You're always on your own fucking program, Bennett. Graham is a team event. If you can't make it work with your male classmates, then you should at least be trying to find some sort of solidarity with the other women here. Find some damn allies. Ask any upperclass girl what their biggest regret is and they'll tell you it's not leaning on the other women. Getting to know each other."

I turn my head to look at her. The rage shines brightly in her green eyes. Rage I didn't know she felt for me. I change my mind; she wouldn't have been a good choice for Regimental Commander either. She wants to lecture me about finding solidarity with other women, yet here she is, tearing me down. A poor helpless knob. Her mentor knob, no less. She's supposed to protect me, teach me about how to survive here. Instead, she's pushing me into the deep end. This isn't four years ago when she and Ward and Craft were knobs. The school, the Corps, were still trying to figure out what to do with women at Graham. What uniforms to wear. What our half-press drawers should look like during inspections. What the size of our band of gold should be. They had no upperclass women as examples. To seek solidarity with. To be their advocates. Now we're everywhere and part of of this school.

Who does she think she is? And whatever Ward told her.... I'm not even going to finish that thought. Coleman doesn't see how I'm accepted by my classmates. She only sees us for five minutes during formations.

"You think being on Corps Squad is about being lazy and getting out of stuff. Let me tell you something—Nicole has worked her ass off, both as a cadet and an athlete. When she's not with her company, she's at practice or working out to be prepared. All so she can proudly wear that 'C' on her singlet, and represent this school around the state, the country even. She wanted to do both, yet there're only twenty-four hours in a day. Something had to give..." She pauses, drawing in a single breath. "But none of that really makes sense to *you*. Because if it did, you would've accepted her invitation to join the cross country team. You would've thought of someone other than yourself for a change."

I clinch both my fists flush at my sides as they absorb my anger. She doesn't know anything about me. She doesn't know anything about my life or what I've been through. I've spent every day of the last three years thinking of someone other than myself. Every single second after the semi missed the red light. In hopes, that maybe, *just maybe* I can rewind that one moment. But that only happens in movies. All I have instead are tear stained pillows and a father who I'm trying to connect with. She doesn't know why I'm here. Yes, she's my mentor yet she hasn't once truly gotten to know me? Not like Chris, who's at least attempted to get to know me. The *real* me.

Her anger boils over at my stoicism. "Get the *fuck* out of my room."

Chapter Twenty-Four. *I have a suggestion and I'd like to run it by you.*

"Preston said he's really close to getting the financial files we identified three weeks ago!" Max says, *no*—nearly shouts at me with a wide grin, as I enter the upstairs room at Tad's.

"Uhm…hello to you, too."

Max just waves at me and continues. "Do you know what this means, K? We'll be able to not only identify who WQ is, but we'll also be able to…."

He's off and running on a tangent meant to get me up to speed on the latest progress in his investigation. Just three weeks ago we sat in this very room, mending our friendship and going blind in the face of stacks of spreadsheet-covered pages. My eyes still ache at the memory. But for all the time we put in, I can't muster up the energy to care just now. I know it's important.

"Kensley….*Kensley*! Are you listening to me?"

"Of course I was. I was just thinking." I playfully swat Max on the arm in hopes of distracting him. "You might have some more info about the donors soon. See? I heard you."

He presses his lips together but doesn't question me further. "I'm headed back to campus now. The upperclassmen on the *Commodore* are all on General Leave so this'll be a good time for me get some research done without interruption. Or anyone looking over my shoulder. Plus, I've gotta write an article for the upcoming edition, too."

"Oh…okay." I lower my head, hiding my disappointment. As much as I don't want to hear or talk about the LAMC Foundation or donors right now, I also don't want to be alone with my thoughts about Coleman's accusations. There's no telling what dark forest of ideas they'll lead me to.

"I need to do some research too and the Internet in the library is faster than the one here at Tad's."

Max laughs. "No kidding. Who still has dial-up?"

Campus on Sunday always straddles that fence between reality and the hereafter. Cadets are still walking around in uniform and doing all the normal cadet stuff. The campus is still grey. The air still tinted with the faint smell of marsh. But Sunday brings an otherwise absent calm to campus. There's no class to hurry to. No formation. Nothing to shine. Nothing to clean in preparation for a room inspection. And less upperclassmen shouting at you or asking you rhetorical questions like - *Where the fuck are you going, knob.* Looking not for a response but a way to quench their own boredom.

The library at Graham is mainly for studying. It's not a place where cadets are supposed to "hang out" and sit idly in a corner over lattes. I head straight for the four rows of twenty public computers immediately to the right of the circulation desk.

Ward.

Doesn't she have her own computer in her room? I immediately veer right, swallow the sour taste in my mouth, and move to the magazine area to the right of the circulation desk instead. I take a seat on one of the brown leather couches and pick up the first magazine I see. There's no doubt Coleman already told her about Craft asking me to be on the cross country team, and my response. And then Coleman galloping around me on her Lipizzaner stallion as she tossed her wisdom to me like a queen throwing scraps to the hoard. I bet Ward laughed at it all, with that annoying, saccharine-infused laughter of hers and topped it with - *I told you so.*

Graham doesn't know what it wants. I try to blend in and get punished for it. Part of me—the spiteful part of me, almost wants the LAMC Foundation to raise enough money so Graham can revert to being all-male again. It would teach all these girls—Ash, Reagan, Coleman, Craft, and of course Ward — a lesson. Their definition of assimilation is not the right one. We have to blend, fade into the grey. When a locked-on female cadet finally shows up with the focus and determination to *earn* her rank, what happens? Coleman yells in her face with a kind of unbridled rage that even I can admit was a little disturbing.

Finally, Ward gets up from her computer and heads upstairs.

I sit down at her abandoned terminal, the only one that's come open. I shift uncomfortably in the plush seat, still warm from Ward. *Gross.* After I log-in with my student identification, I loiter on various web pages reading about random news from across the world, celebrity gossip, movie openings that I can't go to, really just aimless clicking around.

A stall tactic.

I bite my lower lip, then pretend to stretch to sneak a look around me. All the cadets seem to be engrossed in whatever rabbit hole they're following on their screens. There's more privacy here than in my room.

No Ash or Reagan pretending to read their glossy magazines or constant visits by Dane or Wade.

Deep inhale. Deep Exhale.

My shaking fingers garble the word *missed* at the first attempt.

I strike the enter key.

Stress. I have to suppress a snort of laughter. Where do I even begin?

Hormonal imbalance. I don't even know what that means. I'm nineteen years old, not knocking on the door of menopause.

I quickly close the browser before I can read further as, out of the corner of my eye, I spot Ward thumbing through a thick, blue-embossed reference manual. She must be late on her assignment. Why else would a senior spend her Sunday in the library? *Oh, because she has no friends*, I think meanly. Serves her right.

The tension in my muscles signals it's time to go. I hit the log off button, and grab by cover and knobby bag. I'm out the door so fast that if I were to turn around, my chair would probably still be spinning.

***

"All knobs fall out around the company number," Coleman commands after Thursday evening formation that week.

In less than thirty seconds we arrange ourselves in our usual tight semi-circle around the number fifteen. Geez, the same knobs still haven't figured out where the deodorant aisle is. Thank goodness for my body spray that I got downtown.

"Bring it in, knobs. Just a quick announcement." Coleman bellows. "Barton Hall is going to start holding rank boards in a few weeks. That means each company is going to start looking at various positions, too once the key leaders are selected.   So if any of you knobbies are interested in company clerk, meet in the squad room after evening mess. That'll be all."

"Okay, form up so we can march over to mess," Trevino orders. "I didn't get like this from eating air." A low roar of laughter erupts from us knobs. I really hope Trevino is company commander next year. It's between him and Johnson, I think. Unless they bring in someone from another company. But that would only happen if there's no organic talent —a huge embarrassment for the company and that senior class. Fifteen's company has the talent and temperament. Trevino is not only more tolerant of girls at Graham but he has a sense of humor too. I know he got mad at me for my haircut only because he had to. If had been really upset he would've PT'd me for sure.

I waste no time heading to the squad room after evening mess. The usual suspects are already assembled—Callahan, Singleton, Lawrence, as well as a few I've never pegged as ambitious—Doss and Wade. Wade? He's *so* laid back.

"Pretty ballsy of you to be here, Bennett." Callahan sneers. "Tours aren't looked upon favorably."

"Whatever."

"Oh no, you forgot," Singleton chimes in dramatically. "It's the *neeeeeeeeew* Corps."

The others laugh in response.

"Oh yea, good point. Blatantly violent the Blue Book and you can still be a first semester company clerk. Quotas and all." Callahan nods his head in feverish agreement. "So maybe they'll *give* it to you after all."

Fuck you. Nothing is *given* to me.

The tension in my jaw keeps me in line. I still need them to survive, like it or not. They'll hate me enough when I get clerk; I don't need to add fuel to the fire.

"Welcome knobbies." Trevino steps into the squad room with a ghoulish smile. We brace harder than we ever have, at his entrance. He's flanked by Gibson and Lawson. "Just so there's no confusion, you're all here to roach—."

"Jose, you can't say that shit anymore. Remember? Wright *just* talked to us about it yesterday," a voice calls in from outside the screen door. Johnson.

"Shit. I forgot. Okay, okay…so ya'll are here to…to *try oooout*— god that sounds lame, for company clerk, right?"

"Sir, yes, sir." We answer in unison from the depths of our diaphragms.

"Okay. Just didn't want to have accidentally walked in on a book club or something."

I bit the inside of my mouth to keep from laughing.

"Sir, no, sir," Callahan bellows. That was rhetorical, you idiot.

"The try-outs will start Monday morning.' Trevino turns to smile at Gibson at getting it right. "A couple of ground rules so you can use the weekend to prepare: Ya'll are going to form up on-line together from here on out. Regardless of what platoon ya'll are in. Next, ya'll need to have the same brand of everything. Undershirt, socks, underwe— Oh, shit." Trevino pauses, realizing that we can't all very well wear the same brand of underwear, or the same style. Singleton's words—*new Corps*— mockingly ring through my mind. "Forget the underwear. Basically, you guys need to be shit-hot on your knob knowledge and blitzed. All day. Every day."

"Sir, yes, sir."

"You'll take turns shadowing Lawson on clerk duties each night. Gibson will help out too. We'll put a schedule together. Spencer, Caleb, anything to add?"

Gibson speaks first. "Make sure you can really afford to do this, knobs. Not just now as knobs, but as sophomores. It's time consuming. Sometimes you're up late—."

224

"Or up early, because Barton Hall is breathing down everybody's neck for some admin shit," Lawson finishes.

The upperclassmen all nod.

"Don't do this cause your Dad or brother or third cousin twice removed was a clerk and you've got something to prove," Gibson adds. *He's talking to you, Callahan.* "That's all I got, Jose."

"Thanks guys. Tim, you want to add anything?"

Johnson presses his face against the screen door. "No. Nothing from my end, Mr. Trevino." Every knob knows not to call an upperclassman by their first name until Recognition Day, but we also all know each other's first names. Johnson physically cringes every time his first name is used around knobs.   Such a tool.

Trevino sighs before turning back to us. "Any questions knobs?" He looks us over. "Now's your chance."

"Sir, no, sir." Even if we had a question, no one would dare ask it.

The heavy wooden door shuts with a thump.

"Okay, let's get started. What brand of undershirt is everyone wearing?" Callahan asks taking his usual de facto leader role.

"Wait…" I blurt out unnecessarily and unplanned. *Shit.* In my eagerness to usurp Callahan from his role, I didn't think this through.

They turn to me in annoyance.

"We should write this down on a list." It was the best I could do.

"You mean like this *one*…" Singleton responds holding a sheet of lined, loose-leafed notebook paper.

My faces tingles with embarrassment.

"Back to the subject at hand." Callahan regains the groups attention.

They were nearly equally divided between Hanes and Jockey. Callahan, being a Hanes wearer, makes an executive decision that everyone else must be as well. No one protests, of course. The same discussion is had about our black socks and about the brand of the shoes we've worn all year. Thankfully we all had the same brand cause I sure as shit was not going to break in another pair of shoes. Nor break in the shine.

"Okay, let's get Hanes for our underwear too. And the same *style*," he continues, turning to me in challenge.

I cross my arms in silent protest. "Hanes makes women's underwear, too" The need to corporate stronger than my emotions.

Callahan smiles satisfactorily. "Remember guys, we're the future leaders of this company, of the *Corps*. Let's start acting like it," he says, his gaze trained on me. "Although it might be too late for some."

Dick.

———

Trevino said try-outs for Company clerk don't officially start until Monday, but I know we'll be closely watched from here on out - especially me. The spirit run after parade today will be akin to the Olympic Trials, the judgmental eyes of the upperclassmen like imaginary television cameras recording my every stride. *Oh, is Cadet Bennett struggling with sprints? She's less push-ups than her male classmates too. I've seen a clear decline from last month, Ron. And now a word from our sponsors.*

"Any plans for the weekend, Kensley?" Ash asks out of the blue as we're getting ready for classes.

"Um…no. Not really." I can't very well tell her I'm helping Max expose the secret donor for the LAMC Foundation.

"That doesn't sound very fun." Is that genuine sincerity in her voice? She has always been nicer to me, especially when Reagan isn't around. "But then again…there are limits to how much fun we can have as knobs, right?"

"What are you doing?" Quickly moving the attention off of me.

"Oh, nothing big. Wade and I are going to a movie. And then of course getting supplies for the banner for Corps Day." She giggles unnecessarily. *Shit.* The Corps Day banner. I've become so reliant on Callahan telling us when to buy supplies that I didn't think of just taking initiative and getting some myself. I've got to do better.

"Wow—that's pretty courageous of Wade to go to a movie with two girls. What did you guys pick for him?"

"Um…" She turns her face away from me. "It's actually just Wade and me going to the movies." I hear the blush in her voice. I don't know why she's shy or coy about it. It was only a matter of time before she or Reagan dated another cadet. It's a normal social interaction at any other college, but an automatic outcast stamp on your forehead at Graham. Hard pass for me.

Nausea accompanies me to my morning and afternoon classes. And through parade. It might just be the warmer days, although there is a lot riding on everything from here on out. A lot.

I quickly devour a power bar while changing out of parade uniform into PT uniform.

At Trevino's instruction, we form up into our own little squad at the rear of the other knobs in formation. All of us - even those not seeking company clerk rank, dressed alike in Graham-issued blue cotton shorts, matching t-shirts, and white socks. Those of us seeking rank clearly distinguishable from our equally matching running shoes.

"We love…fifteenth company. We love…fifteenth company." We chant over and over again breathlessly as a warm up. My thigh muscles scream their own chant as we step into high knees.

"Get 'em up, knobs. Get those knees up!" The upperclassmen around us demand.

Coleman and Lawson are in front of us. Trevino is to our left. And whatever other upperclassmen want to join us are scattered around. PT on

Tuesday and Thursday is mandatory. Spirit runs are not. Lawson, as the company clerk stands in front of the platoon next to Coleman. He raises the guide-on—a wooden pole, affixed with a periwinkle pendant announcing the company number in white—straight into the air. It's the signal that Coleman is ready to go. Trevino halts our marching in place and calls us to attention.

"Forward march." We follow Coleman out the battalion and begin a slow and steady jog behind her and Lawson.

We head straight to the soccer field next to the infirmary. The grass is soft yet slightly moist under our feet. Not soaking wet, but just wet enough for it to matter when laying down for sit-ups or flutter kicks that I know await us. We stake our claim to the north section of the field, much to the annoyance of the no-see-ums - South Carolina's state insect, already there, who have no mercy on our exposed skin. Each bite is a reminder that we're unwelcome guests and that I forgot to put on bug spray. No telling how long we'll be here. Spirit runs are measured in rounds of exercise and not time. Five rounds of pushups here. Twenty sit-ups there. A set-up fireman's carry. Sprinkle in some flutter kicks. Sprints across the field against an upperclassman for poor performance or being slower than your classmates or just because.

"Form back up into formation, knobs."

Huffing as one, we're at a jog again around campus, heading to the next plot of unoccupied land—the parade deck.

The power bar seemed to have helped my nausea. My pacing was good on my push-ups and I was able to keep from going to my knees, unlike Ash and Reagan. And even though I still felt weak carrying Ash on the fireman's carry (girls are always paired with girls, much to my annoyance), at least I didn't drop her like she did me.

After more rounds of physical fitness on the parade deck, we form up again for our final run through all of the battalions.

The guide-on and Coleman leads us into Alpha Battalion, as we raise our exhausted voices high and shout, "We love…fifteenth company!" Over and over again. The addition of our clapping further announcing our presence. Voices high. Enthusiastic. Announcing our company's presence and place in the Corps. Running in near perfect formation. This is where the spirit run truly gets its name.

One lap. Two laps. And out the battalion onto Bravo Battalion.

Tired of being in the back with the rest of the clerk aspirants, I attempt to wrangle a spot in the middle of the formation. (Assimilation, right?) Yet just as I move into formation, I feel the waistband of my shorts cinch tighter. It takes a few seconds to register the firm hand grabbing my shorts.

"Where the fuck do you think you're going?" A voice I don't recognize snarls in my ear as he pulls me back from the middle of the formation. The force of his push towards my previous place in formation causes my feet to betray me and I become a slave to gravity, landing face forward in the Bravo Battalion sally port. My right palm instantly aches from absorbing most of the force of my fall. The painful sensation of a shoe making contact with my low back eclipses the agony in my palm. Others have a chance to avoid me. Yet the company—*Coleman*, keeps moving forward through Bravo Battalion without me. A few faces turn around to look like on-lookers of an accident, yet none stop.

"You alright, Bennett." Corey offers his hand, Gibson and Goodman by his side.

"Sir, yes, sir." My right knee feels like it took a hit from a sledgehammer. Clearly my palm couldn't save all of me.

"Maybe she should go to the infirmary," Goodman suggests. "Her knee is bleeding. It's not a lot—probably not enough for stitches, but better safe than sorry."

"Hold up your knee, Bennett." Gibson instructs.

I attempt to hold my balance as I bend my aching leg into a 90-degree angle.

Gibson bends down ever so slightly and inspects my knee as if I'm a piece of meat at the counter of a Soviet butcher. "Hmmm…yeah, I agree with Eric. I mean, you're the XO and all, but still."

Corey takes a few seconds to consider the situation, as other companies pass us after their two laps within Bravo Battalion.

"Okay…Eric, take her to the infirmary. Stay with her until I can get Allen or Pitchford there."

"No problem."

I don't want to go to the infirmary. No knob *ever* wants to go to the infirmary. We'd rather walk around with an exposed bone than be labeled as weak or accident-prone. And especially not now.

But I know my protest will be futile. And I dutifully hobble along side him.

Chapter Twenty-Five. *Then they came at me again.*

"All clear." Reagan shouts at the knock at the door.

Darron enters the room. Barely. He keeps the back of his heels on the threshold, for fear of catching cooties, I suppose. I roll my eyes at him before he even speaks. "Hey Bennett…I just came by to tell you that it's your turn today for clerk stuff. Lawson said he'll find you after morning mess." He turns to leave before I can say anything.

My eyes close with relief. I'm still in.

I was worried my fall in the Bravo Battalion sally port was an automatic ouster from the clerk try-outs. Everyone else seemed to have been asked to accompany Lawson to Barton Hall, or been invited into Johnson's room with Lawson at night with the door closed. Each emerged, red-faced and drenched in sweat, but with a gleam in their eye from the unofficial PT session—a right of passage; a system. Callahan and all the rest have gained entry into a boys' club that remains closed to me no matter how much I've been trying to join. Upperclassmen's fear of getting pulled for hazing or *worse*, sexual harassment, stands in the corner like the grim reaper. My only consolation—if there's any to be had—is that no other girl cadet has been PT'd either. I kept Reagan and Ash from it after their stupid highlights, and I haven't heard of any other girls coming close.

Lawson comes to my table towards the end of morning mess. "Let's go, Bennett."

I toss a questioning look at Coleman. I may want to be a clerk, but I'm still aware I need my mess carver's permission to leave. Not to mention, the gaudiness of a sophomore ordering a knob around who's sitting at a senior's mess doesn't escape me.

And it doesn't escape Coleman either. "You haven't given me the news of the day, Bennett. You can leave after that."

Her glare measured looks straight ahead and never at him. Lawson continues to stand next to Coleman. As I recite the news of the day, he fidgets with his cover and clipboard. He rocks back and forth on his heels in silent annoyance. A battle between telling her off and respect for the rank structure within the Corps plays out in front of me.

"Thanks. That'll be all, Bennett." After I recite the top headlines.

Lawson walks ahead of me as I walk at attention, squaring my corners, out the mess hall.   "Pretty slow on your knob knowledge there, Bennett. I better not be late for class," he spits at me, taking his anger out on me.

I offer no reply.

"Meet me at the mail boxes. We certainly aren't going to walk to Barton Hall together." Didn't think we were. I assume my normal knob pace, leaving Lawson behind.

"And step it out," he shouts after me. Evidently not his annoyance.

The morning clerk duties are pretty simple. Check the fifteenth company mail slot for "any and all paperwork" the Commandant's department may have placed in there for us. Check the mailbox again after lunch and again before evening formation. If it requires immediate attention, mark it as such and give it to Trevino immediately. Sometimes you'll just have to put it on his desk in his room if you can't find him. That's it—for now. Lawson said he'd explain the evening procedures to me after evening mess. And with that, he leaves me alone in Barton Hall.

Asshole.

I have a feeling he's leaving something—okay, maybe a lot, out. I triage the mailbox's contents looking for anything marked urgent. Nothing. I stuff the papers and manila folder in my knobby bag and head to morning classes. As instructed, I hurry to Barton Hall again before lunch formation. I arrive feeling over-heated, nearly panting. My damp undershirt sticks to my clammy skin. Probably just the change in temperature. It's nearly March after all.

Nothing in the 15th Company's spot since this morning. A sense of annoyance already fills me with the thought of being back here again in 45 minutes - after lunch. I wonder if Lawson was just being a dick when he told me to check the box before *and* after lunch. It's a near impossibility to walk from one side of campus to another and make it back on time for anything. I could ask the others, but they'd probably just think I was complaining or trying to get out of clerk duties.

"Sir, Mr. Trevino, sir, Cadet Private Bennet requests permission to drive your room, sir," I announce after knocking on Trevino's door before lunch formation to give him the papers from this morning. The screen door swings open and Johnson steps out.

Great.

"Bennett, what month is it?"

"Sir, March, sir."

"So that means…let me think. You started matriculation week in August, right? That means you've been here for five, six…no, *seven* months!" I stare at his rhetorical charade blankly. "And in all of that time you've yet to learn that you have to ask *both* inhabitants of a room fucking permission to enter?!"

"Sir, no excuse, sir." He knows damn well that the mesh screen doors make it a challenge to see who all is in the room.

With two large steps, he's directly in front of me. Close enough for a whisper to vibrate against my cheek. The faint smell of stale coffee on his breath.

"Right. Take the easy way out. That's how you've spent your *entire* knob year. Taking the easy way out. Running to Barton Hall or a tactical officer or your mommy whenever an upperclassman slightly raised his voice at you to remind you of your basic knob duties." I wince at his words. "You and your kind ruined this school. A hundred and fifty-two-year tradition just flushed down the fucking Ashley." The hatred shines in his eyes, dark and deep. "When I become company commander, you'll spend your entire sophomore year a private. There's no way you'll carry the guide-on at parade at *my* school."

I brace harder and bit the inside of my mouth. A retort loaded and ready. Yet Coleman's words echo in my mind. *Don't argue with them.*

"But let me tell you about an even better future." He pauses to see if anyone is within earshot on the galleries. "For me, at least. The LAMC Foundation is going to make Graham great again. While you were busy playing cadet, we were busy raising money all around our alumni community. With Warren—I mean *the honorable Judge Quante*—the Foundation was able to draft a compelling and legal framework for the transition. Oh yeah. It's happening, sweet pea. So better start thinking of what college you'll go to next year. You'll be packing your little dollies up before you know it." He snickers. "You'll be able to tell all of your little friends at your tea parties at your new school about that one time when you went to military college. Man, I cant *wait* to see the look on your face and the rest your fucking kind." He steps back. "What the fuck did you want again?"

"Sir, the mail, sir." I thrust my left arm forward, manila folder and loose pages in hand.   He shrugs them off without a second thought before slamming the door shut.

I'm stuck holding the mail as the bugle announces formation. Damn it.

I run down to first division to line up for formation.

"Figures you can't complete a simple fucking task." Lawson snatches the papers out of my hand as I run past him.

Chapter Twenty-Six. *They were making me mean and angry.*

I can't go to Tad's today. Not even on a Sunday. I'm tired of talking about the fucking LAMC Foundation and tired of this place.

For once I am thankful for Ash and Reagan's social life.

The room is mine.

Quiet. Space to finish Gish's assignment.

Every so often, a door slams or a stray voice on the loud speaker breaks the silence, but for the most part, Graham is silent.

It's nearly two o'clock in the afternoon and I haven't seen the light of day. Haven't spoken to or answered another human being. This is just like when we first moved to New York during my sophomore year. In a city of eight million people, I was always alone. Isolated. Abandoned. I can't breathe. The walls are pressing on my lungs in a terrifying, inescapable way. I need to get out of this room.

"Hello, kid." Dad's voice crackles through the receiver clutched in my hand.

Knobs aren't allowed to have phones in their rooms; our only option is to use the phone room across from the post office in Lackey Hall. There's always a line. Three hundred and twenty or so knobs queuing for six pay-phones. And then of course there are the glass doors. Your always on display begging for interruption from an upperclassmen walking by. Always someone looking. *Judging.*

 This is my first call from here. Ever.

"Hi...did I, um...call at a bad time?" I fumble with the metal chord in my hand, as I keep my voice from shivering while thinking of something - a reason to call.

"Oh, um, no. I'm just surprised to hear from you. Everything okay?"

I cover the mouth piece with my hand as I let out a long sigh. It's obviously a bad time.

"Nothing's wrong. Why would you ask that?"

Silence exchanges through the line for a few seconds. Dad, the lawyer and orator, fills the space quickly with talk of the weather, parade, and homework. I tell him all about the clerk try-outs but not what Johnson said to me. Or anything about the LAMC Foundation. He tells me to keep my head up and about the days of his youth, when he too sought to be clerk. I wish I could see his face so I could be sure that he's proud of me.

Proud of this decision, Graham.

Proud of me as his daughter.

"Are you coming down for Corps Day?" I ask already knowing the answer. It's the last of the three big weekends at Graham.

He sighs before answering. "I don't think so, Kensley. Work is keeping me pretty busy. Besides you'll have plenty to do as well."

"I understand. Been there. Done that."

The minutes on my phone card run out before we formally say goodbye.

A drop of loneliness rolls down my cheek as I replace the plastic receiver into the cradle.

———

"What do you even find fucking attractive about her? A *knob*." Callahan's attention on Wade as I enter the squad room.

It was only a matter of time before Wade and Ash's dating wasn't a secret anymore. And if any of our classmates didn't already know, Callahan would make sure to confront Wade in the squad room so that they would.

"It's none of your business what I do in my fucking private life," Wade fires back, his fists opening and closing at his side. "I don't tell you what to do in *your* free time."

"This isn't about your private life. Nothing here is private. It's about unit cohesion—."

"Oh, give me a fucking break. You didn't come up with that yourself. Your daddy or uncle brainwashed you into thinking women 'ruined this school.' Welcome to 2001, motherfucker! Where women will be your coworkers, hell…even your boss." Wade curses, nostrils flaring.

"That may be true. And I don't have a problem with any of that. I have a problem with guys dating in *my* Corps. 'Cause when you break up, we—" he gestures to the room, "are gonna have to tolerate the fucking aftermath. The silent treatment, the moodiness, the sulking. And *that* goes against unit cohesion." Callahan bites back with a tight, satisfying smile.

"Your Corps?" Wade catches the earlier insinuation. " Who the hell do you think you are? Whatever. You're an idiot," Wade retreats out of annoyance.

"I second that," I echo, to my surprise. *Shit*

The room freezes.

Callahan whips his head in my direction like an owl hearing the rustle of a mouse. Hunter and prey. "Oh, what do you have to say Ms. I-want-to-be-a-company-clerk."

Eyes are either on Callahan or me or both of us, heads swiveling back and forth like spectators at the US Open.

If I don't answer him, he'll have won. Even if only by default.

"Wade should be able to do what he wants."

"Well unit cohesion also applies to not falling during spirit runs."

"Motherfucker, didn't you fall up the stairs on our *second* day here?" We all keep score.

"Seriously? That's what you pull out of your hat?" he asks with a smirk. "You're just choosing sides with Wade because you wish he'd taken an interest in you. But with that haircut…who could blame him?"

The room erupts in laughter. Bile rises in my throat.

"What? Nothing to say, Bennett? Truth hurts, doesn't it?" He pauses, more for effect than anything else. "You're a walking contradiction. You pretend to have this tough exterior. That you can do the same number of push-ups as me. Run as fast as me. Want to be treated *juuuuuust* like me—hazing and all. But in the end, you're just like *aaalll* the other girls at this school. You want a separate system where you're only compared to other girls. It's easier to be a big fish in a little pink bowl, than a fish in *our* bowl…where the only outcome for you is to be devoured."

Adrenaline roars through my veins. How dare he compare me all the other girls on this campus? He's the one floundering in the little bowl. Not me. He has no idea what kind of shit I deal with on a daily basis. I don't even have a bowl. I'm gasping for air half the time in a dirty puddle. Comments made in passing. Salutes from upperclassmen not returned. Those name tags added on your field jackets a few months ago, ordered by the administration after some upperclassmen threw rocks at one of us. We want nothing more than to be part of the fourth class system. To be part of the Corps. To be part of Graham. The long grey line. If we have our own system, it's only because we were never offered the ticket to yours.

Fuck this guy.

"You're a coward, Clint. And a bully." He recoils slightly as I take a step closer to him, my words no longer on a leash. "I'm sure if I did my research about your military high school days, I'd learn that you were the one who was devoured. Always getting picked on with your 2.0 and go GPA. Now at Graham, it's a fresh start for you, isn't it? And you don't even have to be *that* good."

The room takes on the mood of a locker room at Callahan's expense with bursts of "oh shit" sprinkled in.

He stares at me with crossed arms. He knows he can't back down. And he has more to lose.

"So we are taking our gloves off, I see." He takes a step towards me and I to him, signaling confidence. "You have *some* fucking nerve talking to me about a fresh start, Kensley E. Bennett." His voice flashes like lightening before the thunder. "You aren't the only who can do a little on-line research. You claim you're from New York but that's just where you spent the last two or three years." He looks slowly around the room, assessing that he has everyone's attention in the small space. A villainies smile overtakes his expression. "It's where you went to go hide after…" The tone and pitch of his words lowered to a near whisper. "…after you *killed* your mother."

His cruelty is reflected in the eyes around me.

"Yeah. Oh yeah, *I know*. I know what you did. Being from South Carolina, Kensley, you should know people talk about the things the papers are gracious enough to leave out. Who's being devoured now." He leans back against the metal rack, smug and victorious.

In the ensuing silence, you could've heard a roach scurrying across the hardwood.

His words pierce through my heart, my soul, my world.

Numb from the shock of his utterance, I stand frozen in front of him.

In front of all of them.

Instantly *judged.*

Yet none of what he said was a lie.

"All of that's true," I whisper into the room.

I was driving when the semi missed the the red light. We were just going out for a quick trip to the mall. We were gone less than an hour. But all it took was a few seconds for her to be gone forever, leaving me alone with a father who spent nights roaming the halls of our house in Columbia, a specter of his former self. Kids at school, even my closest friends, shunned me as if death was a contagious disease they would catch if they sat next to me. My grades began to suffer. I failed a class. Then another. Pretty soon I failed the entire year. But I didn't care. The only thing I cared about was the burn of alcohol in my throat, the numbness that overtook my mind as it raced like fire through my veins. That's why we moved to New York. To get me away from my bad choices. It was the first step towards absolution. Towards being whole again.

The second was enrolling at Graham.

But not for me alone. For her.

At the excitement of gifting me *Lords*.

Of how it keeps me connected to her.

Normalcy.

And for him. Maybe if I wore the same uniform as he once did; if I marched across the same parade field as he did; if I ate in the same mess hall; if I suffered the fourth class system the same way…Then just maybe he might see himself in me again. See me again, period. But the wicked sharpness of this double-edged sword has been cutting through me all year: Graham is what I need, but my mere presence here means this place is not the same as it once was, and my penance is not as complete as it could be. If Graham was to recreate me, it had to be untarnished, like when Dad was here.

"You're just like the fucking rest." Callahan breaks the silence.

"Fuck. You!"

Fueled by months of anger, frustration, annoyance, of being silent. "I uphold Graham standards more than you do asshole. But I'm—." I inhale deeply settling in for battle. "— And I'm still better than you. Because I did more than just shine my fucking brass all pretty. Or suck up to the upperclassmen. And I certainly am not like the fucking rest of the women here." Triumphantly I jab my right index finger in my chest. "I was the one who reported the shit that was going on in the Field House, motherfucker." "Me. Not you. Not any other cadet. Just plain old me."

Only Callahan asks what everyone else is thinking. "What the *fuck* does that mean?"

"Just what it means. It was one of the worse kept secrets on campus. So it didn't take much to figure it out. And when I did...I just slipped a note under Wright's door on a Sunday afternoon," I announce proudly. "It was already a distraction and it was going to give women a bad rep. It had to fucking stop."

I lean against the half press with a self-righteous glower. "Who's upholding standards now, bitch?!"

"That's a pretty interesting story, Cadet Bennett." Coleman's voice seeps through the screen door. We were so caught up in our own knob drama, we never heard the lone bugle note calling us to formation. Lost in our own battle, our company commander had to come get us. There she stood on the other side of the screen door, encircled by blurry faces of who knows how many upperclassmen, our drama had an audience.

"You're all late for formation. Roll out. Bennett, report to my room after mess."

***

"Enter," Coleman shouts from the other side of her door. Coleman never came to take her seat as mess carver at dinner. She marched over with us, but then disappeared. Yet here she is in her room. Alone. The light of her desk lamp throws ominous shadows across the floor.

"Explain yourself." A demand before I even close the door.

"Ma'am, no excuse, ma'am."

She lets out a laugh. For a second I envision throwing a bucket of water on her and clicking my heels three times. "For fuck's sake. Don't be a fucking coward now."

"Ma'am, this cadet private..." but I don't finish. I don't know how to finish the sentence. I don't know what she wants me to say. It's pretty simple—I saw wrong-doing on campus and reported it. End of story. Anyone would have done the same.

"Fine," she snaps. "I'll explain. Fill in the parts that I get wrong." Coleman takes a seat at the end of her desk and crosses her arms. "You didn't report what was going on in the Field House to uphold standards. Stop fucking lying to yourself. To me. To *everyone*. You did it to hurt the women who were already here because *you* didn't think they deserved to be here. Blah, blah, blah. Same story with you all the time." She stares at me waiting for a response. A denial? When I offer none, she continues. "If not, you would've used your chain of command and reported it to me first. Or even Dehenre. I checked with her at dinner, by the way. You didn't go to her. You've only ever wanted one thing: approval from your male classmates and male upperclassmen. And maybe a little by the administration, too."

I break my brace and look over at her, leaning against her desk. There, in the dim light, the pool in her eyes reflects a hundred tiny insults. "After all of these months, Bennett…you still don't get it. Graham isn't about parades or who had the shiniest brass or even who had the highest rank. When you decide to take that first step through the sally port, you make a conscious decision to adhere to Graham's value's of honor, duty… and the other cadets - no matter how *you* feel about them. You join a *family*. A family cares for each other…looks out for each other…respects each other. They're people you can depend on for the rest of your life, Bennett. When you receive this …" She holds up her right fist, turned at an angle for me to clearly see her band of gold. "…that's your commitment to the family. You can call up twenty years from now and chat with, as if you saw them yesterday."

Those words. A thickness forms in my throat.

I've heard them before. Dad. And now, *Coleman.*

I did everything they asked me to do.

242

I did everything I thought was right.
Yet still I got it wrong.

Chapter Twenty-Seven. *I had perfected a bland personality, a bland appearance, and a bland record.*

"Hurry up and change out of parade uniform and into PTs, knobs," Trevino instructs as soon as we come back from parade. "Douche detail time." If we could, we all would've let out a groan. Not only was the parade today a little longer because of Corps Day, but we've also got to make sure our rooms are presentable for tomorrow's open barracks. Singleton said he's picking up the banner from his parents' tonight. I'm not even sure what it looks like or if Coleman and Ward's names are on it. They started designing and painting it without me. I offered and kept asking, but some how I was left out of the process.

West and I grab a large garbage can from fourth division and fill it three-fourths of the way with hot water in the men's bathroom as they have open bay showers. We carry the garbage can to the end of the gallery, where our classmates eagerly wait with straw brooms. Water sloshes out of the can with every step. Our tennis shoes are heavy with water. My fingers cramp from my grip on the handle.

"Fucking be careful. I don't feel like dropping this thing," West snips.

"Don't snap at me. You're dumping water out of your side too."

"Knobs!" We both freeze in place, still holding the can by the handle. "You must have a lot of fucking time on your hands to hold a discussion right now," Matthis says sarcastically. "Look down there. See your classmates waiting?"

"Sir, yes, sir."

"Well, since you already decided they can wait till you finish your little conversation, they can wait a few more minutes. Hit the deck!" West shoots me an eat-shit-and-die look. (As if I were the only one talking.)

We set down the trash can. I try to inconspicuously dry my hands on my blue PT shorts but as soon as my right hand touches the wet cement floor, I realize how idiotic and futile the attempt was. The concrete slick and unforgiving.

Matthis assumes the push-up position with us, per Graham tradition.

"Ready. Down. Up. Down. Up… We'll do this for twenty." I'm not concerned. Push-ups aren't a weakness for me. I've always gone over the maximum score for women—and *men*—on the PT test. And I'm not going do my knob duties any less just because my my classmates are icing me out. If anything, the more I "put out," the more they'll see that I do belong here.

"Down. Up. Down. Up…."

I steal a glance to my right and look down onto the quad. I pause for a moment—getting out of line with Matthis's cadence. None of them are doing push-ups with us. With *me*. They're just standing there. Bracing. Waiting. Looking. Any time one knob in a company gets dropped for push-ups, the others are supposed to join in. Now they've taken on the look of an angry mob. Holding not pitchforks, but brooms.

"Getting tired, Bennett? Down. Up."

"Sir, no, sir." I lie. My chest strains with each push up.

"Down. Up. Down. Up. Down. Up. Down. Up. Down. U—*shit*. Did you hit your chin?" My right hand slips on the wet cement and my chin hits the gallery floor first.

Then my right elbow.

Then my right knee. It instantly remembers the fall in Bravo Battalion during the spirit run.

Then the rest of me. I wish it happened that slowly, but it didn't. I was soaked and flat on my stomach on the cold wet gallery floor before I could react.

"Get up, West. Go get Trevino."

I ease myself up on my aching elbow and knee as quickly as I can. Trying to save face. I didn't fall out of weakness. Just bad luck on the fucking wet cement. Matthis looks at my elbow and is about to tilt my chin up when he realizes he didn't ask permission to touch me.

"What's going on?" Trevino demands as he steps onto fourth division.

"They were talking on the galleries, so I dropped 'em for push-ups. Her arms gave out and well, she hit her chin on the gallery."

"Uh-huh," Trevino says, looking me over from two feet away.

"I think she might need stitches. But I can't tell. I'm a Poly Sci major," Mathis says grinning. "Plus, didn't want to touch her and be accused of hazing or some shit." His grin disappears.

"No worries. You did the right thing," Trevino assures him. "Allen—get up here and take your classmate to the infirmary." Trevino's booms through the Battalion and down to the quad.

"Sir, yes, sir," Ash's falsetto voice sings up from the crowd.

"Sir, Mr. Trevino, sir. This cadet private—," I begin to protest. This would be my second trip to the infirmary in less than six weeks.

"Save it, Bennett." Trevino cuts me off. "You hit your head. I'm not going to answer to Colonel Wright if you end up with a brain injury or some bullshit like that."

Ash and I walk to the infirmary, where the same nurse who saw me a few weeks ago checks my vitals and chin. Ash waits in the hall, occupying herself with the stack of left behind magazines. Ash and Reagan have taken to a near silent treatment since my …..confession in the squad room.

Thankfully, no stitches need. "You may have a scar." Something I can live with, surely. After a brief physical, the nurse considers me fit for duty.

I reach down for my still wet shoes and stop. My hands are trembling.

How the hell did I end up here?

I thought I had my life back on track. Graham was the first step.

Right shoe. I swallow the knot in my throat.

But maybe in some twisted irony, this is supposed to be my future. Stumbles and falls to teach me resiliency, To teach me how to make it through - on my *own*.

Ash pokes her head into the door. "You about ready? The nurse said you were cleared." Her voice cold, her tone distant.

"Yeah…sorry. I was just putting my shoes on."

"It's fine. It's just my parents are probably already waiting for me outside the sally port."

Right. They're here for Corps Day. "What are you guys doing tonight?" In an attempt to extend the conversation.

"Oh, just dinner. I think, um, Wade's going too." A shy smile crosses her face. "How about you?"

"The usual. Tad's. Max'll be there."

Her face lights up at the mention of Max.

"Don't even go there. You know we're just friends. Nothing more. Contrary to popular fiction, men and women *can* be friends," I tell her, half laughing as we leave the exam room and the infirmary. I ignore her eye roll.

Of course the douche detail is over by the time we get back to the battalion. Most, if not all, of the battalion is already changed and on their way to general leave. I let out a deep sigh and begin to change into leave uniform for the brief walk to Tad's.

"Do you want me to make you a sandwich, too?" Max yells at me from the kitchen.

"Depends. What kind?"

"All we have is turkey sooooo…"

I join Max in the kitchen. From the looks of it, the kitchen is being used to prepare a three-course dinner for five. Utensils, bread, meat and cheese litter the counter. Max is a firm believer in seeing all of the ingredients at once instead of pulling them out one by one. I don't tease him about it anymore, but it's still humorous to watch. Besides, there's something to be appreciated about consistency. And dependability.

"How'd you know it was me?" He hands me a plate. "I never said I wanted one."

He shrugs. "You'll eat it. I knew it was you because Tad's at some alumni event and Stacey hasn't been over in months." Right. She pretty much stopped coming to Tad's after we got pulled.

I take a bite of my sandwich. It hits the spot. (I hate it when Max is right.) "Tad is at *another* alumni event? He's getting involved a lot lately."

"You know it's getting down to the wire. For Graham too. Not just the LAMC Foundation. We've got what—six more weeks until Recognition Day and then the of school?" We walk to the den and sit on opposite ends of the sofa.

"Speaking of…did you make any more progress?" I ask, leaning forward. Eager for a distraction.

"Yes and no. No—in that Preston wasn't able to get any records for me after all. Something about privacy or whatever. I didn't understand it all. But yes—in that he was able to get an attendee list from the last event the South Carolina chapter of the LAMC Foundation held. I did look at the photos on the website, but none had names underneath." Max pauses to wipe mustard off his lip. "I cross referenced the list to the spreadsheets we reviewed though."

"That's great," I proclaim. "It's more than you had a few months ago."

Max gives me a half-hearted shrug. "I don't know. I'm pretty frustrated with it all. I hoped to have the big donor identified already."

"And then what? I mean…don't take this the wrong way. I know that was the plan all along, but what was supposed to happen after that?"

Max looks at me blankly. Clearly he doesn't have an answer. Judging from his expression, I don't think he even considered the question. He just liked the project, the journey. And the trust Preston had in him. A *knob*.

"Well, I would expose him - WQ. Big donor dude," I blurt out, startling Max and me. "I mean, why not?"

Max looks down at his plate. "Uhm…sometimes …sometimes that might not be the right answer. At least not at first." His voice trails off. So much for the a distraction.

"So you …*disagree* with me?" No sense in beating around the bush.

"Um…look K. We don't need to talk about it. You did what you felt was right and—."

"No! I'd like you to at least say it. Yes or no." He's not getting out of it that easily. "You owe me that."

"I don't owe you anything, really. We're all entitled to our own choices and opinions," Max says with a slight redness in his face. "Okay. Fine. Yeah, I disagree with you. Happy? Dont get me wrong. I'm not saying I agree with the shit that was going on in the Field House. I knew about the room from people in my company, by the way." He purses his lips. "I just think there were other ways to handle it. You could've talked to me. You could've gone through your chain of command. Let the Corps handle it. Instead you slipped some *anonymous* note under a door in Barton Hall. And it blew up. You didn't think about the consequences it would have on the cadets. The innuendoes made about Corps Squad cadets. About other women in the Corps. About any male cadet that talks to another female cadet whenever —"

I hold my hand up. "Wrong. It didn't blow up. It never made it to *Caroline's Corner*. That should tell you it wasn't *that* big or important in the grand scheme of things. You're just saying all of that because Malone has brainwashed —"

"—You're so naive. It never made it to the paper because General Gentry made sure it fucking didn't."

My heart stops. His words a punch in the face.

"The school couldn't afford negative publicity like that, K. Not when so much is at stake. You of all people should understand that." He pauses to take a sip of tea and catch his breath. The coolness of the tea seemingly stoking the remaining embers in his voice. "Remember a few weeks ago when I said Caroline had been in to speak to Preston about a job? Well, she got it. It wasn't an outright quid pro quo, but…"

"Don't fucking talk to me about not understanding the stakes. You're a *guy*." My eyes are heavy with anger. "I have a lot more at stake than you ever will."

"I wasn't implying that you don't understand the stakes. Just maybe that you didn't consider *all* of the consequences."

I explode. "What. The. Fuck. I sure as shit understand consequences. This is more important to me than you realize. I need to be here."

I begin to sob into my hands.

Max comes to sit next to me on the sofa. His voice is soothing. "Okay, okay. I'm sorry. I kind of dragged you into this rabbit hole of an investigation. But you slipping the note under Wright's door was kind of a dick move. There's a—."

"I know." I whisper faintly. "You're the first person I've admitted that too"

Max looks at me in surprise.

"That includes myself."

"Thank you for trusting me." Max pauses, searching for a way to lighten the moment. "I knew you'd been distant the last few weeks. I didn't know if it was just cause you were doing more PT sessions cause of the Field House thing or because….well, I thought it was because you were kind of seeing - not sure if that's the right term, that upperclassman."

I chuckle. "Harvatin? Fuck no. I'll admit that I flirted with him for a bit but only cause he did the same. And it was only as friends —"

"Are you serious?" Max's eyes grow big. "Well, there's a bit of irony for ya. That dude fucking hates—I mean really *despises*—women at Graham. He's got a 'Save the Males' sticker on like, everything he owns."

My head shakes in disbelief. "No he doesn't."

Max has it wrong. They're probably old stickers. Chris just kept those out of nostalgia. Or irony. Chris was just applying to Graham when the school was knee-deep in lawyers and the Department of Justice. Not to mention, the pressure he put on himself to be like his stepdad, Warren.

Warren.

Callahan's boasting in the squad room.

Johnson on the galleries.

Chris's anger at Coleman.

Quante.

"Warren Quante," I blurt out excitedly.

"What? I'm confused."

"No. Sorry. Shit. Warren Quante could be WQ. Our mystery donor. He's a judge." I tell Max all about how I figured it out. Chris losing his dad. Chris getting mad at Coleman when she brought up his dad. Everything. It makes perfect sense. A judge—even one in retirement— would want to stay anonymous to avoid any ethical questions about his past rulings. He'd open himself up as an easy target against discrimination suits if his bias against women was made public. Any defense attorney would have a field day if his client had been a woman.

"Daaaamn!" Max jots it all down in his little notebook. "Do you know what this means? This is huge."

———

Yet Two weeks after our discovery, there's no mention of the big donor in the *Commodore*.

None whatsoever.

Nor is there mention that Caroline is now on the *Commodore* staff as a independent advisor.. Maybe they're waiting to announce it at the beginning of next school year. Or maybe it was all a ruse to get Caroline not to publish the story.

But there's plenty of focus on me. Seniors have stopped returning my salutes around campus. It was hit-or-miss before, with a few stalwart "Old Corps" believers ignoring me and every other woman's salute on campus. But now it's like they're all going out of their way to salute every knob, male or female, when the gesture is offered alongside a "good morning" or "good afternoon." At first, I was shocked at the disrespect; at the break from military protocol. Then I just became irritated. Finally I just accepted it.

"Callahan, Bennett, Doss, Singleton, Lawrence, and Holden, meet in the squad room after dinner formation tonight," Coleman announces at breakfast formation. A tingle runs through me. They've made a decision on who's going to be company clerk next year. We weren't called in alphabetical order. I was named second. As in second semester company clerk. It's not what I wanted, truthfully. Maybe sometimes things do work out.

I spend the day's classes drafting and editing the email I'll send to Dad tonight telling him of my selection. Or maybe I should call him. No, an email will be better just in case he is busy.

"Guess they made their decision," Lawrence babbles uncomfortably into the silence. One by one, we entered the squad room without saying a word to each other.

"Yep. Makes sense given that Trevino will be CO next year," Callahan utters.

What? How does he know? I bite the inside of my cheek to keep my expression neutral. Casual as if I already knew.

The screen door screeches.

"Good evening, knobbies," Trevino drawls. Blurry faces assemble behind him on the galleries. They've all come to watch. Fervent eyes looking.

"Okay…this ain't the Oscars or anything like that." I clench my fists tightly to keep from laughing. "We had our rank boards last week, and it turns out Barton Hall liked what I had to say, so I'll be the Company Commander next year."

"Sir, congratulations, sir." A few offer.

"Thanks, knobbies." Trevino smiles. "So with that, Callahan and Holden will be my clerks. Callahan, first semester. Holden, second. Congrats, guys." With that, he walks out.

The door slams shut.

Sadness instantly consumes me.

Singleton, Doss, and Lawrence take turns congratulating Callahan and Holden, and leave the room. I quickly congratulate Holden before moving onto Callahan. I muster all the strength I have into a tiny smile as I extend my silent hand to Callahan.

It's left frozen in midair.

Unmet.

Callahan walks past me. Chin high. "Guess the best man won!"

Chapter Twenty-Eight. *My time in the city was up and the long seasoning was complete.*

Dehenre stands at the head of the conference room with that annoying sparkle in her eye. "Okay ladies, take a seat please." Hopefully this'll be the last all-girl meeting we have this year.

It's only knobs again. Thirty of us total. Those who arrived early snagged a seat around the large wood table. The rest of us stand around. With no upperclassmen present, we bask in the joy of being able to lean against the wall or the back of the chair freely. Shoulders relaxed.

Ash and Reagan, as usual, are standing together on the other side of the room. They're chatting and giggling with some other girls. Every so often they'll shoot a quick glance at me, as if the tiny micro-photos will make one complete photo.

"We're just a few weeks away from Recognition Day, which is *so* exciting for lots of reasons. But for me too, because it'll be my first Recognition Day. And you guys—." Dehenre's voice cracks as her eyes well up with tears. "I'm sorry. I promised myself I wouldn't get emotional." The room responds with a stereotypical "awww," the same response lobbied at cat videos on the Internet.

"I'm just so damn proud of you guys. *Really*. General Gentry's goal at the start of the school year was to have all of you make it to Recognition Day. And here we are, *so* close. Just four weeks away. With everyone still here. You know I can't tell you when Recognition Day is exactly—tradition and all. But I can at least tell you how proud I am of you." As soon as she finishes, Dehenre is encircled like a teen pop star, as usual, by her groupies. In the excitement, I easily stride to the door, hoping to get a jump start on my English final. It's a take-home.

From among the group of girls, Dehenre's voice calls out. "Kensley, wait outside the room for me, please." You've got to be fucking kidding me? This woman always wants to talk to me.

"Can you believe it? The end of the year is finally here," she beams at me with the same enthusiasm she had with the other girls as we walk to her office.

"Yes, ma'am. It's been a long year." I try to look as disinterested as possible.

She smiles her motherly, warm smile. "Sorry to spring this on you with such short notice, but Cadet Harvatin wants to talk to you. He's in my office waiting."

I think I'm going to be sick.

"Are you okay?" Dehenre touches my shoulder. "You went pale all of a sudden."

I swallow my pride and probably a bit of my lunch. Now's as good a time as any.

"Yes, ma'am. I don't think I drank enough water today." I already know what this is about. He's the one person who hasn't talked to me about the Field House investigation. Yet the one person who should.

The door to Dehenre's office is closed. I take one last deep breath before entering.

Chris is sitting in Dehenre's chair behind her desk. Feet up, as if he owns the place.   Clipboard in his lap. Pen in hand.

"Ah, perfect. I was wondering if Dehenre forgot to send you up. Have a seat, Cadet Bennett," he says, as if we've never met. Was Max right?

I sit down obediently. Let's see where this goes.

He lets out a sigh. "Okay…at this point, everyone knows you're the one who slipped this note—" he holds up a half sheet of white paper with a couple of typed sentences on it, "under Wright's door, right?"

I nod.

"Good. Then—."

"I don't want to talk about the note or the Field House."

My brazenness catches him off-guard. "Excuse me, *knob*?"

"Don't give me that. I thought we were friends." I remind him just as easily as I remind Ash to clean the room. "Why do you always act so hot and cold. One minute you want to be chummy and the next, you treat me as if I'm invisible. Or worse …as if, as if our conversations meant nothing. As if I mean nothing." I surprise even myself at the honesty. The vulnerability.

He takes his feet off the desk, settling in for the sparring. "That was then, Cadet Bennett. This is now. And tomorrow. And the day after that." Beads of sweat appear on his forehead. "Shit is complicated." He runs his fingers through his black hair. "This isn't a fairy tale. I may have a sword and all, but I'm far from perfect. Believe me." He tries not to chuckle at his joke.

Oh, I believe you.

He wipes his forehead and lets out a frustrated breath. "Look, I'm graduating in like…three weeks. Heading off to the Army. I didn't mean to lead you on, if that's where this is going. You're around guys twenty-four hours a day. I think you just misunderstood things."

I hold onto the sides of the plastic chair like a parachute.

"Yea, we shared some things about ourselves." He let's out a sigh. "I was just checking up on you cause it seemed like you needed a little attention. But …but we aren't friends."

And with that, he walks out of the office.

I don't cry. I don't even feel like crying. I don't know what I feel at this moment.

Oh yes, I do.

I sprint to the bathroom down the hall.

The smell of my own vomit mixed with lemon disinfectant seeps into my nostrils. My clammy hands reach for the dry, scratchy toilet paper from the holder. I catch a glimpse of my miserable reflection and slump back against the wall of the stall. Defeated.

I wipe my mouth with toilet paper and flush.

My heart is still thumping against my grey uniform shirt as the bathroom door swings open.

Leather loafers echo against the white tiles in rhythmic steps towards me.

"Here, knob year can be more stressful for some than others." A bottle of water appears from underneath the door.

I take it and open the door.

Ward.

Just what I needed. She's everywhere I don't need her to be.

"Ma'am yes ma'am. Thank you, ma'am."

She takes a seat on the brown leather couch in the bathroom and crosses her legs. "Let's cut to it. I know you better. You aren't stressed. It's not like I haven't seen you in my battalion all year. Walking around like you've got more to prove than the rest of us."

My face flashes embarrassment.

"Like *youuuuu* know Graham, the Corps better than those of us who've been here longer." She drums her fingers against her crossed legs.

I take a sip of water and lean against the wall. The plastic wall cool on my back.

She twists her band of gold around her ring finger. Taunting me. Ward gets up from the couch and straightens her duty shirt. "I should've told you this sooner, Bennett…" She leans down so closely that I can tell uses the same perfumed body spray as I. Her tone soft but resolute, she whispers into my ear. "It's never too late to quit."

The door closes behind her with a soft thud.

My body slides down the wall in one movement.

Her words burn in my ear.

I knew on Hell Night that Graham was wrong for me. But it was too late to walk away. Besides, where would I go? I'd be just another statistic on the road to assimilation. What will I tell my Dad? My friends? I needed Graham more than it wanted me.

Hell Night.

I wanted to be hazed.

Out of tradition, to be like my male classmates, to be different than the other women in my class or at Graham. Period. To show them women *do* belong here. That we can do all of the things. That we didn't ruin this school.   To truly be part of the grey fabric that weaves together traditions.

The *Old Corps.*

That's what I wanted on Hell Night. And it's what I've wanted the entire year.

We didn't know exactly when it would start. Or how. All we knew is that it would happen sometime in the first few days after we reported to Graham. We slept every night fully dressed in our PT clothes, shoes hanging over the end of the bed, blue cotton shirt and shorts sticking to our clammy skin in the Charleston summer. Our racing minds keeping us from sleep. We slept on top of the blankets on our racks.

The ominous dong-dong of bells, the opening bars to "Hells Bells," came out of the silence and cut through the night on the third day.

It's played at every Hell Night since time immemorial. It was the same that night as it was for those who occupied this room before me, and even when Will McClean attended his fictional version of the college in *Lords.*

For all of us, the bells signaling the start. The *beginning.*

"Get up, knobs. Party's fucking over." Voices echoed within the battalion. Screen doors banged open and shut like a drum solo. The clanging of wood on metal trash cans. Perfectly choreographed. Eager hunters who had laid in wait. Waiting for the signal.

"Hurry up and get down on the fucking quad."

"You better not be late."

This was it.

I was going to be part of it. *Finally.* I'd pass over the threshold just like all the men who came before me. Filled with anticipation, fear, and eagerness, we rushed downstairs, taking care not to slip in the dim light.

We formed up on the quad in a perfect platoon. Thirty knobs. Bracing. Waiting.

"I won't take no prisoners, won't spare no lives…"

"Close your eyes, knobs." The battalion instantly blanketed in silence and darkness.

Goose bumps rippled my arms in the damp Charleston evening air. My breath quickened. Beads of sweat rolled down my spine. Bodies passed—next to us, between us, behind us—indistinguishable. Only specters of air.

Metal ground on the concrete floor as someone pushed the gate of the sally port shut. Camera flashes dance behind my closed eyes. I bit the inside of my cheek to keep from smiling. Another body passed behind me. A puff of warm breath wafted against my ear. "Brace."

The music stopped just as abruptly as it started.

The loudspeaker crackled overhead in its place.

"Graham Class of 2004, tonight is the start of a nine-month-long test. A test of your courage, strength, and conviction to endure all that we place in front of you. How you overcome those challenges—individually, and as a class, speaks to your true nature as a person and ultimately as a Graham cadet. It will not be easy but then again, you probably already knew that; or you wouldn't have chosen to be the man in the arena whose face is marred by dust and sweat …and blood; who strives valiantly, … who errs. Who will come short again and again because there is no effort without error and shortcoming. Those who actually strive to do the deeds; who come to know great enthusiasms, great devotions; who spends himself in a worthy cause; who at the best knows in the end the triumph of high achievement, and who at the worst, if he fails, at least fails while daring greatly, so that his place shall never be with those cold and timid souls who neither know victory nor *defeat*."

Ward's voice went silent, fanning the anticipation of what was to come.

"Class of 2004, the fourth class system… is *now* in effect."

The hunters were unleashed.

The dong-dong of the bells started anew.

"I'm coming on like a hurricane…"

The sensation of the bodies around us—passing between us, returned. Faster. Angrier.

Yelling. Shouting. My eyes shoot open. Angry faces inches from mine, blurring into one. The faint scent of peppermint gum. Of sweat.

"Is that the best you can do? Get your fucking chin in. Shoulders back." Who shouted what words or the intended target is lost in the haze of the humid air. Lost in the guitar riff. Lost in the confusion. Lost in the excitement. Lost in the masochistic yearning and giving.

The chaos around me—upperclassmen shouting conflicting instructions, wood on metal, the jungle's serpentine—all brought calmness within. *I'm ready.* I was ready to be part of fifteenth company. Part of the fourth class system. Part of Graham. The old Corps.

"Get up to fourth division knobs," a Texas drawl demanded. We ran across the quad to the stairs. "Oh by all means…take your sweat ass motherfucking time, ladies," another voice spat in our ears.

As soon as the first knob in line took a step onto the stairs, we realized this wasn't going to be easy. Or fast. "Are *youuuuuuuuuu* fucking kidding me, smack? You're going to step onto *my* fucking stairs without asking for permission first?" The upperclassman at the top of the stairs shouted sarcastically. The shiny brim of his cover masked his eyes, shielding his identity. His white gloves gleamed in the faint light. His costume a perfect fit.

"Sir, no excuse, sir," the knob answered. *When in doubt.*

"You don't know who the *FUCK* I am, do you? You've been here for three days with nothing to do. Just laying around your room. Getting fat and nasty. You had enough time to memorize your chain of command. Oh it's going to be a *looooong* nine fucking months for you," he lamented without taking a breath. "Get out of my face. You're wasting my fucking time."

"I'm gonna get'cha..."

This went on until finally one of us got it right. The same process was repeated for three more divisions, sometimes with multiple upperclassmen - strangers still, on the stairs. White-gloved hands thrust in your face like a blades. A dare. A judge. Upperclassmen switched out the minute one of us got it right. And so the search for the right upperclassman's name began afresh.

If you weren't in the driver's seat on the foot of the stairs, you were dropped for push-ups or sent to run satellites around the battalion. Thrust into the web of upperclassmen from other companies. Faces and names you definitely didn't know.

But driving the stairs and doing push-ups on Hell Night was par for the course. Easy.

"You're only young but you're gonna die."

I hungered for the suffering. The kind Will McLean saw transpiring in the dark corners. The kind he longed to stop. That's what I had to have. I needed to have. Longed to have. No matter the cost.

I purposely flubbed the words as I recited the Graham cadet prayer.

"What. The. Fuck. Of course *you* fuck it up." Johnson stood in front of me with a satisfactory smile punctuated with a laugh. "Enjoy your satellite around the battalion, Bennett."

I took off in a cantor counter-clockwise towards sixteenth company. In the confusion, and busy with their own festivities, I went unnoticed. Disappointed, I rounded the corner and headed towards seventeenth company. There too, I went unseen. I made another turn towards fourteenth company.

Halfway in between fourteenth and seventeenth company, a voice called out. "Knob stop!"

My feet obeyed without hesitation. I turn to face the voice leaned against the gallery walls. The room across from me was open. Shadows of air chairs and silhouettes hanging by their arms from full presses danced in the glow of the moonlight.

This was it. My Virgil illuminating the path.

"You got me ringing..."

The voice stepped off the wall and out from the shadows and noise. "What do you think you're doing, running around *my* Battalion?"

"Sir, no excuse, sir."

"Do you know who I am?"

"Sir, Mr. Kent, sir. The Delta Battalion Executive Officer."

His eyes looked me over cautiously. Weighing the consequences. "Do you want a *real* Hell Night?" His whisper sent a shiver down my spine. Honey in my ears.

"Sir, yes, sir."

The screen door of the room opens. An upperclassman beckons me inside.

I take a step.

"What the *fuck* kind of answer is that, knob?" Ward's voice came through the noise without notice, her face sharp and harsh even in the shadows. "I got this Marion." *Shit. The token Regimental Commander. I read all about you before I got here.* She stood inches from me. "And just WHAT do you think you were off to do…" She looks down at my name tag. "…Cadet Bennett?"

"Sir, I mean…*ma'am*, no excuse, ma'am."

She looks me over. Judging me for my decision. For my motivation.

"What you see there…" She nods towards the room. The shadows now in mark time march unison, rifles held high above their heads. "…in the recesses of secrecy, hidden from review and accountability, isn't the way to earn her place here, Bennett." She narrows the space between us with one stride. "You earn your place by being a good classmate, studying, and most importantly setting an example for those that'll come after you. It's both a burden and responsibility for those of us in these early years of assimilation. Unwritten. And that…" Her head turns left to the open door again emphasizing the point. "…is *not* how we do that."

Chapter Twenty-Nine. *The blaze had been spectacular and infinitely satisfying.*

The next morning, I don't go with Reagan and Ash to the squad room for morning formation.

Instead, I remove my company number from my shirt collar and place it on my desk.

I toss my cadet ID next to it, for someone's clipboard.

I walk out of my room, everything I want to take packed into the knobby bag at my side.

Upperclassmen hurry past me on the galleries, down three divisions.

I walk straight out the front sally port of Delta Battalion without anyone stopping me or asking where I'm going.

Already invisible.

Already forgotten.

Yet no longer looked at or judged.

The lone bugle calls the Corps to breakfast formation, like it has in days past and will in days future.

Acknowledgements.

As I sit down to express my gratitude to those who have supported me on this writing journey, I am reminded that writing a novel is never a solo endeavor. It takes a village, and I am fortunate to have had an incredible community of friends, classmates, and mentors who have encouraged and inspired me along the way.

I would like to extend my heartfelt thanks to Megan Gentry ('02) for planting the seed of a story arc idea many years ago, and for recently reminding me that as we get older, the gap between caring and not caring gets smaller. Your friendship means the world to me.

To Jose Negron, my ride-or-die battle buddy since Thanksgiving 2010, I am grateful for your unwavering support and camaraderie and equal love for "hustlin'".

I would also like to thank Jim Woodward for his daily calls, which have become a highlight of my day. Your kindness and thoughtfulness have meant the world to me, and I appreciate your presence in my life.

To Carlos Bennett, I thank you for being a listening ear and a source of comfort. Sometimes, all we need is someone to hear us out, and you have been that person for me. Thank you for being "fam" and for being there when it matters most.

I am grateful to everyone who set aside time throughout the years to read some early drafts. Big shout out to Brian Laslie ('01) and Erica Stark for taking the time to read and provide feedback. Your input has been invaluable, and I appreciate your honesty and insight.

To Ann Thomas Ronayne and Keenan Grigg – your humor and sarcasm were a blessing at school.

A huge thank you to Mrs. Margie and Harvey Dick ('53) for opening their home to me and other cadets. Their stocked kitchen and den served as a respite for not only clean laundry but meeting others like Neal and Cooley.

To my friends, Class of 2001 Citadel classmates and fellow members of the Corps, I would like to extend my thanks to all of you to include - Dan Ruttenber ('01), Dion Trahan ('02), Brandy Perry Baker ('01), Mandy Garcia Patrick ('01), Eileen Guerra Quinn ('01), Crystal Spring Haney ('01), Craig D. Wilson ('01), Jennifer Causey Phifer ('01), Deonn Crumley Baker ('01), Morgan Lynn ('01), Lisa Lugo Weber ('02), Dena Abrash Elrod ('01), and Dr. Vlasta Zekulic ('02). Your friendship and support have meant everything to me.

I would also like to thank Kelly Gosnell for her tireless efforts in recruiting women to The Citadel in the early years and for providing a safe space for us to vent and share our experiences. Your dedication and passion have made a lasting impact, and I am grateful for your presence in my life.

Finally, I would like to express my deepest gratitude to Tony Lackey ('61), MGen John Grinalds, Chip Nimmich ('76), and CSM Sylvan Bauer for their guidance, wisdom, and support while in the "leadership laboratory". Your influence has shaped me in ways that I am still discovering, and I am honored to have had the opportunity to learn from and be inspired by each of you.

Apologies to those who I have missed in mentioning. Please know that your lack of mention does not void your influence.

Thank you all again for your love, support, and encouragement. This novel would not have been possible without you, and I am forever grateful.

-Melanie